LIPSTICK

Also by the author

Unlawful Justice (2017)

The Mogul (2018)

The Heist Artist (2019)

Bhendi Bazaar (2019)

Doosra (2019)

VISH DHAMIJA

LIPSTICK

HARPER
BLACK
An Imprint of HarperCollins *Publishers*

First published in India in 2019 by Harper Black
An imprint of HarperCollins *Publishers*

Building 10, Tower A, 4th Floor, DLF Cyber City, Phase II,
Gurugram Haryana – 122002, India
www.harpercollins.co.in

2 4 6 8 10 9 7 5 3 1

P-ISBN: 978-93-5357-283-9
E-ISBN: 978-93-5357-284-6

Typeset in 10.5/13.7 Adobe Caslon Pro at
Manipal Digital Systems, Manipal

Printed and bound at
MicroPrints India, New Delhi

'Hello, Zoe!'
'Hello.'
'How does it feel?'
'Oh, it feels good to be back!'

Author Note

Lipstick is the third book in the Rita Ferreira series. After the success of *Bhendi Bazaar* and *Doosra*, I received a lot of requests from readers to

- write more thrillers featuring DCP Rita Ferreira, and
- keep them dark.

Although there are references to the previous Rita Ferreira thrillers, this is in no way a sequel. It's a standalone story, and I've tried to keep it as close to reality as I possibly can while writing fiction. If you've read any previous books in this series, you'll know that I try to follow all police procedures – I research on the web, I speak to IPS Officers, but sometimes I have to stray from the facts (a) intentionally, so that I do not give away any confidential information I have access to and (b) inadvertently, due to gaps in the information. You must understand there are many police procedures/rules/information, which are *classified* that no police officer will share.

It gives me immense pleasure to inform you that – thanks to the belief and labour of Story Ink – Rita Ferreira would soon be adapted into a multi-season premium web series by Abundantia Entertainment. Watch this space!

As always, I'd like to thank a lot of people who helped me write *Lipstick*: my wife, Nidhi, for being my best critic; Patrick Whittick for giving it the first round of edits; to team Siyahi for suggesting changes and sharpening my draft into a finished manuscript, and then the editing team at HarperCollins for giving it the shape it is in. I simply cannot thank my fortune enough for being in such good hands.

I thank all my readers who encourage me to keep on writing. I hope you enjoy reading this book.

Love, lots of it.
Vish Dhamija
Find me on:
Facebook: www.facebook.com/VishDhamija
Email: vishdhamija@gmail.com

Serial killers don't stop. Until they are stopped.

– Vish Dhamija

La plus belle des ruses du diable est de vous persuader qu'il n'existe pas

– Charles Baudelaire, *Le Spleen de Paris*, 1862

(The finest trick of the devil is to persuade you that it does not exist)

PRELUDE
1993

I wish I were Adam or Eve; then I'd have no parents – at least not earthly ones.

My mother never really liked me. I have a feeling that she never wanted me in the first place. I was either a mistake or something forced upon her by my dad and society. Her disgust with me was fairly transparent. Perhaps I reminded her that she wasn't only tied down to a husband, but also to a child. Leaving a husband was one thing, but leaving your child …? To her, I was a toe-rag, and I accepted it as I accepted so many other facts that I learnt in the science or geography class. I was thirteen, and a loner since as far back as I can remember, and contrary to whatever anyone might tell you, I quite enjoyed my solitude. At school, I made every attempt to keep social interaction in check; I was like another small boat on the Dal Lake on a busy summer's day. Watching, listening, observing, but always striving to remain inconspicuous. Being the only child of my parents, there was no sibling interference to impinge on my privacy.

Money was never a problem in our household. My mother was a senior finance manager in a pharmaceutical company and my father, the retail head in a consumer appliances company. Both of them made shedloads of money, but they had little time to appreciate it, save for buying electronics and updating cars, which were more to demonstrate their financial status amongst their peers than anything else. To be honest, they hardly had time for each other. Or me. They worked obnoxious hours to put the proverbial food on the table that no one had time to eat anyway. The secret to the success of their marriage was, ironically, their absence from each other's lives. We seldom ate as a family, except on some weekends when either one of them wasn't travelling. The dinners were all the same. They began with the usual drab meal and ended in some pointless argument that one of them would start. During the few meals when the two weren't snapping at each other, they would resort to dropping broad hints about how hard they slogged to provide me with the best education, the best opportunities, the best of everything. Blah-blah-blah! Of course, I appreciated that I didn't have a dearth of toys or comic books or music, but it wasn't just me they were labouring for, were they? They were competing within their own peer groups and climbing their respective career ladders; it was their rat race and I just happened to be another one of the meaningless trophies they had picked en route.

Unfortunately, my school results weren't bad. *Hard-working and above average* was how the teachers put it. Only partly true, since I hardly worked for it, although I still made it into the top quintile. I didn't need to put in much effort for what they taught us at school or tested us on and that left me with a lot of time on my hands. I could have easily topped the class, but I had no intention of granting my parents another feather to flaunt to their friends. Which was a tad unfortunate because, had I been a laggard, I'd have – just might've – received more attention from them, even if for the wrong reasons. Also, I was meticulous to a fault. I didn't break my toys; kept my room clean. I simply did not give them any reason to focus on me. Well, except for the chronic bed-wetting, for which, after a lot of screaming, shouting and threatening (on their part), they hauled me off to a doctor. He diagnosed me with *nocturnal enuresis*. According to the doctor, it was neither a physical ailment nor an emotional trauma: he assumed that there was no way I'd have emotional issues when I was being brought up in such an exemplar family environment. Instead, he labelled it a 'developmental' issue, and we let it pass, although my mother continued to rant and rave most mornings about my ailment when she fluently cursed my father and me. Just how my father shared the blame was something I couldn't figure.

Some of my parents' friends thought I was a bit withdrawn; but then any child whose parents engaged in verbal duels no less than thrice a day – like the devil himself prescribed it – would invariably tend towards taciturnity.

Like Calvin had Hobbes, I too had an imaginary friend. I say 'imaginary', but he was actually quite real. I talked to him, we played, we did a lot of things together. In time, I realized that this other person who was always alongside me, was my alter ego. *Mini-me, Mad-me, Crazy-me, Needy-me.* I called him 'Nutty-me', since I infinitely prefferred 'nutty' to 'crazy'. I'd say one thing, and Nutty-me would contradict me. We'd argue. He was the evil one of the two, a sneaky devil always pushing the boundaries when I was frightened or trying to make a sensible decision.

Being a loner made me a voracious reader and I rarely toed the line with regard to age-appropriate books. Dad had a penchant for pulp fiction that he picked up on his travels. I relished these more than I did my own books. Most of these contained one or two raunchy scenes, which gave me immense joy, and of which my own books were totally devoid. That – I vividly remember – initiated the discovery of my hitherto latent desires. My mind fizzed with questions and the body stirred in response to the provocative text. It made me stop and take notice of the subtle changes occurring within my own body.

Although I still had no desire to be drawn into the inane and juvenile conversations of my classmates, Nutty-me and I enjoyed watching girls. I was too shy to talk to them, but liked looking at them, especially the slightly older ones, since their bodies were more in line with the ones detailed in the books. Nutty-me helped me find opportunities where I could covertly admire their skirts hike up when they bent forward or sat down.

'*Lie in wait by the foot of the staircase that the girls use*,' recommended Nutty-me.

Rummaging through my father's fiction shelves, I found something that rocked my world. A letter addressed to my mother from someone who was apparently her illicit lover and, going by the sordid details, now pined for her sensuous body, and it certainly wasn't my father's handwriting. It appeared that the man who wrote this letter had had more than one steamy encounter with her to describe in minutiae what made her red-hot in bed. I noted that she indulged in sadomasochism, enjoyed bondage and other kinky perversions – whatever! Although it was revolting in a sense, much as I tried, I couldn't help visualizing the erotic act. It ran like a continuous film in my brain and, despite my naïveté on the subject, I realized I was mentally editing it to suit my embryonic, nonetheless lambent, libido. The tighter I squeezed my eyes shut to get away, the clearer and brighter the words became – like they were being seared onto my eyelids – and perverse as some might find it, it became a huge turn on for me.

I mentioned it to no one; who could I speak to, in any case? And what could I tell them anyway: that my mother was a dirty, depraved deviant that enjoyed … kinky stuff? And although it was pleasurable at most times, it bothered me no end, especially with all the missing information. I didn't know how old the letter was, as, despite its wealth of detail, it lacked a date. Although it didn't look very recent, it wasn't ancient either becuase I could see that it was from an inkjet printer. The paper hadn't yellowed or cracked at the creases. I had no idea how my father had got hold of it and what had been the immediate repercussions – why hadn't he divorced her?

'*He's a pussy*,' Nutty-me was furious. '*Maybe he has a harlot on the side as well.*'

I wondered about the man who had written the note. I wondered if my mother was still – on the pretext of travelling on work, *wink, wink*! – clandestinely meeting him for her carnal pleasures.

The discovery of that letter changed my life; I could interpret the unfriendly vibes my father exuded whenever my mother was around. It spelt out the context and I started comprehending his snide comments whenever he had an argument with his adulterous wife. My hitherto peaceful solitary existence was filled with unwelcome noises, but I couldn't put the genie back in the bottle … no one could.

ONE
1 July

Every metropolis around the globe has rush-hour traffic on weekdays – in the mornings, when people leave for work and their children set off for school; and in the evenings, when they flock home.

But not in Mumbai. Mumbai's rush hour is 24/7. It's the most populated megalopolis in India, and although the number of people is only marginally higher than in Delhi, Mumbai's denizens have to make do with one-third the area of the National Capital Region.

It was 9 p.m. and Deputy Commissioner of Police, Crime Branch, Rita Ferreira was stuck in traffic. She was cursing herself for having left office so late when she had known the party was to begin at eight. But then she had been called into a last-minute meeting at the precinct, so it couldn't be helped.

She was riding shotgun with her police constable cum chauffeur, Kuldeep Singh. It was one of those extremely rare occasions when the two were invited to the same event. As the white Volkswagen Jetta threaded through the traffic, Rita fiddled with the radio. Kuldeep was one of the most reticent men she had ever had the misfortune to meet. He was the envy of the other drivers in the force because he drove the amazing Miss Ferreira. From the rumours that were rife, she was aware that, although constantly heckled by the other police officers, he had never once retaliated or said a word for or against her, even in jest.

Rita Ferreira was Mother Nature's ace: a blessed metabolism in her gene pool with a bit of calisthenics and yoga at the crack of dawn kept her in top form, and a stunning form that was. Her face wouldn't register beautiful on the Phi and Golden Ratio proportions that model scouts used, but she was seriously sensuous. Thirty-*something* – Rita never quantified the something – five-foot six in her stockings, tawny and toned. Curvaceous enough to warrant a double take wherever she went. With that physical description she shouldn't have joined the police. Anyone who didn't blend into the background in mufti shouldn't be in the force. You couldn't hide a peacock amongst the crows. But she had defied that. She had joined the police and had been eminently successful.

The radio was tuned to 98.3 FM Radio Mirchi, and a fun item number about the poor and much-maligned *Munni* played while Rita lowered the mirror in the visor to check herself one last time before the car turned into the venue. She looked at her watch. 9.40 p.m.

Kuldeep stopped the car and, as usual, waited expectantly for Rita to get out before he parked the vehicle.

'You're coming in with me, aren't you?'

'Yes, madam.'

'Then park the car, and we'll go in together,' Rita indicated a vacant slot on their right.

'You go on ahead, madam, I'll join you after I park.'

'No. You were delayed because of me, so we'll go in together.'

The occasion was Senior Inspector Rajesh Nene's farewell party. He had been the senior-most member in Rita's team and had initially been deeply sceptical of a woman leading the Crime Branch. In the course of time and several cases later, he came to realize and appreciate her dedication, commitment and her astute powers of deduction that helped solve crimes. Nene became a reliable associate and a big asset. He had forgone all promotions because he was reluctant to move away from Mumbai. 'Family reasons,' he had claimed. His voluntary retirement at fifty-one would be a great loss.

'Ma'am,' he boomed over the din of the party, 'I had given up on you.' Nene still looked young for his age, with a full head of curly L'Oréal black hair. His five-foot eleven body was ram-rod straight. He raised his glass half-full of whisky.

'And why would I miss this opportunity, Rajesh? Sorry I'm late, though.'

'I'm just glad you could make it. What will you drink, ma'am?'

'Whatever you're having …' Rita discovered that Kuldeep had already made himself scarce despite walking into the party with her. *Cheeky!*

There were about thirty people in the large hall, but mostly men. A reminder to Rita that she was in a job that was traditionally a man's domain. She spotted two other direct reports.

Senior Inspector Vikram Patil, marginally older than Rita, was clearly the next in the chain of command, now that Nene had retired. He was from the State Police cadre and a strong contender for the post of Assistant Superintendent. This advancement was in the offing and the meeting that Rita had attended just before starting from work today was about personnel. Vikram Patil's name had been put forward for a promotion. A gentle giant, Patil towered over Rita. A few years ago, he had gone on a strict fitness regime and had lost some thirty kilos. Today he was lithe and lean.

'Blended or single malt, ma'am?' he asked.

'Whiskey with an *e*, if there's any.' Rita had a predilection for Bourbon, Jim Beam to be precise.

'Let me check.'

'I'll ask someone to get a bottle of Jim Beam for you, ma'am,' said Nene who had overheard this exchange although he had been chatting with another guest.

'Forget it Rajesh, I'm an equal opportunity drinker – I'll have any whisky. Vikram was only pulling my leg.'

'No ma'am, I insist. You're my guest for the first time.' Nene was at least six drinks down and Rita had no desire to wrangle. Although she would have loved to drink anything that was offered – even Vodka – she figured that waiting another ten minutes wouldn't hurt.

How was she to have known that the gods had something else entirely on their minds?

Rita chatted with Vikram as Nene walked away. Vikram was a tad tipsy as well. Inspector Jatin Singh, who was the other aide-de-camp to Rita, strolled over to greet her. It was common knowledge that Jatin had aspired to join the movies and that his brigadier father had nipped this hankering in the bud. Jatin was a couple of inches shorter than Patil and, in addition to looking like a Greek god, was a sharp dresser. This evening he was in full sartorial splendour in a linen suit with a pale blue, open-collared shirt. There was nothing after the initial hello. Just a vague smile and she realized that he, too, was quite inebriated and perhaps didn't want to unwittingly commit a social solecism.

Rita suddenly felt out of place in a room full of plastered policemen. She espied two other inspectors she had worked with, Akhil Mathur and Ravi Mathur, clearly wasted, having a loud argument over something trivial with some other policemen.

From a distance, she saw Rajesh Nene triumphantly wave a bottle. She waved back at him with a smile and just then, her iPhone started to buzz.

Rita was still single and an orphan, her parents having passed away some years ago. The only person who called her at odd hours was Ash Mattel – he lived in London – but she knew that he was on a flight tonight, winging his way to Delhi for some workshop. Given that almost everyone she worked with was here at the party, her phone ringing at this hour – past 10 p.m. – wasn't a good omen. If the caller couldn't wait to call in the morning, it asserted that there was something burning somewhere. And if you were in the police force, you knew that the fire wasn't lit up for a barbeque.

'DCP Rita Ferreira,' she said, glancing at the number. It was a local Mumbai mobile phone but the caller wasn't in her phonebook.

'Good evening, madam,' said the voice at the other end. 'I'm Senior Inspector Vinod Shukla from Worli Police Station. We were called in an hour ago about a missing person's enquiry, which turned out to be a homicide at Dr Annie Besant Road. I'm at the scene of crime, and it looks like the work of the person you've been looking for.' Rita's heart raced as Vinod Shukla gave a quick summary of the victim and the tableau.

'Give me the exact address, I'll be there …' Rita looked at her watch, 10.18 p.m., they were in Juhu Vile Parle Gymkhana Club, approximately twenty kilometres to the location of the murder, '… in about fifty minutes. Close the place down; call in the forensics, the doctor …'

Her demeanour or tone of voice might have given it away because Vikram, Rajesh and Jatin looked at her. The question came the moment she hung up.

'What's happened ma'am?'

'He has struck again.'

The first murder had happened in Kandivali nearly nine months ago. Gina, a slim twenty-five year old, had been found dead in her one-bedroom apartment, tied up on her bed, gagged and wearing a dog collar. She had been asphyxiated with the leather collar after being violated in both her vaginal and rectal orifices with her own hair brushes. The perpetrator had ruptured her ante-mortem, delivering pain that was a clear indication of the rage and mental instability of the perpetrator. However, no bodily fluids had been found in either of the orifices, which meant that the killer himself hadn't actually penetrated his victim.

Four months later, the second victim, Radha, had been found in an identical position as the first. She was only twenty-two and had also been violated in the same fashion in her apartment in Andheri. She was as petite as Gina and her end had been just as agonizing. Brutalized while still alive and then strangled with the dog collar that her corpse still wore like a degrading trophy.

Another commonality between the two victims was that they were both commercial sex workers. Hookers usually took the tricks to a rooming house that was short-let for such paid-for rendezvous. But in both these cases, the client had somehow convinced the girls to take him to their own homes so no one would see the murderer with the victim prior to the killing.

The autopsy reports had been identical. Two things stuck out as extraordinary matches: both women's lips had been severely bruised. On closer examination it appeared that the women had been either forced to apply a dark red, almost crimson, lipstick – or the offender had applied it on them and then had savagely eaten it off their lips like some ritual before gagging them. Some of the colour had spread beyond the lips, to the chin and upper lip. The two lipstick shades – which at first glance had seemed similar – were in fact one and the same: Maybelline Jewels Refined Wine. Although both Gina and Radha had been light skinned, two girls having similar tastes in lipsticks could not have been purely coincidental.

The maniac killer hadn't raped the women. No penetration. Perhaps he was incapable. Perhaps he got off on making women suffer. The Mumbai police force hadn't been able to avert their untimely deaths, but the least they could do now was ensure that the perpetrator didn't claim any more lives.

Both Gina and Radha walked the streets soliciting clients at the curb. More often than not, the rendezvous was either at some seedy hotel or hot pillow joints and – sometimes, albeit rarely – at the john's residence. It was common knowledge that most guys preferred not to pick up women in the vicinity of their homes. In such a scenario, the girl would need to travel a longer distance to fornicate at the customer's place. This entailed a higher degree of risk – what if the man took them to a house full of other randy men? Ergo, most working girls avoided that unless the financial reward was considerably higher.

What had bothered the local police stations investigating the past crimes was that no foreign male hair, bodily fluid, skin residue or print had been found at the scenes of the crimes; consequently, no DNA had been recovered. Nevertheless, the killer hadn't cared about leaving his dental impressions behind, although he had been careful to wipe off his oral fluids from the lips of the victims with a strong bleach to remove any traces of DNA. And while teeth marks were as individualistic as fingerprints, they weren't the easiest to track down. The police had no dental records of existing criminals on file, forget those of the millions of law-abiding citizens in Mumbai. It would be a rare occurrence if dental records could lead them to the teeth that did the damage. No one was pinning their hopes on them or holding their breaths.

The case had been escalated to Crime Branch and an executive order had been issued by the Commissioner of Mumbai Police to all precincts in and around Mumbai that any new incident that resembled the two previous murders must be directed to DCP Rita Ferreira for enquiry and investigation.

And hence, the call to Rita now.

'I'll come with you,' Vikram said as she disconnected the call.

'No,' she said bluntly. 'You are plainly under the influence of alcohol and there's no way you can be on official duty.'

Jatin didn't even bother to offer. He was definitely intoxicated. Rajesh Nene, even if he wasn't drunk, had retired. There would be a vacuum until she found someone to replace him.

'Ma'am, I'll come with you.'

Rita raised her eyebrows since she didn't recognize him.

'Madam, myself Sub-inspector Harish Chandra Bhatawadekar, but all my friends call me Harry.'

'Hello, Harry,' she shook his hand.

'Ma'am, I've been meaning to talk to you. I had planned to make an appointment to meet with you tomorrow. I know Senior Inspector Nene has retired and you have an opening. I'd like to join your team.'

Rita looked at a man who was just about as tall as her. Late twenties, shaved head, unusually broad shoulders and built like a bull, but with a remarkably child-like face. He wore khaki cotton chinos and a white T-shirt. No gun. Before she could say anything, he softly added, 'And I don't drink.'

That sealed it.

'I have worked with Harry in the past, ma'am,' said Nene, 'I can vouch for him. I swear he will be a good fit. We used to call him Idiom Kumar then …'

'*Idiom* Kumar?'

'Oh, his penchant for Hindi idioms got him that nickname. I bet you'll hear some soon. But honestly, he'll be a great fit, ma'am,' Nene chuckled.

'One thing at a time, then, Harry. Welcome aboard on this case. We'll see how we get you into the team later – I'll need to speak to the powers-that-be.'

'Fair enough, ma'am,' Harry said.

'All right then, let's go,' Rita said. She apologized to Nene and left a word for Kuldeep to enjoy the party since she was taking the car. He could imbibe freely and take a cab home.

'What do you know about this case, Harry?' she asked as they walked out.

'Like I said, ma'am, I was planning to talk to you tomorrow and so I've already done my homework.'

'I'm impressed.'

As they walked towards the car, Rita counted her blessings that day: one, as she had been delayed at the meeting she hadn't had time to change into away-from-work clothes, so she was in her standard work outfit, blue, skinny jeans and a long-sleeved, collared white shirt; two, arriving late at the party meant she hadn't had a chance to grab a drink; and three, finding young Harry, an abstainer.

'This way, Harry,' Rita gestured towards her car and unlocked the VW. Harry removed the cover from the red beacon and climbed in. The police cherry started rotating brightly on the roof as Rita reversed and exited the parking lot. Then she turned the siren on. Within the confines of the car, Rita realized that Harry was a smoker. One could use Dettol to wash one's hands and brush one's teeth with Colgate or Patanjali's Dant Kanti, but the smell of cigarettes obstinately clung to one's clothes.

'So how many do you smoke in a day, Harry?'

'How—' he began.

Rita waited him out.

'A pack a day. Do you smoke, ma'am?'

'No. I used to, but I've quit now.'

TWO

Rita slewed right at Gulmohar Road and sped past Narsee Monjee and Mithibai colleges. The traffic wasn't too heavy and with the flashing light and siren blaring on her car, people quickly made way.

'So tell me about yourself,' Rita said, to take her mind off the macabre incident that they were headed towards.

'I joined the force five years ago. I was at Juhu Police Station for the first four years and only recently moved to the Head Office. I partnered with Senior Inspector Nene on a case. He was the one who suggested I speak to you to see if I would fit into Crime Branch ...'

'Why Crime Branch?'

'I prefer investigating to executing orders. I think I have an analytical mind and I enjoy solving puzzles and mysteries. But I'd rather let my work speak for itself to *my-own-mouth-sweet-parrot* ...'

It took a while for Rita to decipher what Harry meant. She had to directly translate Idiom Kumar's idiom back into Hindi word for word: *Apne Munh Mian Mithu Banna.* Then she burst out laughing.

'I see why you got the nickname.'

'I was a student of Hindi literature, ma'am. I loved the idioms. The trouble is, if I say them in Hindi, they aren't half as interesting, and most people don't stop to listen. But I'm happy to drop my habit if—'

'No, I didn't mean that. I think it's a quirky way to be heard, and to make people smile.'

'You're correct, ma'am. It is to add humour to an otherwise mundane existence.'

Everyone's a comedian. Rita understood. Humour lifted the shroud of darkness for a while. Harry wasn't unaware that he sounded ridiculous; he just let people think whatever they wished.

Rita zipped along the straight Swami Vivekananda Road.

'So you're single?' the question slipped out before she realized it.

'Yes, ma'am.'

'Girlfriend?'

'No. What about you?'

Rita saw no point in telling Harry about her broken affair with Karan – the two had split since Karan moved to the US to work in consulting.

'I have a part-time boyfriend.' Why was she opening up to Harry when she hadn't even mentioned her relationship with Ash Mattel to Vikram or Jatin? Maybe it was different with Harry.

Vikram, Jatin and Rajesh were already in the department when she took over. The three men were sceptical about her becoming the departmental head. They had seen her as a woman first, a leader second. Harry, on the contrary, had shown keenness to join the department knowing she was the boss. But still … she realized she should put a stop to the conversation.

But Harry was confused. 'Part-time boyfriend? Never heard of that. What do you do the rest of the time?'

Rita smiled, but didn't say anything. Ironically, she wondered if talking about the murder would have been simpler and safer.

Harry smiled back. He was smart enough to understand she had already said too much.

The car came off the Bandra-Worli Sea Link, turned left and raced towards Dr Annie Besant Road.

They didn't have to look for the apartment block. The police had created a temporary barrier to stop and check every vehicle passing by.

Rita slowed down to a halt and pulled out her badge.

'Third building on the left madam,' the constable said after the salute.

'Thanks.'

As they alighted from the car, Rita realized she didn't have her Smith and Wesson. She usually donned a cotton jacket, to cover her shoulder holster. But she hadn't carried a gun tonight since drinking and guns didn't go together. Instead she had locked it in her drawer back at the precinct. But it didn't bother her. She didn't think she needed one tonight. There was little chance of the killer still hanging around in the vicinity. In any event, the local Worli Police was there.

The building was a new and plush multistorey block. It had a lobby on the ground floor with a concierge desk behind a glass door. Someone had to buzz visitors in. A security guard in a pale blue faded uniform stood by the door that was now wedged open with police personnel walking in and out. There was a phalanx of khakis around who recognized Rita as she walked in, followed by Harry. After the salutes and good evenings, one of the uniforms said, 'Senior Inspector Shukla is on the seventh floor waiting for you.'

Rita nodded and walked to the elevator.

'Thank you for coming so quickly, ma'am,' Shukla, who was outside the apartment, hurried towards them as the elevator car opened, 'I'm SI Vinod Shukla. I was the one who called you.'

Rita shook hands with him and introduced Harry.

Before they entered the apartment, Shukla updated the newly arrived officers with the basic details. The victim was Anu Singh. 'I got her name from the post in her apartment, and the photograph on her driving licence. The police have already carried out a preliminary inquiry and found out that she ran a clothing boutique near Churchgate. Her husband is travelling, and has been informed. He's on the next flight back, so should be with us latest by tomorrow evening. No known boyfriends or extramarital liaisons that we know of, yet,' Shukla recited from the sheet of paper he had pulled out of his pocket.

'Where's the husband?'

'In London.'

'When did he leave?'

'Yesterday morning.'

'Convenient, isn't it? Husband travels, has an alibi; the wife gets killed, and the serial killer we've been looking for gets the blame.'

'Are you serious, ma'am?' asked Harry.

'It's plausible. The fact is there is a serial killer in town and the tabloids have printed more than they should have; we can't dismiss the possibility of a copycat killer, or of the husband being involved. I'm not being a cynic, but it's too early to rule out anything. He is certainly a "person of interest" at this moment.'

'The husband, Shekhar Singh, took the morning flight yesterday to London on a work trip, and was due to return a week from now,' Shukla explained.

'Any signs of a break-in or forced entry?'

'None, as far as we know. It seems that Mrs Singh let the killer in willingly, which is perplexing. Either the killer was known to her or he masqueraded as a messenger or delivery man ...'

What were the chances of a coincidence like that? Rita thought, but didn't voice her suspicion. She glanced at the lock on the main door. There were no marks or scratches to indicate that it had been picked recently. There were no windows that opened into the common-area corridor that could be broken into to enter. It was outrageous to even think that someone would have scaled the wall from the outside to break into a window on the seventh floor anyway. 'What about the security guard on the ground floor? Where was he yesterday evening?'

'It's more like a reception, ma'am, and it's only manned until 7 p.m. After seven, the occupants of the building have to let their visitors in. The guard you might have seen downstairs was called by the police after they arrived here ...'

'So either the killer tailgated someone into the building or the victim let him in.'

Shukla nodded.

'Why do you think the murder is related to the past cases that we've been investigating?' Harry asked.

Shukla looked at him disdainfully. He didn't expect a junior officer to question him, but he obliged him with an answer anyway.

'Same MO. The victim was naked, lying face down and spread-eagled, her arms and legs tied with ropes to the bedposts at each corner. Strangled with a brown leather dog collar around her neck. Found with the handle of a huge hairbrush inserted into her rectum, and a curling iron thrust into her vagina. We could see ruptures in the surrounding areas on her body, but I'd rather let the details be provided through a postmortem report,' he said.

'Face?' Rita asked.

'It's apparent that she wore a bright red lipstick that's been scraped off her lips as in the case of the previous vics. Bite marks are evident on her swollen lips. The mouth area appears to have been swabbed with a strong bleach post that.'

'Damn it! The bastard is clearly taunting us.'

Everyone understood the repercussions. It was only a matter of time before the media descended on the scene. An hour max? They'd have big microphones and bigger cameras and an even bigger list of questions.

'The victim's handbag contained a purse full of cash, credit and debit cards. There's jewellery in the house as well as a safe that hasn't been broken into. Nothing seems to be stolen,' Shukla confirmed. 'Hence, robbery can be ruled out as the motive.'

'Let's go in and see. Do you want to wait here or join us?' Rita offered an out for Shukla, who she knew had already been to the room once.

'Nothing left in my stomach to puke after the first visit, ma'am,' Shukla grimaced. Rita liked his self-deprecatory attitude, although he had shown slight derision at being questioned by Harry. Roughly her age, Shukla was tall, burly, clean-shaven and had a buzz cut. He hadn't had any qualms about admitting that he had been queasy after seeing the dead body; no unnecessary machismo. Much like her.

If Shukla hadn't been her colleague he was – if not husband material – at least good for a quick romp. Rita realized that she was deliberately buffering herself with erotic imagery to avoid being traumatized by the grisly sight she was about to see. The scene of murder wasn't something anyone ever got accustomed to, but it was part of the job in their line of work. The victim hadn't asked to be murdered and therefore her side of the story needed to be articulated by the results of the police investigation. Shukla asked a junior officer for a couple of kits: gloves, shoe covers, plastic cap for hair and a white paper suit. He motioned to her and Harry to enter the apartment and followed them in.

Anu and Shekhar Singh's spacious three-bedroom apartment had been luxuriously appointed without being conspicuously opulent. Pale ivory walls with classy paintings, a mix of modern leather sink-in sofas and traditional carved and polished wooden furniture adorned the place. At the far end of the living room was an eight-seater dining table. A stuffed deer head mounted on the wall above the dining area – maybe taxidermy, maybe fake – seemed eerie in the eating area, Rita thought. She wondered whether it was Anu or Shekhar who had decided on a dead animal as part of the décor. One end of the room had bookshelves. Mostly hardback fiction, some self-improvement, a few biographies and travel guides. Someone was a voracious reader here. She noticed from the tired spines that they had all been read at least once. A massive sixty-five inch Samsung television was on the wall with Bose surround-sound speakers. A sumptuous lifestyle by any standard, but then if Shekhar Singh was doing well enough to travel abroad for work, and Anu ran a successful business as well, it was only to be expected. The apartment felt comfortable and lived-in. *A broken one now*, thought Rita. A credenza against one of the walls, held several photographs of a couple – presumably Anu and Shekhar Singh

– good-looking and stylish, although he looked a good eight or ten years older than his wife.

'He's forty-three,' Shukla said, reading her mind. 'She was thirty-two.'

'Who found the body?' Rita asked.

'One of her friends, Rashmi Sharma, called us. She had been trying to call Anu since the afternoon, as the two were meeting for dinner tonight, but the victim's phone was switched off. The friend said that it was very unlike Anu not to answer her phone or call back. After trying in vain to contact Anu, she called Shekhar, who was having a similar problem getting in touch with his wife. Rashmi called us and here we are. I've sent an officer over to take Rashmi's statement.'

'So you broke into the apartment?'

'No, ma'am, we asked a neighbour on the first floor to call the receptionist-cum-concierge to return to the building. The locking mechanism of the cabinet that holds the master key requires at least one resident in addition to the concierge to open it. No single person has access to the master key.'

'Does he know anything we should know?'

'No, ma'am. We checked. He had left the building at seven last evening. Although he was here all day today, he didn't see Anu Singh, but that wasn't unusual. He doesn't see all the residents every day. He left work again at seven today and only returned when we called him. We're checking his alibi.'

Rita glanced into the kitchen that was next to the large living room. There were a few unwashed dishes in the sink. There was a large American fridge-freezer and glass cupboards that displayed expensive crockery. Rita became aware that she was dawdling; the rest of the apartment could be surveyed later. In any event, the report she would read from the crime scene experts would cover it all. And, as typical of her, she would obviously visit the scene of crime again.

The doctor who had been summoned arrived and after his initial assessment, said Anu Singh had been dead for more than eighteen hours. The official statement would only come after the autopsy. So would the cause of death although it was quite apparent.

A chill ran down her spine as she resolutely turned towards the bedroom and entered with Harry doggedly following close behind. Shukla was still in the living room talking to his team. She threw him a glance and he gave her a wry smile, but said nothing. The unmistakable reek of death permeated the room – an almost unbearable combination of blood, urine, sweat and the decomposing body. Fortunately, as the air-conditioning had been switched on all the while and the house being airtight, the flies and maggots hadn't arrived to dine on the deceased.

Rita knew what to expect; she had seen photographs and read accounts of the previous two murders, but she still wasn't prepared for the horror of the diorama before her. The local police had put up temporary lighting in the room that harshly highlighted the naked corpse lying with her face turned towards the door; her dull, empty eyes bulged and were speckled with red dots denoting burst blood vessels as a result of the strangulation; the mutilated lips silently begged for mercy. A strong stench of bleach lingered in the air too. The assailant had once again dabbed the mouth area with heavy-duty bleach after gnawing off the lipstick. Whatever he mixed in the bleach erased his physical presence from the scene. DNA was an extremely fragile chemical compound and stronger chemicals like ammonia, hydrogen peroxide and sodium hydroxide would – if not completely destroy the DNA – contaminate it enough to render it unusable for chemical reactions needed in Polymerase Chain Reaction (PCR) for DNA profiling. The evil son-of-a-bitch certainly knew his chemistry.

Rita squeezed her eyes shut for a moment and let it all sink in. She had, over the years, cultivated the handy skill of grasping a scene with a photographic memory. She could pluck details out of her memory as and when required. Unfortunately, each macabre tableau remained seared into her brain for all eternity. She stepped closer and noticed the chafed skin on Anu's ankles and wrists. She had obviously fought hard against the ropes. The blue nylon cord that had been used to restrain Anu still lay there, although her lifeless limbs had been released by the police after taking in situ photographs. The cord had been looped around all four limbs to tie up the victim. There was no blood but the mattress was soaked with other fluids. Anu had lost control of her bladder at some point during her ordeal. Rita was now close enough to see the victim's sightless stare, the pupils rolled back with only the whites visible – a possible result of strangulation or perhaps the victim was desperately trying to look at her attacker while he was squeezing the life out of her. Rita noticed that Anu Singh's body was well-toned, much like her own, only a little shorter. She felt a rivulet of cold sweat travel down her spine. Anu's body had been stretched so hard by the restraints that her ribs showed from under skin that had angry abrasions in places. Her back and hips were streaked with crimson welts like she had been whipped sadistically. The skin was lacerated in areas and the blood had darkened and congealed after she had died. She had been assaulted both premortem and postmortem. The shoulder-length, coffee-coloured hair seemed to have been grabbed and yanked out by the roots, and spread around the bedroom. Anu Singh had until recently been an attractive woman.

Having missed dinner at the farewell party, Rita's stomach was empty; else she would most certainly have cast up her accounts at the sight of the corpse.

Rita swore softly. The police had let yet another woman down, she realized. She took a deep breath to calm herself.

'You okay, ma'am?' Harry asked.

She nodded and looked around for any whips or belts, but there were none. Either the police would find something in the search of the premises or the killer carried the tools of the trade with him. *Did the killer carry a briefcase around?* She saw the clothes that Anu Singh would have been wearing before the assailant stripped her. They would be collected, tagged, analysed and put into evidence. The bathroom drains were dismantled to see if the perpetrator had disposed of anything of consequence unwittingly, but they found nothing.

'No one in the neighbourhood heard any noise or saw anyone enter or exit the apartment; no strange vehicles had been parked in the vicinity; no strangers had been seen lurking …' said Shukla from the doorway of the bedroom. It was safe to assume the victim was tightly gagged throughout her ordeal. No doubt, the offender removed the gag after the woman died to put the lipstick on, and then took it away with him.

'The usual then? How does everyone in the city go blind to their surroundings when it's critical? On other occasions, tongues just can't stop wagging – whose wife was with whose husband at a party …' Rita scoffed. She wasn't talking about anyone in particular, just chattering to take her mind off the grisly spectacle before them. The naked body of Anu Singh lay exposed in plain sight. Death, especially a violent one, took away everything, including the person's dignity; never mind whether one was a common streetwalker or a respectable businesswoman. Anu Singh had just become another statistic in the police files.

'We'll get the killer this time, ma'am. No one, not even the devil himself, can be so thorough as to not leave one single tell-tale clue,' Harry sounded optimistic.

'Famous last words ... by the look of it, he's made a "clean" getaway at least twice before that we know of.'

The police had found previous two bodies in situations that suggested sex, but no semen had been recovered from the crime scene or in any of the victims' cavities. The killer had meticulously cleaned up after the deed leaving no spillage or clue whatsoever. Or maybe used a condom. At least the lubricant of a condom would be have shown up in postmortem if this ultra-cautious killer had penetrated an orifice. However, there was no sign at all of any kind of penetrative sex with the victims, which, albeit strange, wasn't unheard of. Twisted brains often found sexual gratification in the kill, rather than in the actual act. Anu Singh's autopsy would reveal if he had broken his pattern and provided his DNA.

The Medical Examiner and Crime Scene Unit still worked on the scene. Fingerprints were being dusted and the apartment was being thoroughly and minutely searched.

It would be a day or two before the complete reports came in.

'Dr Mehta, when do think Dr Khan will carry out the autopsy?' Rita asked the ME; she had worked with Dr Khan on a case previously.

'Later this afternoon, I think.'

'Ask someone to give my office a call please, one of us will attend the autopsy.'

'Yes, of course, Rita.'

'Thank you. Let's go,' she motioned Harry. 'Keep canvassing the area,' she instructed Shukla. 'We'll take over the case, but you're responsible for securing the scene of crime until you get further instructions. I suggest you ask two of your team members to stake the place for some time. Discreet, plainclothes. And please get the crime scene units to submit all reports as soon as they can.' She looked around one last time. Everyone moved in slow motion at a crime scene. It was a battle between time and precision. No one wanted to obliterate evidence and as a consequence, fuck up their career. Time, for once, was not a priority.

'Absolutely, ma'am.'

'And please, as soon as everything is documented, cover her up.'

Handshakes, salutes and then Rita and Harry were out of the apartment. It was 2.30 a.m.

THREE

Rita wondered whether there was any point in going home. There was little chance that she would get any sleep. In any case, she would have to return to work early to start the investigation and then attend the autopsy in the afternoon. Would it be better to go to the office now, get the ball rolling and then go home? This wouldn't be the first time she would have worked through the night.

'Where should I drop you?' she asked Harry, who looked wide awake too. Youth had its advantages, even if he was only five years her junior.

'Don't worry, ma'am, just drop me off anywhere on your way and I'll take a cab home.'

'I'm heading back to Crawford Market; I think I'll get started on this case.'

Crawford Market was one of the most prominent markets in South Mumbai. Named after the first municipal commissioner of Mumbai, Arthur Crawford, it was the first building in India to be lit by electricity. With so much halo and history, the area surrounding the market had come to be known as Crawford Market too. Mumbai Police headquarters was opposite the market square, and the top brass of the police force was based here. Crime Branch, too, was stationed here under the leadership of Vinay Joshi, Joint Commissioner of Police, Crime Branch. DCP Rita Ferreira was one of Joshi's direct reports.

'I'll come with you.'

'You don't have to ... I think you should go home, catch up on a few hours of sleep and return with a fresh mind in the morning.'

'It's already morning, ma'am, and I really want to be part of the investigation from the word go.'

'Okay, but let's stop somewhere on the way for a strong coffee.'

Mumbai is a city of many cities. It affords luxuries to its hard-working denizens that a lot of residents in other cities can only fantasize about. For starters, Mumbai is a 24/7 city. The elite can drive into a five-star hotel to a coffee shop and order a cappuccino at any part of the day or night in any major city. However, in Mumbai, even the roadside tea and coffee carts operate 24/7. Rita stopped at one of them and the two long arms of the law alighted, stretched, yawned and picked up coffees.

The coffee was dismally awful, but the caffeine kicked in strongly enough. Mission accomplished.

The office building was devoid of all life at this hour of the morning and an unnatural lull had settled on the precinct. No computers. No printers. No office staff. No chirping, no one gossiping. No humming of machines. No mingling whiffs of various deodorants and perfumes other than the lingering smell of stale food that the staff consumed during the day.

Rita had a small, utilitarian office on the first floor with a desk, a phone, a computer, a swivel chair behind the desk and two chairs for visitors. Upon a small sideboard perched her cafetière. She sat down and gestured to Harry to take a seat too.

'We need to set up an Operations Room. Up until now it was Jatin, but now that you've joined the team, the responsibility will be yours.'

Rita was particularly fastidious about the Ops Room from which the investigation was run. All the documents – evidence reports, witness statements, scene of crime photographs, every investigating individual's investigation logs and reports, and all the timelines – were held in the same place and made available to the team assigned to the project. Moreover, the person manning the Ops Room was also responsible for (a) the encryption and digitalization of information, (b) saving this to a common hard drive so the team could access to it from everywhere and (c) generating executive summaries for the powers-that-be.

'Thank you, ma'am.'

'Commandeer the large meeting room at the end of the corridor,' she indicated the left wall. 'Collate all the information we have on the two previous murders, and we'll add the reports we receive from Anu Singh's murder as the investigation progresses.' The summary reports from two previous police stations – that had investigated the past murders – were full of assumptions and conclusions that were bound to be flawed, but they still needed to be included.

Harry saluted her and left.

Rita brewed herself another coffee and sat down. Images of Anu Singh flashed across her mind: her pain, her fear and her violent death. Two other women had suffered the same fate before her but, as Rita hadn't been roped into the cases then, she hadn't seen their corpses first-hand; the previous two victims had come to her only as files, a series of numbers.

The pattern was unmistakable. It was the same twisted bastard, no doubt. But he seemed to have taken a leap now, brazen and immune to the risk of being discovered.

The incident at Dr Annie Besant Road had been different: although the modus operandi had been similar to the previous two incidents, the victim had been of a different profile. Mrs Anu Singh, whilst in the same age range and general physiognomy as the previous two homicides, ran a successful business and was married to a well-to-do management consultant, who had been out of the country on a business trip at the time of her murder. The two murdered hookers could have unwittingly picked up a client who was into sadomasochism and things could have inadvertently gotten out of hand. Possible. Prostitution was a flourishing, albeit ravening, racket. Only cash and no tax. Most upmarket escorts had pimps; they took their commission and vetted the clients. But self-employed hookers catered to the lower-to-middle end of the market. From everything Rita had gleaned from the files, both Gina and Radha had operated in that realm. The poor girls selling themselves had to make snap judgements at the kerb and unless the guy resembled devil, with gleaming red horns on his head, they would take on a complete stranger if the price was right. That made them easy targets. From the killer's perspective such self-operating hookers were low-risk. No one cared about these girls. Their families had disowned them long ago. The neighbours, if any, shunned them and wanted them out of the neighbourhood as soon as possible. With no one chasing them for a closure, the priorities of the police would have shifted to the next case even before the hapless girl's body was cold. These were girls the police and the rest of Mumbai had already given up on. It was easy to blame their deaths, their ugly end on kismet. Karma. The simplest explanation: they were hookers who picked the wrong client and things went out of control. It wasn't as if these women had deliberately opted for this profession over opportunities of becoming doctors or cricketers.

In retrospect, the local constabulary had categorized Gina and Radha as victims who had been in the wrong place at the wrong time and their deaths were pure happenstance; an occupational hazard.

Nevertheless, irrespective of their lifestyles and status in society, they had the right to justice. As one of Rita's favourite fictional characters – Michael Connelly's Harry Bosch – always said: '*either everyone matters or no one matters.*'

The attack on Anu Singh was definitely premeditated and targeted. Someone had fantasized about making out with her before offing her. Someone had lured her into being a victim of his lust and she had inadvertently signed her own death certificate. There was nothing random about this murder.

But Anu Singh's murder was the killer stepping out of his comfort zone.

He had upped his ante by moving south, indicating that it wasn't the just streetwalkers from suburbs that were at risk. Everyone in the poshest parts of Mumbai was too. This galvanized the forces of law and order. It would now be as high profile a case as could be. Serial killers were one of the most frightening of all criminals. They were psychopaths who selected their victims at random. The next one could be someone that one cared about, and that scared everyone for their wives and girlfriends and sisters.

Ironically, as in all other cases of serial killers across the globe, when the previous investigation had run dry, the Mumbai Police, too, had wanted their killer to strike again and slip up. This was in the hope that a victim could escape and report it, and provide evidence against the attacker. But it wasn't to be in this case. Regrettably, Anu Singh had succumbed to her assailant. Rita could only hope that there would be no more.

The fingers of dawn started to lift the blanket of night. Rita knew that the days ahead wouldn't afford much downtime. It was time to take a power nap and get ready to face another day. She checked in on Harry. He had started work in the Ops Room, but had eventually given in to sleep on four chairs aligned in a row.

Rita quietly shut the door and left the building. Thick grey clouds covered the sky. It was the lull before a storm; there was no wind at all and nothing moved. The monsoon had been sporadic this season, with the heat and humidity unprecedented for this time of the year in Mumbai. Rita could feel the perspiration trickle down her back and between her breasts. It was coming to twenty-four hours in the same clothes that, besides the sweat and grime, had the pervasive odour of death clinging to them. A cold shower was long overdue. As was sleep.

As she drove to her apartment in Bandra, her thoughts returned to Anu Singh. What if – a worm of anxiety slowly but surely unfurled in her brain – what if it was no more than a simple case of 'wife murder'? It wasn't beyond the scope of possibility. Yes, it was evident – given the parallels – that the three homicides were, on the surface, the work of the same person. However, nothing said that Shekhar Singh couldn't be the one they were looking for, although it would be too easy if he were. Then again, it wasn't something unheard of. Kill one or two females in the same fashion before offing your wife and the police would never suspect you. Isn't that what Jeff Bridges had done in the film *Jagged Edge* – disposed of a female in the same manner much earlier, and hence the whole case swerved in his favour on the single premise that he couldn't have been the one? He fooled his own defence lawyer with his clever ploy and almost got away until Glenn Close pulled down the curtain.

Of course, Shekhar Singh had an alibi, and that alibi needed to be checked.

She thought of calling Harry, but remembered he was sleeping. For all she knew, if she woke him up he might come out with some rude idiom. She smiled as she drove into her apartment block on Linking Road. She sat in the car and typed an email message to him instead: *We need all intelligence on the victim's husband. Travel, financial, extramarital activities ... etc., etc., first thing when you wake up.*

Rita's apartment was a brighter version of a Scandinavian furniture catalogue. While all the inside walls were ivory, one of the larger ones in the rectangular living room was painted blue to add a splash of colour. The living room was the only one carpeted wall-to-wall, since she was a music junkie like her father, and music sounded better when it didn't deflect off bare flooring. The apartment had minimalistic furniture with two single mattresses stacked together to serve as a divan and the large cushions casually and tastefully strewn on the mattress-on-the-floor seating made it appear colourful and comfortable. At the far end of the room, the wide French window opened into a small balcony. Customized shelves filled with vinyl records – mostly from her father's collection – adorned more than half the wall facing the blue wall. The other shelves on the wall contained paperbacks bought with unfulfilled intentions to read, as she never found the time to do so. Sandwiched between the two shelves was her most prized possession: a 1980's Bang and

Olufsen stacker – record, CD, cassette player and the amp – also her father's. There weren't any pretty pictures of her, just one of her parents next to her music player. She extracted *Sketches of Spain*, gave the vinyl a wipe and put it on. Miles Davis' *Concierto de Aranjuez* came alive as she took off her clothes and carried them into the bedroom.

As she showered, she acknowledged she could only clean her physical self from the residue of the murder; her mind continued to dwell on the case. She couldn't imagine how the paths of two hookers, who operated at the lower-to-middle spectrum of the sex-trade ladder, would have crossed with a well-to-do boutique owner. For that matter, there had been no evidence in the files to suggest that even Gina and Radha knew each other or were in any way connected. Gina and Radha operated in different geographies: Kandivali and Andheri were separated by ten kilometres. It wasn't like there was some 'Hookers' Club' where the two socialized over a drink to exchange client info. But there had to be a common denominator between the two prostitutes and Anu. Logically, the predator and prey had to come together somewhere before the hunt began. There just had to be an intersection point somewhere. But the question was: *where*? And how soon could they find the connection, and catch the killer – by police definition: any unknown, unidentified killer was generally assumed to be a male until they had reason to believe otherwise – who had cold-bloodedly killed the vulnerable women. In any event, the corpses in these particular cases exhibited every sign of being the work of a male, but that constituted almost half of Mumbai's population. Or if one assumed the population to be composed of four-person households with one male being a child, it was still twenty-five per cent of Mumbai's twenty million. Also, at present, there was no evidence to prove that the killer was not an inhabitant of the city – someone who took the train in, stalked and killed his victims, and took the train out. For now, everything she had added up to zilch.

The iPhone chimed earlier than she had anticipated. It wasn't the alarm she had requested Siri to add; it was an incoming call. Still dazed from exhaustion and lack of sleep, she answered the call, without looking at the caller ID.

'Sleeping late or waiting for me in bed, sweetheart?' Ash Mattel aka Ashwin Mittal, had, after a long battle with autocorrect, thrown in the towel and anglicized his name. He was a psychiatrist by profession and helped the Metropolitan Police in New Scotland Yard with the profiling of criminals. Ash, it seemed, also had a doctorate in cheesy one-liners that had put off Rita initially, but she had gradually come to accept this shortcoming. He was the *part-time* she had mentioned to Harry. Ash and Rita had been together at St Stephen's, Delhi, for one year before he left to study medicine at Cambridge. They didn't know each other well while in college, but at a chance reunion during one of his trips to India, while Rita was in the middle of a difficult case, he had officially helped her to profile a criminal. He had remembered her from their college days as the girl in the black bikini at the pool, and she remembered him as the guy who had dropped out of the graduation course. They hit it off and caught up every time Ash was in the country. He was divorced. Rita and Ash were good friends and had made a marriage pact to wed if they found themselves still single when they got to forty. For the time being they were happy to continue as friends with benefits. Ash Mattel was tall, balding and manly with flaring nostrils like a horse. The only way to describe him was by the oxymoron ugly-handsome. He looked more like Amrish Puri than a doctor, yet there was a certain something about him that Rita found incredibly attractive. He was Mr Charming when it came to words, whether cheesy or classy.

From the quietness in the background, Rita surmised that Ash was in his hotel room and not an airport lobby. He had been a gentleman and waited until it was daylight in India before calling her. Little did he know that the new case had altered Rita's sleeping schedule.

'Hi Ash, I got home very late last night,' she said groggily, adding, 'in fact, it was five this morning when I came in.'

'Oh, partying without me, are we?'

'Naw. I had something important to attend to.' Rita sat up in bed. The time on her bedside clock showed 8.57 a.m.

'Is there someone more important than me?' Mr Cheesy carried on.

'Yes.'

'Who?'

'Everyone.'

'Touché. Is the subject of your attention dead or alive?'

'You're dead right; it is a murder case.'

'Can I be of any help?'

Ash had a security clearance from Mumbai Police; he had worked on cases in India before. He was listed as one of the official consultants although he didn't charge for his services. He could anonymously use the gen gained here to solve cases at other places. Quantico had recently added him to their list of criminal profiling advisors, so Ash was also working for the FBI in the United States of America.

'Actually, you can. Where can I fax you the details?'

In the age of high-speed internet connections, most people wondered who used facsimile. However, an old-fashioned fax machine was still considered one of the safest mediums of electronic communications. A photograph of a sheet of paper transmitting through telephone cables had the least chances of being intercepted or diverted.

'Let me find a secure line and call you back.'

'When are you coming to Mumbai?'

'I'll be with you on the sixth. And then I'm all yours.'

Four days to go, Rita mentally calculated.

INTERLUDE
Summer 1994

The past year had been extremely frustrating. My body grew bigger, my voice deepened and I sprouted disgusting hair everywhere. The admiration I had for the boy in the mirror started to dissipate with the new hirsute image. I felt I was losing control of my body and its functions. At times, erections happened several times a day for no apparent reason. On other days, when I wanted one, I simply couldn't get it up. As puberty set in, I found to my consternation that my bed and underpants were wet again in the mornings but figured – after reading up about this phenomenon in the library – that what I'd had was called a nocturnal emission, or wet dream. Reading about puberty provided me insight into masturbation. It was a true awakening, but a catalogue of unanswered questions accompanied it. Was it the right thing? Was I doing it right? Did others do it too? Did girls ...? I was self-conscious and more nervous when there were girls around. I wondered whether girls grew unwanted hair as well, and if they did, where this grew, as they didn't appear to have any on their faces or visible body parts.

Then the summer holidays started.

Summer had been unusually hot with temperatures touching forty-plus degrees centigrade. After ten in the morning, a forlorn kenopsia prevailed across the streets and the apartment complex where we lived. Most working people had left by then and the kids – the socially inclined ones – congregated at each other's houses to play indoors. It made me wonder at the sadistic attitude of schools, ending the annual sessions at the height of summer, when we couldn't enjoy life half as much as we could have, had the break been in mid-winter. But it was moot for me. The other kids in the apartment block – they belonged to various schools – had stopped asking me to join them after their initial approaches were thwarted by my less-than-pleasant rebuffs.

We lived in South Delhi on the first floor of a vast apartment complex. It had four units on each floor of the five-storeyed block. The smaller blocks in the complex had more apartments per floor. My parents had, at the right time, bought a large three-bedroomed flat with a large balcony that could be accessed from the living room. The balcony could easily accommodate a single bed, but ours only had a wicker two-seater, clothing rails and some potted plants. The balconies of two adjacent apartments were so close that one could easily jump across the three-foot parapet to get into the neighbour's balcony.

The apartment next to ours had been left unoccupied for a month. The new neighbours moved in just as the summer break began and my life changed forever. They were a young couple. Tina and Kapil Aggarwal. They introduced themselves in the common area by the landing on our floor. Kapil was twenty-five or so, and he sold computers for a company. He was a mousy character, his face the colour of Assam tea and his hair a strong Americano – obviously hennaed for some reason; perhaps he had greyed prematurely. Tina, his wife, was a stunning twenty-three old made in the same mould as my gorgeous mother. The similarities were stark: petite and shapely. As I would find out soon enough, their similarities didn't conclude on the physical front. Their personalities and carnal appetites were identical as well. Their mutual dislike for each other was instantaneous. Civil hellos were exchanged. And that was it. Dad once asked whether we should do the neighbourly thing and invite our new neighbours over for tea and snacks to welcome them, but the idea was quickly quashed at the dining table. And that was that. Dad didn't raise the topic again. Tina wasn't coming to our place

Tina was a sizzler. She wore shorts to beat the summer and her legs were as unblemished as her face, with skin like porcelain. I caught my father stealing a look at her every once in a while whenever we bumped into them in the common areas or on the staircase and Tina's eyes stayed on my father a tad longer than I'd have expected. I could sense my mother's hackles rise. My parents were spoiling for a fight, but it never happened in my presence. I was already five-four and bigger than her, but Tina completely ignored me – the adolescent with the obnoxious peach fuzz and acne.

I could see why she had that massive chip on her shoulder; she was aware of the effect she had on men. She had a thin, high-cheekboned, oval face with big brown eyes, an aquiline nose and shoulder-length, straight coffee-brown hair.

I could never look straight at her for fear of uttering something stupid. She was so slender that I was confident I could easily lift her in my arms. Or at least I thought I could. Or maybe imagined. The problem was, every thought of her body was so dang exciting that I lost control of the new-found hardening between my legs. She knew she was gorgeous and hence, the conceit. Maybe she thought she had the power. She was captivating enough to have a hold over men, who'd come dribbling if she as much as gave them a hint. Looking down at others came naturally to her. Perhaps she was born into money and regretted having married a loser of a guy. I encountered her twice during their first week in the building and although I made an effort to give her a smile and say 'hi', she didn't even acknowledge my presence. Her attitude towards me was frosty, uninterested. I wasn't on her radar. She mostly wore short skirts or shorter hot pants. Her full lips were always painted dark crimson and she had a habit of running her tongue on her bottom lip, like she was licking her own lipstick and enjoying it. Perhaps, if some prey didn't get attracted to her body enough, her pout could complete the seduction. Or perhaps lipstick was a tasty thing.

The truth about Tina emerged in the following weeks.

She was a social butterfly. Although she hadn't been born into money, she had a knack of attracting it by cuckolding her pitiable geek of a husband. He left home at around eight-thirty every morning and some 'guest' dropped by to see her around ten. The guests – and I had started recognizing three of them by now – all appeared well-to-do, middle-aged men who were either malingering or had flexible working hours. Most days, whoever turned up stayed until late afternoon. There were even times when she hosted two guests – one in the morning, one in the afternoon, but they were always out by four. Perhaps she needed time to clean up before Kapil returned; perhaps she needed the time to recuperate.

The common wall between the apartments wasn't as soundproof as Tina would have liked to believe. Either that or she didn't know I was home. Or possibly, she didn't give a rat's arse about me. I had enough sense to understand what the men were coming for. I deduced what was happening next door, but I did not tell my parents. At any rate what would I have told my mother? That she now had competition in the building?

I was fortunate I wasn't a cat, because my curiosity had started getting the better of me.

FOUR

The Operations Room was all set by the time Rita arrived at work around noon. A detailed map of Mumbai was up on the wall with red drawing pins stuck into three places: Kandivali, Andheri and Worli. The police had let three women down, but she knew she had to park that guilt and move on. More drawing pins were in the little metal box on an open shelf beside the map. Rita prayed that no more pins made it onto the map. Photographs of three young women stared at her, asking for justice. As always there were two sets of pictures of each victim. Before the event and after their life had been snuffed out. Harry must have woken up early and taken a shower somewhere. He looked rejuvenated; he smelt like mint bubblegum. Vikram and Jatin were present as well. Although they hadn't worked through the night, they appeared to be nursing hangovers from the previous night's party. Jatin seemed glad that the task of setting up and managing the Ops Room had been assigned to Harry. It was understandable because although it provided a lot of exposure to the case, but it was grunt work managing all the reports, documents and information pouring in from various sources. Harry seemed eminently capable of handling this side of the work. The team was quickly reassembling, barely a day after Nene's retirement. People left. People joined. Life and solving crimes went on unchanged.

Good mornings were voiced and the four of them settled down. Harry had already updated the other two about the homicide Rita and he had attended the night before.

'We need to split up. The two important things for us to focus on at present are Anu Singh's autopsy and meeting Shekhar Singh,' Rita started.

Vikram pulled out his pad and jotted it down. His was a methodical personality. He always made notes and a task list. He wouldn't rest until he ticked everything off his to-do list. The other two nodded.

'Harry, anything on Shekhar Singh?'

'The Immigration authorities have confirmed he flew out to London on the morning of 30 June. The same evening, his wife was murdered. The rest of the information is being looked into. We should have a file on him by this evening.'

'When does he return?'

'Late tonight.'

'Please ask someone to let him know that he cannot stay at his apartment. He should either put up at a friend's place or check into a hotel. Should he require something from the apartment for immediate use, a police officer should escort him there and make a note of the things he takes.' During evidence collection all crime scenes became sacred monuments; taped and sealed until all alien fibres, fluids or hair were collected and tagged. The investigation only shifted to the labs for analysis post that. 'We'll see him tomorrow morning. Face to face.'

Interviewing a person of interest in a murder investigation on the phone was out of question. Rita Ferreira was a trained IPS Officer who understood that cross-examining someone meant looking beyond the verbal response. The science of kinesics looked at the triumvirate of actual words spoken, the delivery of those words – voice modulation, the unwarranted pauses – and facial expressions that were part of the body language. A telephonic conversation bypassed the vital last factor which was critical in spotting a lie or omission.

Vikram scratched on his pad.

'Anyone wants to volunteer to attend the autopsy?' Rita asked. It was one of the most despised of all tasks, but it had to be done. Sometimes the dead spoke through the morbid pathologists and cracked the case.

Vikram looked at Jatin who looked at Harry who looked back at Rita.

'I'll go,' said Vikram.

'I was only checking; I'll attend the autopsy, *alone*,' she emphasized, 'this afternoon whenever Dr Khan is ready. Jatin, you chase the forensics and scene of crime teams about all the samples that have been collected. Tell them this is a priority, so they had better start moving fast and Harry, you focus on building Shekhar's résumé. Vikram and I will interview him tomorrow. All clear?'

Nods.

Interviewing someone was best carried out in the presence of two people. This was stipulated in the police manual for a whole variety of reasons: two people could spot a liar better, two people could control a conversation better, two people made a better testimony if and when required. Moreover, Vikram could take notes better than anyone Rita knew.

'Anything unearthed from canvassing the area so far?'

'Yes, ma'am.' Harry pulled out a sheet and summarized. 'Although Anu and Shekhar Singh had been living in the apartment block for almost five years, some of the residents didn't know them or each other.'

The snobbery of high society, Rita sighed.

'The landlord of the shop where Anu Singh had her boutique had only good things to say about her. Her customers liked her. There had been no complaints about her by any of her neighbours. She came to the boutique on most days, but there were days she'd go to see designers, so if she didn't turn up to work on a particular day the staff weren't too perturbed. She had no boyfriends or extramarital affairs that were likely to pop out of the closet; nothing insalubrious to dig into.

In any case, an illicit liaison or two didn't warrant a reason to off her.

'Did anyone see any anybody lurking around, a strange car parked in the vicinity while the killer cased the place?'

'No one remembers seeing any skulking strangers.'

This didn't necessarily mean that the neighbours had been unobservant. The killer could have been cunning enough to appraise Anu and the place two, maybe three, weeks prior to the murder. Who would remember a strange car parked three weeks ago? No one. Most people struggled to recollect the clothes they had worn last Monday, so what were the odds they would remember seeing a stranger loitering around weeks before the incident? Nary a chance. Added to the mix was the fact that the person they were looking for wasn't a Grade-A idiot who would have recced the place conspicuously.

'We'll get this bastard, ma'am.'

Rita raised her eyebrows at Jatin.

'Did I say something wrong, ma'am?'

'No. I mean, there isn't another word for this sick fucker, but we should be consistent in how we refer to him, don't you think?' The question was for everybody in the room.

'What else should we call an unidentified subject?'

'*Unsub*? In most parts of the world, the unidentified subject is referred to as an *unsub* until the name is discovered.'

'Unsub it is then,' Vikram said.

'Oh, and before I forget, please fax all details to the attention of Mr Mattel in Delhi. He's on his way to Mumbai to assist us with the profiling of the unsub.' Rita handed the number to Harry.

'Will do.'

'Okay then, let's look at the map,' Rita pointed to the map of Mumbai on the wall.

Kandivali, Andheri, Worli.

Approximately twenty million people lived in Mumbai. The math was hardly any help.

Although theories and statistics could sometimes be an exercise in futility, Rita & Co. didn't have much else to go on at the moment so they rehashed theories and statistics. It was common knowledge that most unsubs did not operate in the vicinity of their homes. It was too much of a risk. Someone might see them; recognize them. There was a possibility that the police doing house-to-house canvassing in the area might chance upon them, and their guilt – however well-guarded – might raise some kind of suspicion. By all accounts, Rita and the team knew this was a careful killer with an above-average IQ; most serial killers were sharp people, and to have got away so cunningly with three murders was in itself a testament to his intelligence. Would he make the mistake of picking up his prey in an area that could lead back to him? Highly improbable.

Then again, how far would someone go to kill so he could get away cleanly?

Kandivali was approximately ten kilometres from Andheri. Andheri was twenty-five kilometres from Worli, and Worli thirty-five from Kandivali.

Nothing gave.

If the unsub was even five kilometres south of Worli, it would mean a trip of over forty kilometres, which, although not impossible, wasn't likely either. It wasn't just getting to the place and enacting the fantasy, it was also about returning. The unsub being in the north of Worli made more sense. For now. However, there was no science to it.

'He could be on the other line?' Jatin pointed out as they debated.

Mumbai's local metro service comprises two heart lines: Western and Central. The three murders thus far had occurred in areas through which the Western line passed. Although there was little chance that the unsub used local trains as his mode of transport, it was an insight that the unsub was familiar with or closer to the Western line, unless he went out of his way looking for victims. Which, of course, could well be the case.

'I agree,' Rita admitted. 'I was acting on a hunch, but I guess it's too early to zero in. Let's not jump the gun.'

Which was wise. Statistically, more investigations were bungled by misinformation rather than no information. A dog on a wrong scent was worse off than a dog waiting for some scent to go after.

'Serial killer surely,' Joint Commissioner of Police, Crime Branch, Mr Vinay Joshi, was the master of stating the obvious. He was a gangling man, almost bald and looked more like a professor than a policeman. Rita always wondered if he was the person Hergé had had in mind when he sketched Professor Calculus. If he was, Hergé had certainly got it right except for the height, as Joshi was far taller than his immortalized caricature. On the surface, Joshi seemed pliable and laid-back, but Rita had known him to be an obstinate mule on occasion. For the most part, he let all his reports believe they were taking the decisions, and it worked in his favour. Rita had never met anyone in the force who had a negative word to say against Joshi.

'Yes, sir.'

'We must tell the commissioner; this is a high-profile case. He must know we are on it before a journalist or some minister calls him for comments.'

'That's precisely why I came to see you, sir. I wanted to update you and Commissioner Saxena about the investigations that are underway even as we speak. We need to brief him so he can handle the media.'

'Good, but Commissioner Saxena isn't in today. Ask my secretary to book time in his diary for tomorrow morning, first thing, please.'

'Will do, sir.'

'Have a good day, DCP Ferreira.' Joshi took a sip of water from the glass on his large desk.

'And sir, Mr Mattel is in India and he has agreed to help us once again.'

'Oh good, he's a bright boy.'

Boy? she chuckled to herself. She wanted to be sure the top brass was with her to use an external consultant. No point in being caught under the fan should the shit hit it. If Ash didn't have clearance to access classified information, Joshi would have certainly objected.

'Good day, sir.'

FIVE

Death is inevitable, but there is no discounting the fact that the angel of death robbed people of all that they ever stood for in their lives, stripped them of all respect and reduced them to the lowest common denominator. Some people could get a better funeral than others but the fact remained: they were dead. For some, like Anu Singh, it was so much more; not only had she been violated and murdered in the most excruciating manner, she suffered the ultimate humiliation of being stripped of her name and given a number instead: J-137/3. Rita had been around long enough to know that *life wasn't fair*. If you've been wronged by life, you'd have to be naïve to think it owed you. It didn't. But as Whitney said, '*it's not right, but it's okay …*'

Anu Singh's cold body lay on an even colder steel gurney, naked, cleaned and prepared for dissection when Rita entered the autopsy suite minutes before 4 p.m. When she had come out of the meeting with Vinay Joshi there was a message for her that Dr Syed Khan, Director of Morbid Pathology, Jamshedjee Jeejeebhoy Post-Mortem Centre in Byculla – a lab leading in homicide postmortems – was waiting for her, ready to begin the postmortem on J-137/3.

It took thirty minutes to travel the four kilometres to the lab. She could have stayed put in her ivory tower and delegated this unpleasant task to any one of the three men in her team who would have done all the legwork without a question. But Rita was unlike other high officials. She was, at heart, still an investigator and she had, in candid social conversations with her friends and colleagues, often mentioned that if she were ever deputed to a totally administrative position, she'd decline even if that cost her a promotion. Or she'd quit and become a stripper. Okay, the last part was said in frivolous conversation and after a few drinks. She wasn't in it for the money anyway. This was her calling.

'Hi Rita.' Dr Khan was an avuncular older gentleman who loved his job and was happiest when he was working on a cadaver. *My patients never complain*, he quipped frequently. He was exceptionally tall and towered over most people. Although his broad shoulders had only just begun to droop with age, he was still athletically built, salt and pepper hair swept back from a wide forehead over a beak of a nose and a square chin that classified him as classically handsome. Patriarchal. Crow's feet had started appearing, but they added to, rather than diminished from his appeal.

'Your timing is impeccable Rita,' Dr Khan looked up as she walked in. Having spent more than thirty years in this job and spearheading the department for nearly a decade, he had conducted more autopsies than anyone could keep a count of and had provided testimonies on numerous cases. He had worked with Rita on several occasions before and chatted with easy familiarity.

Rita and Dr Khan had already donned their disposable surgical scrub suits and facemasks. An intern, who Dr Khan introduced as Mini, joined them to assist the doctor. She murmured *hello* to Rita and immediately got engrossed in preparing for the procedure.

Dr Khan scanned beneath the nails of the stiff. No sign of skin scrapes, no blood, no trace evidence. Then, in one clean motion, he emotionlessly made the preliminary Y-incision that extended from the neck down to the pubis to expose the chest and abdomen cavities that God had so marvellously designed to enclose the heart, lungs, kidneys, intestines …

For the next two hours, he plied his scalpels, knives and surgical blades to make further incisions in the cadaver, inserted retractors to spread the cavities open and used forceps to extract the woman's insides. He poked into her intestines, bowels, kidneys and whatnots while murmuring into his dictaphone all the while. Intermittently, he looked at Rita and crinkled his eyes in a smile, requested Santa's Little Helper, Mini, for other implements, but chiefly concentrated on the task at hand. The stench was unbearable despite the heavy formalin and smell of other disinfectants in the air. The visual was no better, and although Rita had been through this exercise several times before, one could never really get hardened to this.

Dr Khan had once explained to Rita that an autopsy was no different from a surgeon performing a procedure on a live patient; the only difference being the surgeon had severe time constraints – for example, the anaesthesia could run out; but in his case, Dr Khan had no such pressure. J-137/3 wasn't waking up.

Eventually, after he was done, Dr Khan left the cadaver to be closed by Mini and gestured for Rita to walk out with him.

'There's nothing of consequence,' he said when the two sat down in his comfortable consulting room.

She waited for the doc to continue. A homicide shattered all illusions of privacy and personal space. One's entire life became public knowledge as soon as the investigators dug into one's past in pursuance of justice. Didn't someone say, justice was a double-edged sword? A murder exposed your life and innards to the doctor. In any event, the knife always hurt before it could cure.

'It's exactly as it appears. The time of death was close to midnight. The cause of death was asphyxiation casued by strangulation: the victim, J-137/3, was choked by the tightening of the leather belt found around her neck.' Dr Khan had once confessed to Rita that he always referred to his patients by number to depersonalize them; it made his task somewhat easier. Numbers provided the detachment essential in this line of work. 'The supply of oxygen was cut off,' he elaborated, 'as the carotid arteries were squeezed. No toxins or any kind of poisons were found in the body, so I can rule out that the subject was drugged. Yes, she had consumed a few drinks a couple of hours before she died. Blood alcohol concentration was in the range of 0.12, which would definitely bar her from driving, but wasn't a level to render her comatose. I'd say she would have been a bit uninhibited and bolshie, but certainly not unconscious. Not even close—'

'But there's a possibility that she'd have made the mistake of opening the door to a complete stranger?'

'Unquestionably. However, if, as I'm told, she lived in an apartment block with a buzzer at the ground level to admit visitors, why would she? Think about it – how could a stranger go up to her floor without someone letting him into the building in the first place? He couldn't have just walked in and rung the doorbell.' Dr Khan, having worked with the police for several decades, had become more than half a detective himself.

'That's what's bothering us. We've checked with all residents and no one let a stranger into the apartment between the hours of nine and six in the morning. No one. Which leaves only the victim who could have let her own murderer in. Or someone had the keys. Anyway, that's our headache, not yours. Sorry, you were saying ...'

'The victim was gagged. Traces of white fabric have been found on her jaw and chin. The chronology is: the murderer violated her body before killing her. The lips were bleached, almost certainly burnt postmortem.'

'Was the lipstick eaten before or after the violation?'

'I can't tell you that, but I can tell you that the presence of blood in the abrasions on the lips proves that her heart was still pumping and she was very much alive when her lips were bitten off.'

'Any signs that he had penetrated her sexually?'

'No. No semen or residue of condom lubrication in the vaginal vault or in the rectum or in the stomach. All negative. Her insides are lacerated and a mess, since he tortured her with a hairbrush and a metal iron.' Dr Khan detailed the various abrasions in her vaginal and rectal cavities. Both had been forcefully penetrated with hard objects, inflicted ante-mortem, while the victim was bound and gagged but alive. She must have gone through hell before she was killed. Capillaries in the eyes had burst, a clear consequence of garrotting.

Rita could feel the rage building in her. The killer had not only desecrated a woman, he had also inflicted agonizing pain on her. 'When the gag was taken off, why didn't she scream?'

'Perhaps she did but was barely audible since his mouth was on hers. Or perhaps he had held her at gunpoint or knifepoint,' the doctor opined. 'Perhaps she was plain exhausted by that point to resist any further.'

Rita was clearly at a loss for coherent words.

'My opinion, purely assumption, however, I'd say your perpetrator practises what is called *asphyxiophilia*, also known as erotic asphyxiation. Medically speaking, when a person's carotid arteries are being crushed, the deficiency of oxygen and overabundance of carbon dioxide, which heightens the light-headedness, which makes the "gasper" highly sensitive to pleasure.'

'You're kidding me.'

'I'm surprised that you didn't know this ...'

'And I should know that because?'

'You're an educated police officer, a woman of this world, so ...'

'But why—'

'Why should you know this?'

'No, why should anyone do that?'

'Simple. I just told you it heightens the pleasure of the orgasms.'

'Wait a minute! Who gets the pleasure here?'

'The "gasper", the person struggling to breathe, the recipient.'

'Are you saying the victim here let our killer asphyxiate her for pleasure?'

'As I said, it's only a hypothesis, but it's entirely possible, although it could also be the other way around. The killer orgasms as he watches a woman struggle and gasp.'

'Did you find anything on the victim's body that could belong to the killer? Blood, sweat, hair, anything?' All the police needed was one molecule of evidence, although tracing the killer on the basis of DNA from the scene of the crime would be like seeking the proverbial needle in a haystack. Whose DNA would they compare it with? One needed a suspect first.

'Nothing.'

'What about the bite marks?'

'We have them on record as in the previous two cases, but where is the database of dental records to compare them to anything?'

'But could you match these to the two previous cases that I mentioned?'

'I can and I will. The comparison will be in my report.'

'What about any foreign body hair?'

'None.'

'How is it even possible for a man to engage in physical activity and not shed a single hair?'

'Perhaps he wore a mask to cover his face and hair. I'm sorry, but there's nothing that we recovered from any of the three women's bodies that wasn't their own. I will naturally send everything to the forensic lab for further tests, but I wouldn't hold my breath.'

Rita scowled, clenching her fists in frustration.

'I'll send you a detailed report by tomorrow.'

'Thank you, Dr Khan.'

'I won't say "anytime". It can't be a pleasure seeing dead bodies.'

Frustration and fury ate into Rita as her chauffeur took her home. Her worry wasn't unfounded. She knew they weren't dealing with a moron who'd have left any evidence behind. If there wasn't even a follicle of his hair found on the victim whom he had assaulted for hours, what were the chances that he'd have left any prints on the door? However, she hoped that there was something he had slipped up on in this case, otherwise she would have to hope for a slip-up at a future crime scene, which was not desirable because it meant another victim. The investigating team couldn't just sit around waiting forever for the killer to make a mistake when the Machiavellian criminal hadn't made any so far in the three homicides. At this rate, it might even take ten more corpses before the degenerate bungled and left a clue! Not acceptable. They needed to go over everything all over again. Something somewhere had surely been missed. The challenge she had was that her team hadn't investigated the initial two murders first-hand; all they had were handover notes of evidence and analyses from the investigations conducted by the local precincts. Something could have fallen through the cracks and, in light of the recent murder of a high-profile businesswoman, Anu Singh, it would be hard to explain the killer's rationale to the press and the public. As far as the taxpayers were concerned, it didn't matter who had bungled the investigation – either the killer had been caught or was still at large.

Not the best situation to be in, she knew.

The killer's astuteness stunned her nevertheless. Three murders, three victims and not a single clue! A lot of reports still had to come in. Could they get lucky soon?

Fat chance, she muttered.

The new theory of erotic asphyxiation needed to be explored. Did the victims derive a perverse pleasure from being forced to play an erotic game?

With the theory she had gleaned from reading up on both fiction and real cases, Rita knew that sexual gratification was as intrinsic to serial killers as breathing. In the current case, too, they had sufficient evidence to support that premise. All three victims had been discovered in settings that suggested sexual fantasy. However, the absence of semen was an anomaly. Either the killer was extremely careful, or his fulfilment didn't involve ejaculation like normal men. She chuckled at her own stupidity: what was 'normal' about a killer who ate lipstick off dying women's lips anyway?

What had attracted this psychopath to these three women? Could it be the way they dressed? The way they walked? Who they met? Or simply the colour of lipstick they put on – if they put it on themselves. The forensics would report on the make of Anu Singh's lipstick later. The maniac who they hunted clearly had a predilection for a shade of lipstick. Why? They didn't know yet, but she reckoned that the moment they figured out how the killer shortlisted his victims, they'd be halfway there.

'Ma'am.'

Rita hadn't realized that she had shut her eyes and completely zoned out, thinking and devising how to get ahead of the killer. Kuldeep had driven through the gates of her apartment block and had stopped. She alighted, thanked him and looked around. The sun had already set, but there was still a little daylight. The moon had made an appearance, a waxing one-quarter; it would be a dark night, only slightly brighter than the night of the murder.

She doffed her clothes, stepped into the shower and let the grime of the day wash off. As she dried her long hair, she cogitated on the murderer's psychotic fascination for erasing lipstick from his victims' lips with his teeth. What was that about? Was there some significance to the macabre ritual that she hadn't been able to put a finger on? Only one thing was certain: the killer had to be psychotic to deliberately enter Crime Branch's backyard and rattle their cage.

Logging on to her computer she looked up 'erotic asphyxiation'. It was indeed practised by kinky pleasure seekers. She spent the next half an hour going through the details before logging out. She would ask someone in the office to research it in more detail. To her, it somehow didn't correspond with the tastes of the persona of Anu Singh, but what did she know yet? Perhaps, although the killer was kinky, that did not mean that the hapless victim was aberrant as well. Perhaps the killer took inordinate risks to satisfy his sadistic nature. Psychopaths weren't wired to feel fear; their deep-rooted personality disorder blinded them to the threat they posed and were equally uncaring of being unmasked. Rita had apprehended enough killers to know that murderers were phlegmatic towards their victims or crimes.

Rita walked into the living room, flipped the vinyl she was playing yesterday to listen to side B and kissed Jim. Her father had been a social Scotch drinker until the alcohol started corroding his insides. She had promised herself that she would never let that happen to her and had cleverly found a way around this by imbibing, but not Scotch. She knew she was fooling no one but herself; Jim Beam was her poison. She drained a quick one, and refilled. On an empty stomach, Jim descended and sluiced straight into her bloodstream, giving her head a jolt of lightness. *The Pan Piper* sounded even better. It was vastly different from Miles Davis's previous music. This had a distinctive Spanish influence. She called Ash, but the call didn't connect. Surprisingly there hadn't been any call from Ash, which was wholly unlike him. She sent him a text: *call me when you have a moment, even if it's late*, and walked into the kitchen to check for food in the refrigerator. Nothing. Not even eggs. She shut the refrigerator, selected a home-delivery menu stuck on its door with a magnet and called for a pizza.

Rita was still up, reading notes on the previous murders when Ash called around eleven.

'My apologies, I didn't realize the workshop would be so exhausting. The team curating it seems to have overloaded the agenda for today's programme. The session only finished at 9.30 and then we had dinner.'

'That's okay; the workshop was what you travelled all this distance for.'

'No, the workshop is what is paying for the trip. I've travelled all this way just to steal a kiss.'

'Yeah, right. On a serious note, Ash, did you receive the fax?'

'Yes, I did. But I haven't had the chance to look at it. If today's agenda is any indication of tomorrow's, I doubt I'll be able to read and digest what your office has sent me.'

'How long will you be here in Mumbai?'

'As long as you want me to, sweetheart. If you pull out that black bikini you wore in college, I swear I'll send in my resignation—'

'Stop it.' With years of practice, Rita had learnt how to get Mr Cheesy back on track.

'Why? Have you lost the top of the bikini? I'm okay with it if you only wear the bottom—'

'I need you to look into the documents on the flight to Mumbai. And please keep a few days free to go through it with us.'

'I'll even keep the nights free for you ...'

SIX

In her usual gear, a fitted white shirt tucked into jeans and her trusty Smith and Wesson in a shoulder holster under a light cotton jacket, Rita was bright and early into the office to meet the commissioner along with Joshi. But when she got there, Joshi had left her a message that he'd be late, and she should go ahead without him. It was already 9.30 a.m. How late was late for Joshi? It was clear he had wanted to avoid the meeting. Joshi never confronted; he simply avoided situations. She knew perfectly well why he had evaded this particular meeting. If Rita proposed a press conference to update the media about the recent murders, Joshi would want no part in it. Either the commissioner faced the media or delegated it to Rita.

So be it, she thought as she waited to be called in.

Commissioner of Police, Mumbai, Sanjay Saxena or *Sexy* for the rank and file – obviously in absentia – was stylish and old school. He had studied in the Doon School and his English teacher, it seemed, had focussed too much on his vocabulary, perhaps made him learn the entire dictionary by heart. He was born into a wealthy business family and socialized with the *who's who* of Mumbai. He was a scratch golfer and every moment away from the office was spent at the golf course. Always attired like he was meeting Jennifer Aniston for lunch, he looked more like a classy villain from a James Bond film.

Rita knocked and walked in at the appointed hour, 10 a.m.

Compared to the decor in Sexy's aesthetically appointed office, Rita's seemed practical and cheap. The desk and the wing chair behind it were quietly elegant and very masculine. The large L-shaped sofa for visitors and informal meetings had a glass-topped, heavy wooden coffee table in front of it. The carpet was soft and muffled the footsteps, so as to not break his concentration when practising his golf drives. The small putting set with two putters and several balls occupied a corner. He practised during his downtime, which was whenever he didn't have visitors. Five out of eight hours he was in the office.

'Hello Rita,' he greeted her cheerfully. He was dressed in casuals with the kind of sartorial elegance that only came after an hour spent in front of a mirror. He had initially shunned Rita when she had joined as DCP for Crime Branch. Eventually he had unbent towards her when she had cracked a particularly complicated case in *Bhendi Bazaar*. Thereafter he personally picked her for a case that had international ramifications and a bond – albeit very feeble – had formed. He no longer persisted in addressing her by her designation as per protocol. This was perfectly okay by her.

'Good morning, sir,' Rita saluted smartly. Although she didn't need to wear a uniform in her current position, she never once forgot that she was in the force and discipline and protocol were paramount. She glanced at his tidy desk; it had two phones, a computer, one sheet of paper and his iPhone.

'Sit … coffee, tea?'

'Thank you, sir, but I'm okay for now.'

'Tea it is then.' Obviously, the question was rhetorical. Sexy drank tea. So, anyone who visited him drank tea, whatever their preference.

He pressed the buzzer. No one showed up because the catering staff already knew what needed to be brought in.

'So, tell me, what brings you here, Rita?'

Rita updated the commissioner on the murder of Anu Singh and asked if he thought it was the right time to brief the press. Sexy deliberated for a minute and then asked for all the information he needed to field the media's questions.

'The perpetrator's decadence seems recherché. He needs to be stopped tout de suite.' Sexy assured her he would ask his secretary to arrange a press briefing before the end of the week and let Rita know.

Rita knew that *tout de suite* meant immediately. She made a mental note to check what the dictionary had to say about the other French-sounding word *recherché*.

Harry had received the report from the investigators on the ground and handed over copies to Rita, Vikram and Jatin.

Although the investigators had turned Anu Singh's apartment in Worli upside down and inside out, the crime-scene experts got little of value from their search. One of the biggest cunnings of this perpetrator was that he wasn't the typical knife-and-blood loving one, slicing and dicing his victims. Unlike some serial killers in the past, he made no attempt to dispose of the bodies either. He had no qualms about leaving his victim tied to the bed. Using knives was a risky business. In past cases, the knife had sometimes spilled the blood of the killer along with that of the victim. Not so in this case. His MO was strangulation. His sexual gratification further eliminated the chance of being nabbed; he never actually physically penetrated the victim, only penetrated them with toys and objects. He must have taken every precaution not to leave any tissue, skin residue, hair follicle or sweat droplets behind for analysis. Did he carry a vacuum cleaner? In some textbook cases, the killer washed his hands or had a shower before leaving the premises; but in this case, it didn't appear he needed a shower – he wasn't getting soiled at all – nothing was retrieved from the bathroom.

Her friends and neighbours reflected on Anu Singh as a vibrant woman. She was a voracious reader. Interestingly, along with scores of paperback fiction, some erotic literature was found buried amongst her books in the apartment. It wasn't a crime, but it did hint at predilections. The apartment had two manuals of bondage erotica, which made the men rummaging through her residence snigger. However, they could have just easily belonged to the husband who was yet to arrive in Mumbai. Everything was collected and catalogued as evidence, an inventory of which would be sent to Crime Branch at Crawford Market and the think tank could examine it there.

Another similarity in the three murders came to light.

The mobile phones of all three victims had gone missing since their murders. The killer had taken them away and had probably destroyed and dumped them somewhere. The bills found in her home helped locate Anu Singh's mobile phone operator. They were duly contacted with a request to submit the call records on her phone. Perhaps the killer had called her; or had she called him ...?

The home Mac was sent for analysis to the tech team. There had been no evidence of surfing porn sites or dating sites; nothing to indicate that either the husband or the wife were practicing sadism and masochism. Google, Wikipedia, Facebook, Twitter, Gmail, eBay, a few e-commerce sites and some other social networks were the most-visited sites like by any other person, besides Microsoft Word and some Excel spreadsheets with complex calculations and pivot tables. Although none of the regularly visited websites had been logged into as yet, it was just a matter of time before the bright geeks at Crime Branch hacked into them to check for any suspicious activity, but it was still too early to know anything for sure. In short, there was nothing to raise eyebrows, nothing out of character, nothing strange or nonconforming.

The music CD collection in the household mainly comprised country music and old Hindi film songs. Again, nothing unusual. There were no prescription medicine or drugs. A few bottles of expensive whiskies and vodkas, some opened, some still sealed. Yet again, nothing to cause alarms bells to go off.

Something had to give. In the bottom drawer of what was apparently Anu Singh's wardrobe, the police found an incongruity. Anu's clothes had been gone through with a fine-tooth comb by women constables and found to be expensive and branded, of rote for someone who belonged to that financial and social status, some Indian, some western. But one set of starkly dissimilar clothes was stacked in the large bottom drawer beneath a plain cotton nightgown: an ultra-short leather miniskirt and matching undergarments in latex. While it was an anomaly, it didn't actually have the name of the killer inscribed on it. Perhaps she wore the outfit on a special occasion, a fancy dress party? Perhaps they belonged to an earlier time, and hadn't been discarded? Perhaps Anu and her husband indulged in kinky sex, who knew? Or perhaps Anu Singh lived a double life: one with her husband and one for herself. Then again, that didn't mean she deserved to be murdered.

All known friends had been contacted and checked for their alibis to rule them out. Standard operating procedure. There was a common theme when it came to their assessment of Anu Singh: warm, friendly, cheerful and a socialite when her husband was around, but an introvert when her husband was not in town.

The same friends were reinterviewed by other members of the team to check for consistency. Fabricated accounts, when repeated under skilful questioning, tended to show discrepancies, unless a liar had an infallible memory. False witnesses invariably fumbled in the end and got caught out. But in this case, whether or not any of the alibis were concocted, it seemed that either all the interlocutors were indubitably singing from the same song sheet or were speaking God's truth as far as Anu's characterization was concerned. Another dead end!

The investigation confirmed – exactly as reported in the previous two cases – that the apartment hadn't been broken into. The victim had let the killer into her apartment of her own volition. That, or the killer somehow had access to the property. However, considering the glaring distinction in the profile of the victims in the previous two cases and Anu Singh, the investigators – given their limited understanding of the larger picture – surmised that the first hypothesis seemed farfetched. Why would Anu Singh allow a killer into her home? The killer must have had a key. They said they had tried but failed to connect the dots between the two hookers and Mrs Anu Singh.

The only living blood relative of Anu Singh was her brother who had moved down to Perth in Australia. He sounded devastated by the news, but not enough to travel back from

Australia to identify his sister or to perform the final rites. Regrettably, Anu Singh hadn't made a huge enough dent in her sibling's life by her untimely and violent death.

Shekhar Singh arrived on the evening flight – almost twenty-four hours after his wife's corpse had been discovered. As per the instructions from Crime Branch, the local police had asked Shekhar to check into a hotel. He had completed the formality of identifying Anu Singh at Byculla Hospital and was now waiting for the Crime Branch to visit him.

Harry had been good. In fact, excellent. He had, in a limited time, dug up useful information on Shekhar Singh – he was a serial womanizer, and in this particular instance he had travelled abroad with a young female colleague from his workplace. An intern. The two had stayed at the same hotel. A classic, by the book, motive to bump off one's wife.

'All this in a day's work, I'm impressed,' Vikram wowed.

'Yes, Harry, this is incredible. Carry on with your searches. Dig into the financials of Anu and Shekhar Singh. Who held the purse strings, any excessive life insurance policies, you know the drill ...' Rita instructed as she walked out with Vikram at her side.

'Deeply sorry for your loss, Mr Singh, and we truly appreciate you agreeing to see us right away,' Rita began after introducing Vikram and herself.

Shekhar Singh was a large man with a slight potbelly. His thick, straight, black hair was combed back from his forehead. Although his face still bore pockmarks of pimples that he had squeezed in his youth, they did not detract from his manliness. He seemed to have slept in the clothes he was in. His eyes looked reddened behind their designer spectacles. He had either spent a sleepless night or had wept. Whatever it was, he successfully maintained the façade of complete composure.

'Haven't you found out who did it?' He sounded upset, but to say he was grieving would be stretching it.

'Not yet, but we will.'

'Is it true that it's the same killer who has already struck in the city a few times before?'

'Possibly, but we don't have all the facts to confirm this at the moment.'

'Any leads?'

It was a time-tested tactic: the subject wanted to control the conversation by questioning the investigators. To keep the investigators away from whatever they were looking for.

'Mr Singh—'

'Call me Shekhar.'

'Okay, Shekhar, do you have any reason to suspect anyone?'

'No.'

'Any enemies – business or personal who could harm Anu?'

'Anu's enemies or mine?'

'Either.'

'None that I can think of,' he shook his head.

Rita glanced at Vikram. A sign that it was time for him to take over the conversation while she keenly observed the subject. They had done this before on several occasions. Vikram seamlessly took over and questioned Shekhar on his recently truncated business trip: when did he fly out, where did he stay, who had he met, who had travelled with him, what took him so long to return when he had been informed about his wife's untimely death the day before. For the most part, Shekhar had plausible answers. It was a business trip as all business trips were. He was a partner in a firm that secured funding for start-ups, and his trip was to meet foreign investors to present a few new ideas that had recently been pitched to his firm in Mumbai. The inordinate delay in returning – he had boarded the flight twelve hours after he had received the news, despite the extenuating circumstances of his wife's homicide – was due to some fuck-up by his travel agent back in Mumbai who had booked the original tickets. This was a blatant lie. Anyone, and least of all someone of Shekhar's financial profile, would buy a new ticket and not be dependent on a travel agent to try to cut corners. However ignominious the death may have been, it was still one's duty to be by the side of one's spouse's corpse as soon as possible.

'Returning to "enemies",' Rita hijacked Vikram's inquisition, 'was your wife romantically or otherwise physically involved with another man?'

'Of course not.'

Clearly a no-brainer.

'How can you even ask that, DCP Ferreira?'

'I'm sure you'll appreciate we need to check everything to leave no loose ends.'

'She was my wife. The least you can do is show some courtesy and refrain from such insensitive questions,' Shekhar stormed.

'Shekhar, the moment your wife stopped breathing her responsibility passed on to me from you.' *If she were ever your responsibility, that is,* Rita wanted to add. 'While I empathize with you, as a police officer I can't give you a free pass because you are the victim's husband. In fact, statistically speaking, spouses are the primary suspects.'

'And where were you when she was getting killed, DCP?'

'Was she in danger?' Rita ploughed on, ignoring his counter-question. 'Did anyone ever report that she was being stalked or had any enemies that would go to the extreme extent of taking her life?'

'No.'

'Then why would you expect Mumbai Police to be circling your house to guard it?'

Shekhar nodded, like some sense had been drilled into his brain.

'And what about you?' *Strike while the iron is hot*, Rita thought.

Shekhar was neither aggressive nor conciliatory. He remained calm, but the tide of guilt was rising fast on his reddening cheeks. He scratched his neck – a classic sign that the subject was about to lie, prevaricate or be ambiguous.

'What do you mean?'

Rita glanced at Vikram again. Both of them had played this game before. Any suspect, while prevaricating, answered a question with a question to gain time to come up with a plausible lie.

'It's a simple, routine question: are you romantically or sexually involved with someone else?' Rita didn't want to tell him what the police already suspected just yet. She wanted him to be caught out in a lie to gain control of the conversation.

Shekhar remained silent, but his countenance spoke volumes. The remorse of losing a life partner while he and the intern had been humping like bunnies; his conscience would probably gnaw away at him for the rest of his life.

'Are you asking if I'm having an affair with another woman?' he bit out.

'Yes, that's exactly what I'm asking.'

'No way!'

'What if I said you're—'

'I'd say that it's a figment of your overzealous imagination,' he cut in.

'Didn't you take the new intern, Mona Shah, with you to London for the business trip?'

'Yes. She's a colleague who travelled with me, that's all. She stayed in the same hotel, yes, but she stayed in her own room, and I stayed in mine. You can check the hotel records.'

'The hotel may confirm that she was booked into a separate room, but how can they establish where she slept?'

'You'll just have to take my word for it. Or ask Mona.'

'We'll certainly do that. In fact, a colleague of mine is with her right now as we speak,' Rita improvised.

A shadow of trepidation moved across Shekhar's forehead.

'In any case, I'd love to work at your office. Do you buy expensive lingerie for all your women employees or do they have to fit a certain criterion?'

Checkmate.

The police had Shekhar's credit card bills which reflected he had shopped at Ann Summers while he was in London. It could have very well been for his wife, Anu, but his demeanour put paid to that theory.

'Okay, just where is this going?' he scowled. It was apparent he had comprehended that the police had enough evidence of him romping in bed with a floozy while his wife's corpse cooled in the mortuary. There seemed little point in denials when he had been caught with his paws in the proverbial cookie jar. His house of cards was about to collapse, he twigged, and it would be foolish to sustain the façade of *we're-just-colleagues.*

'Where do *you* think it is going, Shekhar?'

He didn't make any attempt wipe the perspiration that beaded his forehead. 'Okay. I admit we had a physical relationship on the business trip; but are you insinuating that I had anything to do with Anu's death?'

'Like I said at the beginning, we have to explore all angles.'

'I'm the victim here. Let's say, even hypothetically, I did have a relationship with another woman, that doesn't automatically translate to murder, does it?'

'Not in itself, no. So, let me request you not to play any more games and hypotheticals with me, and spell out everything, neat and clear, so that we can eliminate you from the enquiry and move on.'

Shekhar admitted to the affair, but it was just for fun, nothing serious. Yes, he had bought lingerie for the intern. Yes, she had stayed two nights in his room, but he still loved Anu. He started going maudlin, reminiscing about his dead wife.

Douche bag, Rita thought.

Rita looked at Vikram and motioned to him to carry on with the investigation, now that the extramarital affair had been brought out into the open.

'Shekhar, we have to ask you this – are you absolutely certain your wife wasn't seeing anyone else?'

'No. I said that before. Do you have anything that contradicts my belief?' he asked.

'Something didn't quite add up when we searched your apartment,' Rita butted in thinking of the dominatrix-style outfit and paraphernalia and that had been recovered. *To each his own*, thought Rita. Nobody had to conform to conservative norms. What had bothered the police was that a similar tendency for kinky sex had not been reflected in Shekhar's belongings. How was it possible for one partner to practice something if the other partner wasn't in the same frame at all?

'What is it that didn't add up, DCP Ferreira?' asked Shekhar.

'Let me ask you straight, and please don't withhold anything from us. Did you and your wife have some proclivity towards sadomasochism, however subtle?'

'Do you mean kinky sex? Not at all, what made you suggest that?'

Rita explained what they had discovered in Anu's drawer.

'That can't be … it's not possible. Anu was a docile woman, she never so much as hinted at such behaviour.'

Well, we don't know the people we think we know, do we?

Rita let Shekhar process this information. He shut his eyes and shook his head in resignation.

'So, what're the new start-ups you're working on?' Vikram started once again when Shekhar Singh recovered his composure.

'Oh, it's a peer-to-peer funding, which reminds me, when can I expect our Mac back. I have personal and official info and other important files on it.'

'Aren't your files backed up?'

'Oh, they are, but the Mac has a lot of confidential info that we cannot afford to lose.'

'Well, it's a homicide investigation; our geeks will have to be absolutely certain that it doesn't contain any gen regarding our investigation before we can return the machine to you. I can assure you that none of your confidential or financial information will be passed on to anyone.'

'It's a new machine so please ask your techies not to pull it apart. I am a geek myself so I know it is fairly common for us to pull apart something if we cannot find what we are looking for.' He attempted a smile, but it was mirthless. 'I'll be more than happy to drop by to provide whatever passwords I know.'

'And Mrs Singh's phone is missing.' Vikram noted and carried on. It was getting late. They had been here for over two hours now, and everyone was tired after the long day. Plus, there wasn't much left to ask. Or gain.

'I am told.'

'Did she have one mobile or two?'

'Just the one.'

'Would you, by any chance, know your wife's passwords for email, social networks, etcetera?'

'No, we gave each other space.'

Of course, or she'd have caught you with your pants down and arms around Mona darling!

'Is there anything you'd like to ask us?' Rita asked, trying to sum up.

'How long before I can go back to my home?'

'We'll let you know as soon as we get the crime scene investigation team out.'

'Thanks.'

'And Shekhar – if there is anything that you think might be useful in bringing your wife's attacker to book please give us a call.'

'Of course.'

'And if you travel out of town, please let us know too, before you do.'

'Will do.'

'There's got to be something on Anu's phone, Vikram,' Rita said as he started his Maruti Gypsy. Vikram was in love with the Gypsy and wouldn't trade it in for any other vehicle that the Mumbai Police offered him. It was like the Gypsy was his second wife. Always sparkling clean.

'What makes you say that, ma'am?'

'The unsub took Anu's phone. Even in the previous two murders, the girls' phones weren't found. It seems unlikely in today's times that two working girls didn't have phones. How would the punters contact the girls for assignations if the girls didn't have mobile phones?'

'What about the computer then?'

'We don't know. The information in our files is still incomplete.'

And it was the truth. The files from the previous murders lacked details. For example, no one had bothered to note the colour of the cords used to restrain the girls. That info could in time be useful or unnecessary verbiage, but it should have been entered into the file. Writing details in files always presented that problem since it was a chore to write down all the minutiae, when there were a thousand and one other priorities. Every place in this world was understaffed, overworked and the criminals weren't taking a break anytime soon for the police to catch up. Additionally, as no one was asking questions or looking for closure, in the case of the prostitutes, there was no rush to painstakingly complete the files. Similarly, there had been no mention of any computers in Gina's or Radha's one-room residences. It was possible that neither girl had one. Perhaps they didn't require one, especially with smartphones these days being so powerful. But that wasn't the point. The fact was that the local police did not think it was important enough to check and make a note of. In this day and age, there should have been a negative mention at least: *No laptop or computer was found during the police's search of the victim's premises.* And now that those cases were months old, who'd remember or ever know. Those details were lost forever.

'What about Anu Singh's computer? If the phone was important, why wasn't the Mac?' Vikram asked.

'As our techies told us, all frequently visited websites have been signed out of. Most home Macs and PCs are shared. So users sign-in-sign-out, and the killer would have either known that, or he made Anu sign out. However, smartphones are personal devices. People don't sign-out every time they switch off.'

'I'll push our tech team to see what they can get,' Vikram sounded convinced.

'Dinner?' Rita asked. She was conscious she had nothing in the refrigerator.

'I was thinking the same, ma'am. I recently discovered a small place in Bandra, not far from where you live. They serve fantastic *momos*. Does that interest you?'

'Of course, let's go. I hope they serve a drink.' Then: 'What did you think of Shekhar Singh?'

'Not a straightforward guy; I mean, he is an adulterer, but murder sounds a bit of a stretch for him, don't you think?'

'Possible, but let's keep an open mind. Let's see what the financials that you've asked for look like, before we give him a clean chit. What bothers me is the S&M paraphernalia we didn't find – his. Funny how sometimes you notice things solely by their absence.'

'True. He admitted he was having sex on the side, so isn't it possible that his wife, too, was having a relationship with someone else?'

'Entirely possible, but nothing we've found so far suggests that. But then truth never unfolds linearly, does it? Let's see what's scattered around in this maze.'

The consensus at dinner was to ask the local police stations in Kandivali and Andheri to send all evidence, all investigation notes and every last piece of information collated from the residence of the two ill-fated girls over to Crime Branch, since the files that they already had were clearly insufficient. Rita told Vikram to get in touch with the mobile operators to check for all call records of Gina and Radha. They needed to reopen and reinvestigate their murders.

Mona Shah – Shekhar Singh's love interest in office – was interviewed separately. Initially, she too denied that she had been rendezvousing with Shekhar, but eventually came around. From then on, the story matched word-for-word including the colour of lingerie bought from Ann Summers.

INTERLUDE
Summer 1994

That summer marked the end of my innocence. It didn't disappear bit by bit like a boulder sinking into a bog; at one point, it was there, the next it had just disappeared abruptly.

It's not just the moon that has a dark side. Everyone has a dark side or, at the very least, dark recesses in the heart. We've all, at some point in our lives, secretly thought of acting out our wildest fantasies, some of them good, most not. There are two main reasons why people don't go ahead with their dreams: either the urge isn't strong enough or they are meek like my own father and Kapil Aggarwal who turned a blind eye to their wives' infidelity. I could never stand weakness of any kind. But then, I had been fortunate to have a friend like Nutty-me.

Nutty-me was stir crazy. He often dropped into my thoughts uninvited, challenged me and, more often than not, pushed me into carrying out *his* lusty, carnal desires. He made me cross the lines. In time, I realized arguing with Nutty-me was a losing battle, a waste of time. I tried. I swear, I tried.

It was Nutty-me that made me jump the little parapet between our balcony and Tina's. For days before I crossed it, I'd sit under it, hidden from the apartment next door, and only peep into Tina's living room through their glass windows. The shameless tart never drew the curtains. Numerous times I saw her totally nude; she'd come into the living room to go to the kitchen for something and then return. Her stomach was like a lower half of a surfboard: flat and it ended in a pointed triangle that was the waxed mons. Nothing in any text I had read or in the pictures of skimpy bikini-clad models in magazines could have prepared me for it. She was celestial, and yet decadent.

'*Jump, you wimp*,' Nutty-me egged me on for days before I actually crossed and got onto Tina's balcony when she was entertaining a guest.

Lust is a devil clad in a Victoria's Secret negligée. Irresistible.

There was a fug, a stale, pungent smell – which I was to forever associate with sex after that – that drew me towards the room. My curiosity prevented any rational thought, but I should have known that my mind was deranged and unable to make the right decision at that moment. And Nutty-me, on my side, emboldened me. But mistakes are what we term our 'lessons' later, aren't they? If I had waited even a minute longer, perhaps the fear would have kicked in and held me back. However, the urges, the passion, the madness took over and I crossed the line; the line was the glass window in Tina's balcony. Today, the windows were wide open. Goddammit!

The man with her was bald with strands of grey, shapeless with love handles and hirsute. As repulsive as the sight was seeing him plunging into her, it was nevertheless erotic to watch a demonstration of what I had only read and visualized in the books until then. To say I was 'stirred' would be the understatement of the century. I was bursting with energy, my heart trampolining from my stomach to my throat and back.

She was on all fours in front of the old son-of-a-bitch as he took her from behind on the large settee. She arched her back to allow him deeper access, her breath laboured like his. He held a belt that was fastened around her neck as he slapped her bum hard. Thwack! Even from a distance I could see the red imprint of his fingers on her flesh, but she didn't make a sound, not a peep. He slapped her other cheek too with equal fervour. How did she explain such marks to Kapil? Or did she not care if he found out? And then she was writhing with pleasure or pain or both. And the old codger panted like a dog that's chased a Ferrari for miles.

As I stared at them from the distance, I heard the two performers reaching some kind of a crescendo. The two gasped and he pushed her forward; both fell onto the settee; he on top of her. His groan of ejaculation amplified in my head and moved south to my groin. It was weird, but it was all happening in front of me.

'Clean your filth with your mouth, you bitch,' I heard him growl as he rolled over, yanking at the leather belt around her neck.

She obeyed by swallowing him. As she finished the task that she had been ordered and brought her face up, he slapped her. Not a playful one, but like a real hard flesh-on-flesh smack. I could see her crimson lipstick around the man's tool.

What kind of kinky behaviour was this? Did my mother like this too? Was that what her lover had written in his note to her? 'Tying' might have just been a cryptic reference to such a game.

The permanence of that transient moment has never forsaken me despite numerous efforts. On the contrary, every effort I ever made to force it out of my memory and my system was met with a heightened pushback. There was no way out, no escape, no eraser to wipe that scene away; it was seared onto my eyelids. I couldn't once shut my eyes and not see it.

I was lost in my own thoughts and missed the guy getting up. I heard the main door slam shut and I gathered that he was satiated and had gone.

Tina still lay on her stomach. Resting, recovering from the onslaught? Her shapely body languid after hours of relentless sex and games, perspiration glistening on the bare flesh like pearls, her breath still in heaves, her rump more beautiful than the most beautiful sight I'd ever cast my eyes on. And the smell. The room smelled of sex, that unstoppable, repugnant smell that filled my nostrils and became synonymous with adulterous sex. What I didn't know then was that the olfactory senses were one of the strongest in evoking one's memory, to make a person love or hate or despise or, in my case, make the blood rush between my legs.

'*Go for her, be a man*,' Nutty-me shouted in my ears.

A strange current passed my boyhood as if someone had run a live wire through my genitals. I could feel a tension mounting, a hardness building, a desire taking over me. A yearning. A hunger. I had to have her. She was insatiable. Wouldn't she love to have more?

I should have turned around, jumped the dividing space between the parapets and left then.

But desire had seized hold of me and propelled me forward like I was on some kind of autopilot. Adrenaline is more powerful a drug than one can imagine.

'*Yay!*' cried Nutty-me.

I tiptoed to the settee. The closer I got, the bolder I got. I had come this far. She wouldn't say *no* to me, would she? My brain was whirling with ideas. All lurid, all wrong. But it was all out of my control.

The first thing I did to take control of her was to take hold of the thick leather belt around her neck. And I tugged it hard. Her neck got yanked, and I heard her choking but I wasn't letting go. I got on to the settee, my knees on either side of her naked buttocks.

'Who—'

'Shut up,' I said, but it was over for both of us.

The intensity of the situation was too much for me. I felt my warmth flooding out. I ejaculated even before I had taken off my clothes. The nitwits would never understand that pleasure resided solely in the brain. Not between the legs. If they had read their biology, they'd have known that sensory glands are wrapped in the synapses in the brain.

And I had yanked on Tina's neck more than I had realized or intended. She was dead. I had, in my own way, made out with Tina when she was already dead … But before she made her final guttural gasp and passed out, I heard her moan in pleasure, I swear.

I have no regrets in life. If you've never taken risks in life, you won't understand me. Tina was a succubus, a demoness responsible for what happened to me. Or what got me started down the path. Without her my life would have forever been incomplete.

#LoveTina.

I didn't know if the men had paid Tina cash or compliments until the police discovered a large quantity of unaccounted for cash in the Aggarwal apartment. Kapil Aggarwal claimed he had had no clue about the money or his wife's predilection. How could a husband not know how wanton his wife was? Especially with all the marks I had seen one man give her that afternoon, how could he miss them? All of them, everyday?

'*He's lying*,' Nutty-me was certain.

The fact that money exchanged hands made the whole episode sit even higher in my now debauched mind.

I was old enough to comprehend what they were looking for and, fortunately, precocious enough to feign ignorance about the activities in the neighbourhood to avoid being the target of any prying into my own private life. If they took me away to question, I knew I'd break. My ignorance was my salvation. Nutty-me guided me to discard the books and play with toys to reinforce their impression. And it said something about their skill that it didn't strike them as odd that a fourteen-year-old played with pre-teen toys.

'*He's a kid*,' I heard them utter a few times.

The investigators were blighted by their blind belief that a fourteen-year-old wasn't capable of homicide; that a fourteen-year-old's libido wasn't strong enough to blind him in the throes of passion. Their theory, not mine, but it suited me fine.

Someone up there in the azure sky loved me. Perhaps that someone had a purpose for me. Perhaps that someone had made me the way I was. And perhaps that someone acknowledged that it may have been a crime, but it was no sin. I was only purging the world of its evil and in the process providing unprecedented pleasure to these women, one final time. I couldn't please everyone, I couldn't cleanse the world in its entirety, but everyone had to do his or her bit, and I took it upon myself to do my part. That someone who loved me up in the sky would certainly take care of everything in the end.

However dark the night got, they said, there was always a promise of the morning.

Truth be told, the police had not one shred of evidence against me or anyone else, for that matter.

A lot of people, besides me, had witnessed random men visiting Tina after her husband left for work. But no one could identify the men or specifically the man who had last copulated with Tina. In the absence of CCTV there was no visual record of vehicles or visitors. The semen in Tina's body was useless, the spank and slap marks on her body and face pointless, since the police couldn't start a search on every denizen of Delhi.

It was all set to be a cold case and after a week of hot scintillating news that the media fed to the readers, it was relegated to the freezer. A snippet here, a mention there. That was that. No fresh discovery, no pointers, no new witnesses, no suspects whatsoever. The police issued a request to people to come forward if they had any information, but no one obliged. The storm had passed and it seemed I had gotten away with it. I won.

I scanned the news for weeks. Nobody told it right, because nobody got it right.

Kapil Aggarwal moved out of the apartment complex. Ironically, the infamy of his wife was too much to bear. A cuckolded husband wasn't someone with whom society empathized. Society pitied and patronized them in the guise of pseudo sympathy. Local journalists wanted to interview him, to help him find his wife's murderer, but they were more interested in her insalubrious activities. What was she like in bed, what kind of lingerie had she liked? What games had the couple played in bed? Did he have inclinations towards his wife's proclivities? Did he know whether the guys gave her gifts? And cash?

I came to know later that he committed suicide.

'*Spineless* ...' Nutty-me scoffed.

Strangely I felt no remorse either. A lingering fear, maybe, but guilt, no. She got what she asked for; he deserved what he got.

I learnt two things. Firstly, in sexual relief, penetration was entirely superfluous. The real thing was control. To have the subject at one's mercy. Secondly, I was fortunate because the police never checked the belt for my fingerprints. But I knew I had to be careful in future. One couldn't rely on sheer luck every time.

My unrelenting desires weren't something I had signed up for. But they took me down a path that didn't permit a U-turn. One way only. Just forward. The thirst became urgent and unquenchable, but I needed to exercise control. If a similar episode occurred in my vicinity, the curtain could drop. Nutty-me wanted me to start talking to the girls in school, but I ignored him for a while. His chatter around me became irrelevant. I could shut him off with a flick, but only sometimes, and he wasn't happy about that.

Sometimes – albeit rarely – I wondered if I had had a sibling, a brother or a sister, things might have turned out differently. I wouldn't have been a loner for starters. The sibling would have kept a check on me. Nutty-me may not have surfaced in my life at all. But that wasn't meant to be, I think.

I couldn't remember a single meaningful conversation with my parents before the incident, and I wasn't letting a homicide in the neighbourhood break that pattern. We continued to exchange silences as we always had. I don't think they had an iota of doubt about my story. The two went back to their bickering soon after and normalcy was restored. Tina had come and gone from our lives. What I didn't know then was that I hadn't escaped. I had sentenced myself to a life that I had signed up for, for a very long time, maybe until the very end.

SEVEN

'Lipstick Killer on the loose.'
'Are the crores funding the Crime Branch justified?'

Front-page news. The media pillory had commenced. They could have been considerate, but why would they be? They had waited a week now and nothing of consequence had been found. The police weren't providing much information – besides one placating little press briefing from the commissioner's office, which was more padding than any real news: '*We are following all leads*', '*We are doing all we can to bring the killer to book soon.*'

For those who followed the investigation, it appeared like the killer was too wily for the specialists in the Crime Branch.

Rita Ferreira was furious although she quite understood the rationale of the media onslaught. A fairly large majority of murders carried little or limited impact. When someone got killed in a remote village somewhere, it hardly made any waves or, if it did, it lived and died in the local pages of the local tabloid. It didn't even make it to the national media. People elsewhere carried on regardless. A serial killer in a city like Mumbai, one where twenty million people lived and worked, changed the outlook of people. It made big news – national, international news – and people across the nation started to panic. Unlimited possibilities played across people's minds. Could they, or a loved one, be the next victim? The story had gone viral, the fear grew palpable and thus, the media was already filling columns, covering and highlighting the incidents, some factual, some fictionally extrapolated to grab attention.

There hadn't been a precise moment in the investigation when it occurred, but somehow the psychopath's fondness for lipstick came to be his hallmark. It was a matter of days before everyone working on the case started referring to it as his signature. It stuck. Despite Rita's initial concern, they couldn't control the damage. News didn't just leak. Nothing was *leaked* to the press; they worked hard at it. Leaks happened because someone tipped people off. In the absence of full details, speculation had taken over. Besides, the media always loved to give monikers, and the 'Lipstick Killer' was better than any they had had in a long time. This was their cherry on the top. A serial killer on the loose made news, but Lipstick Killer gave him an identity, which made even better news.

'What next? Interpol or Sherlock Holmes?'

Rita felt they had surely missed something. She asked the team to go over everything with the finest-toothed comb they had. There had to be some pointer: look again, check everything twice, don't assume anything. They were told to check where Anu Singh purchased her underwear, to meet the shop owners, and ask if she shopped alone or with someone? To drive over the route she took from her home to her boutique every day, to see if there was anything that could have made her cross paths with the killer. Some advertisement that caught her eye and made her call, some place where the killer could have spotted her? Forget a stone, don't leave a friggin' dust particle unturned.

She was sipping coffee in the large conference room that had been commandeered as an Operations Room for the case when Vikram arrived with his coffee. All the various reports – from the crime scene unit to the forensics to the postmortem analysis – were now in, and all of them put together scored a zero. None of them bore any fruit. It appeared that the psycho had pulled off another ghastly murder successfully, not leaving behind anything that could lead back to him. Bummer!

'What about the missing iPhone?' asked Vikram, then gave his unsolicited opinion without missing a beat, 'I don't believe for a second that Anu Singh lost it on the day she was killed. That's too much of a coincidence.'

'This means—' Rita started, '—hold on, and bear with me since I'm trying to think aloud … something tells me that Anu knew her killer. Why else would he be scared about what was on her phone? He didn't take the computer, but he took the iPhone, just as he did on previous occasions. I'm pretty certain he isn't a second-hand smartphone dealer. It might be that there were recent calls and text messages. Let's see when we receive the report from the mobile operator.'

It was hardly an a-ha moment. On the contrary, it only served to highlight the shoddiness of the previous two investigations had been. Why hadn't they called for telephone records to match against? Why confiscate just the phone? To erase contacts? Or texts? Or call history?

'And it might have been the same reason on the previous occasions. Ask for the phone records of all three women. Check for a common number amongst the incoming or outgoing calls. There's a chance that there could be common numbers across Gina and Radha, given that they were in the same profession. In fact, come to think of it, we might find a punter who socialized with Anu but picked up hookers. It's more than likely, and it will be worth looking into if we find one.'

Vikram, ever diligent, took copious notes.

'And, something Dr Khan told me fits now,' Rita voiced her thoughts. She updated Vikram regarding Dr Khan's summary on the erotic technique of asphyxiation, and all that she had read on the web. 'It also ties in with the erotic literature and Anu's underwear recovered from her apartment. So, it's possible that because she had a predilection for a different kind of sexual fulfilment, she got in touch with our psycho and that led to her murder.'

'Without her husband knowing about it?'

'Yes, exactly like her husband having his bit on the side without her knowledge. Isn't it a bit sexist to think that a woman cannot have an extramarital affair when a man can?'

'Fair point, but none of the people interviewed by our teams said anything about the wild side of Anu Singh.'

'She may not have confided to anyone; people don't necessarily talk about what they do behind closed doors. Especially when such fantasies or perversions – whatever we may want to call them – could and would be considered a taboo in her social circles, don't you think?

Vikram nodded. He appeared convinced.

'But you make a valid point,' Rita carried on, 'it would have been difficult for her to find a willing partner in her social circle. It would have to have been a cryptic classified ad in the public domain or some other way, by which she contacted her killer. But this is just one theory, we could be totally off the track because we are hanging all of this on just two elements in the investigation – that the mobile phone is missing, and the victim had some erotic garments at home.'

'But she died of asphyxiation, so that, kind of fits in—' Vikram trailed off as Rita shook her head.

'Or we could be force-fitting it in, we don't know. Perhaps the killer is the one fond of throttling his victims.'

'But didn't you just explain that the pleasure is allegedly increased for the one being strangled, so, what pleasure does our psychopath derive from garrotting the woman?'

'Oh, I wish I knew,' Rita brought both her hands forward like she wished she could throttle someone. 'We don't know what makes the bastard tick; we don't know what excites the victims either. And we have no idea about how he operates.'

The discussion went on for another hour, until they eventually gave it up as a futile exercise.

They eventually hit pay dirt!

Luck is for losers, they said. But, when destiny turned the winds in one's favour, it would be stupid to look a gift horse in the mouth. Rita Ferreira and the team got their break from a re-examination of the first crime scene that the twisted killer had struck. No, they hadn't found any hairs, skin particles, tissues or fluids to match DNA, and neither had the killer left behind a gift-wrapped sample of fingerprints.

It turned out that Radha also owned a computer and it was in her home; but the investigating police had negligently overlooked it.

Although nothing of consequence was scraped from the hard drives of the two computers seized, there was one common factor, the Mac that Anu and Shekhar Singh owned provided the break. It had been a relatively new purchase, bought from the biggest computer retail group in the country called PMC:

Personal Machines Corp. The promise of PMC in the top twenty cities across the country was that they not only sold you a computer, they delivered it to your doorstep, installed it, connected it and got you started. They had won a lot of service awards and were planning to expand their operations further to other, smaller, cities. However, what caught the eye of the investigators was that one particular individual had delivered and helped set up the Mac at Anu's apartment and the Acer Laptop at the previous victim, Radha's place in Andheri. Within ninety days of the installation of both machines, the murders took place. The discovery of this similarity logarithmically raised their chances. Perhaps the perpetrator wasn't as smart as he had believed himself to be. He had finally made a mistake, as they all invariably did.

The man who had installed the machines was one Ranbeer Kumar, a resident of Andheri East. He was now a common denominator in the two homicides, the only one they had. Both the women had allowed Ranbeer into their homes for the installation. The central office of PMC in Nariman Point was immediately contacted. Ranbeer, being a contracted staff member, had submitted his statement of work for reimbursement for the hours he had worked in the two locations. In both cases he had been in the victim's homes for a little over two hours setting up their machines, downloading and installing security patches, etc. It was obvious that he had been in their homes, maybe even their bedrooms. Over two hours spent there would have given him, if he was the killer, ample time to get friendly with the women, perhaps case the place for entry/exit points that could provide him with access later. He had to have found some way, since in neither of these two homicides had there had been a break-in, suggesting that his victims, for some reason, either let the intruder into the property or he had either made or stolen a key or figured out some way to steal in and out of the properties.

'I need every piece of intel on Ranbeer Kumar within the next twenty-four hours, without him getting wind of it. Also, we need to put him under surveillance. The last thing any of us wants is him disappearing before we nab him.' Rita was upbeat. It had been a week since the last murder, and this was the first ray of hope. The pressure had been immense.

'Yes, ma'am.'

'Twenty-four hours of collating evidence before we bring him in. Ask your teams to collect as much data as they can, we don't want any damn defence lawyer to even think that this shyster can walk free on bail. I'm sure the investigation will reveal his links to the third murder too. Send someone to prepare for the imminent arrest.'

Setting up stealth surveillance required a court order in most cases. There wasn't a cop in the world who had never bent a rule in their pursuit of justice. But one had to know one's limits, otherwise police forces around the world would be nothing less than organized crime. This was one instance where everyone agreed they should start immediately and bend the rules a bit.

'Be extremely careful. For now, every search, and even surveillance, should be under the radar.'

Ash Mattel had a couple of hours off from the workshop. The other participants – mainly foreigners – had stepped out of the Le Méridien to visit Janpath that was just around the corner. He had stayed back to read his long fax from Mumbai.

He lounged in bed, reading the reports.

All three victims were good-looking, slim and fit. According to the local police the women were vivacious, outgoing, confident and fun-loving. The only two differences were: the first two victims belonged to the same age bracket and profession, whereas the third woman didn't fit this profile. Their cause of death had been strangulation. The strange part was that no evidence of any kind of the perpetrator's fluids had been recovered from the scene.

The victims seemed to have been chosen at random, the hallmark of a serial killer. He had been wholly unpredictable because the police could find no thread of logic for his murderous rampage. He had been resourceful: he changed localities, which helped him since the two police stations prior to Anu Singh's murder hadn't shared the information from their inquiries and inquests.

A look at the timeline of the murders further confirmed Ash's conjecture. Gina, the first prostitute, had been killed in September of last year. The second victim, Radha, had been strangled earlier this year, in late February. A five-month hiatus. Anu Singh was murdered in June, only four months after the second murder.

The shortening of the interval between murders was a dead giveaway of the serial-killer pattern. Serial killers generally had a 'cooling-off' period; the time when their fantasies of the previous kill were strong enough to keep them in check. In control. The fantasy substituted the real thing. But like any economist would explain, every episode followed the law of diminishing marginal utility. Like a cocaine user who had built up his tolerance would need to increase the drug-intake – more quantity, more frequently – to get the same high, the satiation for a serial killer diminished with each kill and the hunger pangs returned quicker and with a vengeance; the next kill became that much more urgent, and the gap between one killing and the next reduced over time. And, exactly as in the case of the cocaine user where one of the doses became the fatal one, a serial killer, too, took increasing risks until one showed his hand. You could hardly call it an accident. They always increased their speed on the wrong side of the road. It was a given.

The thrill of the kill got stronger and catapulted the killer out of control. He upped his game. He decompensated. He no longer worried about the accompanying risks. That, and with every successful kill, the killer started to believe in his own invincibility, convinced that he could do it and get away with it. It was this cockiness that led to his downfall. The more times he did it, the higher the chances of slipping up. Currently, it looked like he was miles ahead of the police. And enjoying it.

The vulnerability of the victims bore a similarity. The first two were clearly understandable if they were working girls – they risked such predators every day, perhaps several times a day. And although Anu Singh broke the mould, she did not necessarily alter the pattern. There had to be some skeletons in her closet that even her husband wasn't aware of. The S&M outfit was the key.

Ironic, he thought, to know that they had the key, but did not know which lock to open.

Gestalt, the word has German origins. And the meaning well established the mentality of the nation in the way it built some of the best cars in the world. Sometimes the whole was different from the sum of its parts. To figure out the whole, one needed to look at the unified thing. The fragmented clues provided in the faxes weren't doing it for Ash. The more he thought about it, the more he realized that a lot could be slipping through the cracks. As such, it was time to wind up the workshop and head towards Mumbai.

DCP Rita Ferreira was convinced they had their man in Ranbeer, but she also knew that everything they had so far was purely circumstantial. They had nothing in the name of forensics, nothing on camera, no eyewitnesses who had seen Ranbeer stalk any of the three victims. And it also laid bare the fact that Ranbeer was being accused of the third homicide merely by extrapolation and, unless something turned up in the search or the poor sod confessed, there was not even a contentious link to Gina. How in the name of the devil did Ranbeer even know about the third woman, anyone with half a brain would ask. Although, he contracted for PMC, he was a freelancer. Hence, he worked from his home and there were days when he wasn't employed by the company and could have been anywhere. He could have well been around in Kandivali and had spotted the third victim, Gina, a young and pretty prostitute. However, any good lawyer worth his salt would argue that this less than tenuous connection wouldn't hold any water and wasn't something on which to build a homicide case. There were gaping holes in the theory and Ranbeer could very easily walk away from justice. Rita understood that. But she also knew it was her best shot yet.

As Vikram led the brigade out of the Ops Room to carry out the tasks, Rita reflected on the lack of profiling. This was Ash's realm of expertise. Unfortunately, he was busy at this crucial juncture. *What good was a workshop in New Delhi when there was a real killer to be profiled in Mumbai?*

EIGHT

The meeting at the precinct in Crawford Market was held at 10.45 p.m., the day after the team had set up the covert surveillance.

The plan was to travel to Andheri East to arrest Ranbeer Kumar before dawn. A lot less cumbersome that way when the rest of world was still asleep, and the media hawks weren't dogging their footsteps with cameras.

Ranbeer's less-than-virtuous activities had been uncovered following a stealthy, remote search into his computer that revealed his proclivity to violent sex. He had access to both free and paid content, including *snuff* films – that depicted sex and death – via a VPN router somewhere in Russia, paid for through money transfer months ago. He had paid the annual membership fee upfront, so in all probability he would renew it. That, in and by itself, was enough to make the arrest since the particular kind of pornography he consumed was illegal in India and in most parts of the world. One would need to stretch the definition of sanity beyond its breaking point to include anybody of sound mind who watched snuff films. It was generally consumed by perverts who bordered on insanity, the possessed, the psychopaths and the mentally unhinged – a special breed of deviants that relished viewing other people being cut and killed for their sexual gratification. Such content chiefly existed on the dark web, but it surfaced time and again when people like Ranbeer were willing to pay and risk their lives to gain unrestricted access.

Sure, this additional information would add to the department's dossier on Ranbeer and help to put him behind bars for long enough, but only if they got the evidence connecting him to the actual scene of crime.

Rita wanted this monster incarcerated for life and wanted to ensure there weren't any cracks through which Ranbeer could slip. There had been too many instances where the defence had won cases because the compiled information about their clients was erroneous, the VPN router had malfunctioned or the internet connection wasn't secure enough and someone else had hacked into their client's account or IP address or some such cockamamie reason. And in Ranbeer's case – considering he was a computer geek – there was always a chance that even the CBI technicians wouldn't be able to extract anything from the wacko's hard disk. All in all, it could be a disaster.

Under the Indian Criminal Procedure Code (the CrPC), 1973, the Indian police is empowered to make an arrest for a cognizable offence – mainly crimes against persons like homicide, rape, battery, assault – without the need for a warrant issued by the court. Cognizable offences were serious violations set out in the First Schedule of the CrPC, and homicide ranked amongst the top. Consequently, based on whatever info they had amassed so far, the police decided to arrest Ranbeer. They didn't think an armed raid was required, but they carried back-up in any event. Who could guess how a scared, desperate psychopath would react?

This wasn't an exact science, but it was as old a police maxim as there ever was that if a person was involved in a criminal activity of one sort, the probability of him being involved in another genre of crime was generally higher. In Ranbeer Kumar's case, the crime he was known to have committed was exceedingly similar to the one the police were investigating. Consumption of banned, violent pornography could have been a harbinger of sexually motivated homicides. The violent content could have possibly intensified the fantasies in his sick mind. It wasn't definite evidence, but the odds were stacked against Ranbeer. Besides, the police could hardly sit around twiddling their thumbs, when he was their only suspect, and there seemed no harm in tossing someone like Ranbeer into the cooler for a while.

As the clock ticked, Rita, Vikram, Jatin and Harry reviewed their doubts once again.

11 p.m.: Was something overlooked?
11.15 p.m.: Had they missed anything?
11.30 p.m.: They had to take a chance.
11.45 p.m.: They decided to get him.

The pressure was mounting from the powers-that-be and the press had been inciting the public. Sometimes, even a wrong move could change the game in your favour. The only disadvantage was that if Ranbeer wasn't the killer, the media flak would be sharp and bitter despite being fully aware that a pervert like Ranbeer belonged behind bars or in a mental institution. Their largest outcry would be that the Lipstick Killer was still at large.

At the stroke of midnight, the think tank decided that they had what they had and it was what it was. Crap!

Time up.

At 01.50 a.m., Ranbeer Kumar was rudely woken up and arrested.

'Where are you taking me?' he asked, astonished that the police should show up at his residence. He was naked except for his briefs.

'To an adventure tour you nitwit ... to the police station, where else?'

'Why? What have I done?'

'You'll know soon enough.'

Ranbeer's one-room apartment was shabbily furnished. Everything was either torn or filthy and it stank worse than a pigsty. Beer bottles, cans and peanut shells lay scattered on the floor. The focus of the room was a desk with a large PC on it. It was festooned with soiled and crumpled tissue paper that no one in their right minds would pick up without protective gloves. If all he did was sit in front of his computer and watch porn, there would be no awards for guessing what the tissues contained.

His apartment was handed over to the Crime Scene Investigation Unit for a thorough search. Although there was no evidence that any homicide had occurred at Ranbeer's property, the police had pinned their hopes that some kind of evidence would be gathered which could link him back to the crimes. They would be looking for anything and everything. His computer was packed off to the tech laboratory within minutes.

By 03.25 a.m., he had been fingerprinted, photographed and put into a temporary cell at the Andheri East Police Station at Vertex Junction, to be questioned by the police in the morning. To his credit, he acted like he had no clue what was happening.

His first demand was that he wanted to speak to a lawyer and protested that he was being harassed. No one told him anything about the reason for this arrest.

This was a top secret, undercover mission, but the investigative journalists who had parked their asses outside the precincts to scavenge for titbits of news that could increase their viewership and readership had already picked up the scent. It didn't take them long to decipher who had been arrested and for what.

When Rita woke up at six in the morning and saw the newspaper, the news had hit the headlines:

Lipstick Killer arrested in pre-dawn raid.

'What the f—' she exclaimed. She quickly fixed herself a strong coffee and dressed to go to work.

DCP Rita Ferreira arrived at Andheri precinct at nine in the morning. Vikram was already there. With tea and formalities out of the way, both were shown to a room to where Ranbeer waited. The small room had a table and three chairs and that was all – a far cry from the interrogation settings in the movies with a one-way mirror to observe the cross-examination of a prisoner. This wasn't *CSI Mumbai*.

A uniformed constable brought in Ranbeer and checked with Rita and Vikram if they wanted the prisoner to be handcuffed. They declined.

Unlike the stereotypical serial killer of one's imagination, Ranbeer looked anything but threatening. Furthermore, he seemed wholly oblivious to the impending doom that hovered over his head. The guy was twenty-nine, but he looked almost forty. He looked tired, dishevelled, unkempt and if the smell was anything to go by, unwashed for quite a while as well. He was diminutive, a mere five feet four, and undernourished, sixty kilos. How could he overpower the women enough to kill them, Rita wondered. Then it occurred to her that the women seemed to have let him into their lives, he hadn't broken into houses. Perhaps they submitted to his … what? Rita struggled to fill in the blank – the guy had no charm, no charisma, nothing. His nose was an inch too long and his long chin hung straight like a goat's, with the three-day stubble around the jowls. If one put a conical hat on his head and a broom between his legs, he'd be dressed up for Halloween. All in all, he looked creepy rather than menacing. Charm – one had to be a blind primate to be charmed by someone like Ranbeer. But, she reckoned, appearances were deceptive.

Within minutes of his entry into the confined space, the room smelt of sweat and fear. The man was scared stiff.

'I want a lawyer, I know my rights,' were the first words that emerged through his clenched yellow teeth. On the face of it, Ranbeer looked half a sandwich short of a picnic, but he knew all the right lines, which was pretty impressive. Rita rolled her eyes at Vikram to convey her amazement.

'You haven't been charged with anything yet, so why do you need a lawyer?' Vikram retorted in a harsh tone. 'You've watched too much television, Ranbeer.'

'I want a lawyer,' he repeated.

Was he just being recalcitrant by playing the wide-eyed innocent or was he really confused? Was it an act or had they messed up in a big way, Rita couldn't tell; partly because Ranbeer had fear stencilled on his face, but the fear could have been there solely on account of his subscription to the porn sites.

'Okay, Mr Ranbeer Kumar, you will get a lawyer, but let us charge you first,' Vikram stuck to his guns.

'What would you charge me for? I haven't done anything wrong—'

'Then why do you need a lawyer?'

'Why have you arrested me?'

Vikram looked at Rita. She had never seen Vikram flushing with anger. Despite Ranbeer's righteous indignation they knew he was guilty of one crime, at the very least.

'There is more than one reason, Ranbeer, and all of them are grave enough to put you behind bars for life, if not give you the death penalty,' Rita spoke without rancour.

Ranbeer began to tremble.

'Could you tell me where you were between 8 p.m. and midnight and beyond on 30 June this year?'

Ranbeer looked at Rita, then at Vikram. 'I was at my home. Why?'

'Can anyone corroborate your alibi?'

He shook his head. 'I live alone, so I don't see how anyone can do so. But, more importantly, why do I need an alibi?'

'Ranbeer, if you keep answering my questions with your own questions, it's going to be a very long night; so it's best if you simply respond to what I ask you.'

'What is my crime? Why am I here?' he defiantly shot back two more questions at Rita.

'How about downloading and watching banned pornography at home – is that enough reason for arresting you?'

'Why did you ask for an alibi then?'

Rita reflected that the guy wasn't quite as dumb as he pretended to be. He had twigged that he had been brought in for a crime that had occurred outside his apartment. This could mean he knew exactly what he was being questioned about and would prevaricate for all he was worth. But then, on the other hand, this could also mean that he hadn't a clue as to why he was being detained. It was difficult for Rita to ascertain.

'That doesn't answer my question, does it?'

'I don't know what you're talking about,' he muttered noncommittally. 'Do you have any evidence against me?'

Rita realized it was time to segue into the main reason.

'Do you know anyone by the name of Mrs Anu Singh?'

'Who is she?'

'She lived on Dr Annie Besant Road in Worli. Ring any bells?'

'No.' Ranbeer shook his head to emphasize.

'Let me refresh your memory: you visited her in the third week of May this year, to install a Mac computer.'

From Ranbeer's demeanour it was evident that he recognized the name, the twinkle in his eyes conveyed that he even remembered the person. 'What about her?'

'So, you do remember her?'

'Yes, I do, and if her computer is faulty it isn't any of my fault; she should complain to our head office for a replacement—'

'D'you seriously think we have nothing better to do but arrest people because someone's computer is broken?'

'How do I know what else you have to do?'

'I'll slap the shit out of you,' Vikram stood up. He seemed to have finally lost patience with the irritating little sod.

'I want a lawyer,' Ranbeer said plaintively.

The mention of Radha and a computer installation at her Andheri residence elicited a similar response. He recognized the name and had a sparkle of awe for the deceased girl. Could be sexual lust or blood thirstiness. But, nothing about his countenance revealed that he had had anything to do with them beyond that first encounter.

Ranbeer Kumar certainly belied his appearance. He was neither meek nor slow-witted as Rita had assumed. For the best part of the next two hours he was noncommittal and ambiguous to all the questions posed, intermittently asking querulously for his lawyer. And, without him being aware that his stonewalling was working against him, Rita had made a note that Ranbeer was cunning and manipulative, and Rita knew that he had assessed that the police had no concrete evidence against him, a conjecture maybe or thin circumstantial evidence at most, but nothing more, otherwise they would have produced it and immediately sent him to jail.

'When will I be released?' he questioned in response to Vikram's threat.

'Probably never,' Vikram growled. Rita looked at Vikram and gave him a short glare, indicating that he *cooled down. Take a walk.*

Vikram rose and left the room in a huff. If he had been acting bad-cop in the good-cop-bad-cop routine, he had been taking his role too seriously.

Rita looked at Ranbeer when the door closed behind Vikram. What had the police been thinking? That they would bring in this guy who looked like the village idiot and he'd immediately break down and confess?

For ten minutes Rita kept asking questions, but Ranbeer refused to cooperate. He said he wouldn't talk until she got him a lawyer. No, he couldn't afford one, but he would happily sign up with a public defender that the police provided for him – as per the law, that was his right. Every crook, however vile and disgusting, had a right to representation. This wasn't a police state; this was India, the largest democracy in the world.

The fear that had been palpable when Ranbeer had first come into the room, had now more or less subsided. He had, in the course of the interview, transformed into a confident man. Perhaps he had deliberately been playing dumb earlier, and when the ploy didn't work, he had decided offence might be his best defence. A lot of criminals did that. Self-preservation was something that comes naturally to all animals.

There was a knock on the door. Thinking Vikram was back, she mouthed 'come in' without taking her eyes of Ranbeer.

It was Vikram, but he had returned with a slip of paper and passed it across to Rita. She glanced at it only for a second and then rose and walked out of the room.

'Who's the lawyer? What does he want?'

The slip merely said that Ranbeer's lawyer was in the main office, making a ruckus that the police had picked up an innocent man.

'She's in the SHO's office, ma'am.'

She?

Rita marched into the office and stood dumbstruck. Sitting in front of the Station House Officer with her back to the door was the familiar figure of Mrs Isha Thapar.

'Hello, DCP Ferreira,' she smiled politely as Rita came into her vision.

'Isha?'

What was Isha Thapar doing representing a scumbag like Ranbeer Kumar?

'Yes, I'm here to represent my client – Mr Ranbeer Kumar. I've been informed you've been holding him without any charges, am I right?'

'We've yet to bring up the charges.'

'May I know what the charges are to take my client into custody?'

'He has been picked up for questioning in relation to the recent homicide of Mrs Anu Singh.'

'Do you have any evidence linking him to the murder, DCP Ferreira?'

'We cannot divulge that, but we've found a definite circumstantial connection between your client and two of the murders in the last seven months.'

'As far as I know, the only link you have is that my client, Ranbeer Kumar, installed computers at the homes of two of the victims, am I correct?'

How did Isha know that?

'Isha, we also know he visits a lot of violent porn sites, with banned images and films.'

'Have you found any such films in his possession yet?' Isha asked.

'Not yet, but the technical team has taken his computer for analysis. Something should come up soon.'

'Well, DCP Ferreira, are you saying my client is here because he watches pornography or is he actually involved in the two or three homicides you just mentioned?'

'Both.'

'Sorry, he can be a person of interest – based on your information about his predilections – but you have no evidence until you recover any images or their residue from his hard drive. And he surely cannot be your prime suspect in the serial killings either, since you have extremely thin circumstantial evidence here. So, you can charge him on account of him accessing indecent images, which isn't the gravest of offences, until the time you find evidence that he accessed or downloaded banned content that you suspect. Until then, I cannot let you hold my client here.'

Sadly, it wasn't only criminals who discriminated amongst themselves – a burglar thought he was better than a murderer who believed he was better than a paedophile – even their advocates discriminated between the severities of crimes. Isha Thapar would have known that recidivism, and progression from one serious crime to another was an established statistic, but she wasn't going to accept that.

Rita knew she had no legal recourse to keep Ranbeer Kumar. She instructed the SHO to check the documents that Isha had brought and release the man.

'Thank you,' Isha said as Rita walked away to tell Vikram that their little jig was up. She heard Isha sternly warning the SHO like a matador waving the red flag, 'you question my client in my absence and I'll gladly buy you a rope to hang yourself.'

The poor bull – the SHO – knowing fully well who Isha Thapar was – did not rise to the bait.

NINE

Isha Thapar wasn't just another lawyer in a city full of lawyers. She was one of the leading advocates and partner in an all-women firm that carried her name on the plaque: ILK and Company. Isha Thapar, Latika Kapoor and Karen D'Silva. Three classmates from college who, after working for a few years in various law firms across the country, got together to set up their own legal practice in South Mumbai. The firm had initially been set up to fight for the rights of the victims of domestic abuse and dowry deaths; to get justice for downtrodden women. They had tremendous political and media support. While the three names adorned the door, there was no mistaking who held the reins. Isha Thapar. She was a demure woman with an extraordinary presence and personality. Petite with long straight, grey-flecked hair; she didn't bother dyeing her hair. She had a youthful face at forty-three and hardly ever wore any make-up except, occasionally, a light lipstick. She wore chiffon saris mostly, exuding elegance wherever she went. She was highly respected in legal circles, even by judges, irrespective of which side she represented in the case.Isha had been extremely successful as a lawyer. She had been on the cover of several magazines over the years, from *Femina* to *Society* to *Cosmopolitan*. She'd been covered by the *Time* magazine. *India Today* had featured her thrice.

What DCP Rita Ferreira found abnormal was, how in the name of God did Isha Thapar even know a scumbag like Ranbeer Kumar? How could Ranbeer afford the services of ILK and Company? And even if all that had been possible, how on earth had Ranbeer – post his arrest – gotten in touch with Isha to engage her as his lawyer? Was it that Ranbeer and someone else were in collusion and committing the murders together; two psychopaths collaborating? It wasn't common but it wasn't unprecedented: Fred and Rosemary West was an infamous husband-and-wife team in the UK, Wolfgang Abel and Marco Furlan had joined forces in Italy on their murderous spree. There was enough history to ignore the possibility, but nothing so far had indicated that there were two killers.

However, Rita felt a little deflated ever since Ranbeer had walked out. It felt like she had just been poked in the gums by her dentist without the anaesthetic. However, she couldn't resign herself to the situation and intended to update Joshi and Sexy immediately. They needed to know before the phalanx of media bodies descended on the Crawford Market precinct with questions. Isha Thapar was socially connected, and she would certainly talk to the press. Even if *she* didn't, the press would want to talk to her. This episode wasn't over.

'You're on your own now. This was a one-time deal,' Isha Thapar told Ranbeer Kumar as the two walked out of the police station.

'Why did you help me?'

'I owe you no explanations,' Isha flashed a disarming smile.

Ranbeer was nonplussed. He had expected this cool and composed lady, who had materialized out of thin air to advocate for him, to take him to her office and assure him that he was now safe. However, his hopes were dashed; the woman seemed to be washing her hands of him even before he could grasp what had just happened.

'But there's got to be a reason why you came to get me out?'

'Like I said, I owe you no explanation, and you owe me no favours or money, Mr Kumar. You're free to go now, but please get yourself a lawyer if the police contact you again. Have a good day.' Isha walked away to her waiting chauffeur-driven car.

Ranbeer was dumbstruck, but he knew what he had to do next. He needed to hurry home and burn his computer. The police hadn't found any proof of his nefarious activities yet and in getting him out of prison, this God-sent lady had given him a chance to erase all the evidence. He couldn't care less if she didn't want to entertain him any longer. He had no intentions of ever getting apprehended by the police again. He would do what he had to do with the hard discs and disappear from Mumbai.

But it wasn't to be. When he got home, he found the police had sealed his apartment. He would have to wait until nightfall to sneak into his own apartment.

'Hmm …!' hummed Sexy upon hearing Rita's plea. She had come in with ACP Joshi. Rita gathered that the *hmm* signified cogitation.

Commissioner Sanjay Saxena, according to the grapevine, was a politician in uniform. His job description no longer dictated that he don his uniform and chase after criminals on a Royal Enfield. His responsibility was to manage the department, uphold peace in the city of Mumbai and maintain public relations. He was the shepherd and as a shepherd, he didn't want his sheep to stray. He was to also ensure that no harm came to his sheep.

Isha Thapar was much more than a mere social acquaintance. Sexy and she had attended seminars on social injustice, and the upliftment of women – socially, culturally, morally. They had been featured together in the media as two modern-day champions of the underdog. And now, DCP Rita had put him in an awkward hole.

He didn't partner with anyone that didn't come vetted by the entire police and PR machinery. And Isha Thapar had come with the judicial establishment behind her. His silence spoke volumes of the embarrassment the department would face in light of Isha going out on a limb to bail out someone who his star DCP had hunted down on suspicion of his being a serial killer. And even if Ranbeer Kumar wasn't the unsub whom they sought to lay by the heels, this guy had enough to go down as a sick pervert for all the banned content he had accessed or downloaded. Had Isha Thapar been indiscreet or had DCP Rita Ferreira put her foot in it?

'I'd need to make a call,' said the big man finally.

'Yes, sir.'

'Do you mind ...?' Sexy didn't have to spell it out. He didn't want anyone to listen in to the conversation when he spoke to the lawyer.

Joshi and Rita walked out and waited in the outer office while Commissioner Saxena asked his secretary to get Isha Thapar on the line.

'Good afternoon, Ms Thapar, how are you?'

'Good afternoon, Commissioner Saxena. I'd be lying if I said I wasn't expecting your call.'

Smart woman, he thought. She had anticipated Rita rushing to him.

'In that case, I won't beat around the bush. How did Ranbeer Kumar become your client?'

'He's not. Someone else, who's our client, paid our firm to get Ranbeer off the hook.'

'Who was that?'

'I'm sorry, I've been asked not to name the client.'

'By who?'

'By the client.'

'By this anonymous patron?'

'He's anonymous to you, not to us, Commissioner Saxena.'

The commissioner's smile froze on his face, before it dissolved. He realized that his hands were shaking and his lips twitched with rage. He looked out of the window to distract himself from his frustration. Daylight was fading to dusk. He could feel his heart shift into overdrive, but he didn't want to go ballistic. That wasn't his style at all.

'Is your anonymous client an altruistic philanthropist who feels compelled to reimburse other people's invoices or did he choose Ranbeer for his exceptional skill set?'

'I completely understand and am wholly convinced about the reason for my client wanting to defend the accused. I cannot elaborate on my conversation with my client. I can promise you that he didn't hire me to obstruct justice in any way. He hired me to get justice for the defendant and—'

Saxena let the silence hang for a while, before she continued, 'Let's just say he's a Good Samaritan.'

'A Good Samaritan recompensing a lawyer to save a demented killer?'

'Ranbeer is just someone accused and has not been convicted yet. He's accused by your department on mere suspicion, and they have no corroborating evidence that the guy is actually involved in any murders.'

'D'you have evidence that he hasn't killed them?'

'You're forgetting something, Commissioner Saxena,' Isha jested, 'I don't have to prove anything. I don't have to prove that the defendant is not guilty. The prosecution has to prove beyond a shadow of doubt that my client committed the crime.'

'So, you're going to serve me ambiguous morsels from law books now?'

'Not at all, sir. But you should appreciate that everyone has a constitutional right to defence in this country.'

The sky outside was changing from blue to marmalade, the sun had wound up for the day and gone.

'Moreover, I can't tell you anything, as I'm bound by advocate-client confidentiality.'

'You know as well as I do that the clause doesn't apply here, Isha. I'm not asking you to recount your candid conversations with the defendant. All I need to understand is why someone who is unrelated to the entire case would foot the bill for someone who's accused of heinous crimes like these. And how could you be in cahoots with someone like that?'

'That train has left the station, sir, and I'm already on board ...'

'Pull the chain and get off.'

'Are you telling me to give up a case?'

'No, I'm asking you to tell us who this Good Samaritan is who got Ranbeer off the hook.' Saxena didn't think the conversation was going the way he had anticipated. She was a lawyer, very articulate and glib. Up until now, he had always been polite and only made requests. Perhaps it was time to pull the right strings.

'Commissioner Saxena, you're putting me in a spot here.'

'Isha, no one who has ever locked horns with my office has come out ahead.' The threat was delivered in an even tone, but Saxena made the message crystal clear. 'What I'm asking you is not really a request.'

'I know I can trust you ...' The lawyer's tone turned conciliatory. She had jested and taken liberties so far because she knew him personally outside of work with their successful partnership at social events. Any other lawyer would have soiled his trousers upon hearing the underlying threat in Saxena's modulated voice.

The conversation carried on for another ten minutes before he thanked her, and she requested him once again not to let the information get to the media for the reasons that she had outlined.

'Don't worry on that account at all, Isha. Have a nice day.'

'It's a minor coincidence, nothing that should sink the ship,' Sexy began when Joshi and Rita had been summoned back into his office. For a change he sat informally on the L-shaped sofa, his right leg crossed over his left knee, displaying his expensive tan loafers under his natural linen trousers. Ever since Rita had known him, he had always been in mufti, never in uniform. There had even been a momentous day when he had turned up to work in his fancy golfing trousers. 'It wasn't a simple conversation, as you can imagine. Isha, being a lawyer, was being unreasonably protective about her real client who hired her to get Ranbeer out, and I had to make her ratiocinate …'

Rita wanted to smile. Had he spoken to Isha peppering his language with such words? Perhaps she couldn't deal with the impossibly abstruse lexicon and eventually gave in to Sexy's demands?

'Obviously I had to keep our arguments under wraps, which were apocryphal anyway …'

In summary, Isha Thapar had been hired by PMC, Personal Machines Corporation. More specifically, by the head of corporate affairs or PR – Sexy didn't offer a name so either Isha hadn't told him or had sworn him to secrecy – to protect PMC. PMC was all set to launch their Initial Public Offering in the forthcoming months. As the entire business model of PMC prided itself on delivering service to the end user at customer locations, mainly homes and offices, if it leaked out that one of their service staff was involved in anything criminal, they could kiss the IPO goodbye. Of course, Ranbeer wasn't employed by the company, but even by association – since most of the home service was outsourced to contracted staff – their reputation would understandably be compromised. PMC's brand value would plummet and lose its most valued commodity – people's trust.

PMC had been left with no choice. Even if they offered payment in gold, no public relations firm could have saved them if the news had got out.

'Shouldn't they have contacted us, rather than sending in a hot-shot lawyer to act as Ranbeer's counsel?' Rita asked when Sexy had finished his spiel.

'I couldn't agree more, Rita. However, we can't blame them for making an imprudent choice in a frenzied situation. They obviously panicked.'

'I totally agree, sir.' Joshi, who had been a mute spectator all this while, wanted to conclude the discussion.

'How do we know that Isha Thapar is telling us the truth?' Rita rallied.

'Good point, Rita. You didn't think I'd let it pass without affirmation, did you? I know the CEO, Rajat Khanna, personally. I will get him to aver. Leave that to me.'

'Thank you, sir.'

Joshi, pleased that the conversation with the commissioner was over, stood up.

'Just one more thing,' Sexy had something more to say, 'the info on Ranbeer being associated with PMC should not leave this office. I gave my word to Isha. PMC will lay-off Ranbeer with immediate effect, and distance themselves from the deplorable guy, which makes sense.'

'So, can we rearrest him?'

'Not on the murder charge unless you find further evidence implicating him in the crime, since whatever we have so far – his involvement in installing PMC machines – has been torn asunder by his lawyer. However, you can make an arrest on the grounds of accessing, downloading or possessing banned pornography as soon as our experts dig up tangible evidence from his confiscated machine.'

'Thank you very much, sir,' Rita got up to leave as well.

On the way out, Rita repeated the words to memorize them: *Ratiocinate, apocryphal* ... she made a mental note to look up the words in the dictionary tonight.

Rita sat alone licking her wounds. A small defeat, but a defeat nevertheless. Just when she had thought that she had all her ducks in a row, one of the ducks walked sideways to take a dump.

Crap, literally and figuratively!

She returned home after an eventful day: the bust on Ranbeer, Isha Thapar walking into the Andheri precinct to get him released, the call from Sexy and the unravelling of a truth.

All in all, an eventful day, so why crib?

At seven in the evening, she sat on the low bay window seat in her living room, Dave Brubeck's *Time Out* played on the turntable, a bottle of Jim Beam by her side. She had walked in after the day's work, peeled off her jacket, holster, boots and jeans. She hadn't bothered to wear anything under the shirt that she had worn to work this morning.

Rita had been successful once before in investigating and catching a serial killer. And she could sense her past feat already haunting her. She guessed the media would be on her case before the sun came up. They had a notorious tradition of putting people on a pedestal when they succeeded and then riding roughshod over them at the first signs of failure. She knew well that a trial by media meant you were guilty until proven innocent. It was left to you, and you alone, to prove your innocence, and the one way to prove that was with results.

The desperation to succeed was a horrible feeling. She reckoned that fear of failure had driven her into taking the ill-considered step of arresting Ranbeer Kumar. Was she losing her touch, her gut feel? Something over which she thought she had control?

Retrospection was easy; it was also frustrating at times like this. Going by the statistics, and by any book or literature she had ever read on psychopaths, she should have known that serial killers adhered to a strictly regimented modus operandi. Besides having above-average intelligence quotients, they prided themselves on being highly organized individuals. Planning was as important to them as the actual act itself. Of course, the MO was modified over time as they grew proficient and self-assured and then overconfident – which led to their downfall – but they didn't change the MO radically. Their signature on the killings, prima facie remained the same, albeit it did gradually evolve, getting finer and more defined. The crimson lipstick being brutally eaten off the lips of the victims had been this unsub's unmistakable signature.

Just as any artist performing a craft, practice made them perfect and hence, the MO was followed to the T to avoid making mistakes. Mistakes could mean getting caught. It was a matter of life and death. The MO wasn't restricted to the actual kill, it extended to the enactment of the entire fantasy from start to finish. Serial killers were known to act in defined phases: spot a prey, stalk her, lure her, lull her into complacency so she allowed him into her home and into her bedroom, before proceeding to overpower her. In this particular case, the killer had somehow convinced his victims to be willingly tied up, seeing as there were no signs of struggle before the three girls had been restrained – no furniture broken or overturned in the room, no drugs found in the victims' bodies – a clear indication that he hadn't randomly picked up the women. Perhaps that was a conjectural leap, maybe the guy had carried a gun or a knife and threatened to kill the women if they resisted, protested or refused to do his bidding. Still it didn't make sense – there had to be some initial scuffle, at least one of the victims would have attempted to run, tripping over something. There was nothing.

No serial killer just chanced upon his victim. Ted Bundy, the infamous serial killer, researched painstakingly to find safe sites to seize and dispose of his victims. Most went for a certain type of victim. Admittedly, the three women had similarities: Gina, Radha and Anu fell into the light-skinned, petite, active women category. What rankled with Rita most was, what if they had missed some vital clue, and zeroed in on the wrong suspect, Ranbeer Kumar?

She picked up the tumbler, upended the liquid and refilled it. She sashayed to the refrigerator, topped up her drink with ice and on the way back to her seat, flipped the record to side B. It was warm and sultry even though she was only in a shirt and not much else. The window to the balcony was open, so the mellow music melded with the whistling of the wind. She undid a few buttons at the top to let in some air between her breasts.

She took a generous sip of Jim – 'kissed Jim' as she called it – and wondered what Ash would think. Her team had detained Ranbeer Kumar because he was the common link between Radha and Anu. However, this fact had also become his defence, so therefore this was where she and her team had gone wrong. If his MO was to target the women for whom he installed computers, how did he find Gina? It was too much of a deviation from his regular routine. If he had picked up Gina from the kerb, then Radha would have also been picked up in the same way, which made Anu an outlier because she didn't walk the streets soliciting clients. It had to be one or the other. There was little chance that the unsub would use two MOs to identify his victims. Moreover, considering the deftness with which this unsub operated and carried out the murders – not a shred of evidence, no fluid, not even a single strand of hair – it would be disrespectful to his intelligence to assume that he would make the mistake of leaving a trail that could be linked back to him in any aspect of his diabolical scheming. He would surely have calculated that the police would eventually figure out that the computers were installed by the same person. Therefore, such an obvious suspect couldn't have been the killer; ergo, it positively wasn't Ranbeer Kumar.

Well, if she was going to gamble on mere hope she ought to have been prepared to accept disappointment. Hope was always underwritten by uncertainty so it could go either way. Sadly this time, she had been left holding the short end of the stick.

She took another sip of Jim and realized with a start that she had finished her third drink. This had to stop, she knew. Gulping down bourbon subconsciously was a harbinger to alcoholism. She decided she would drink consciously and responsibly from now onwards and poured herself two fingers of Jim to start over. She added ice, switched the music to an old Hindi film's: *Haadsaa*; Mumbai had been Bombay then.

The only silver lining in this entire botched-up day had been that Ranbeer Kumar wasn't some upright citizen who would go whining to the media and cause further embarrassment to Mumbai Police. He was vile anyway, and he would be arrested sooner or later on charges of subscribing to banned pornography. Unfortunately, criminals never left behind well-defined pieces of a puzzle for the police to fit together. All there was were warped and distorted clues that made no sense whatsoever. Some did that deliberately, while others were too deranged to make sense of what they did. But Ranbeer couldn't be condoned or overlooked. It was her job to investigate and arrest, it was the court's job to determine whether the doer was sane or not; whether he needed to be incarcerated or committed. He was not to be ignored. *Theirs not to reason why* ... thank you, Lord Tennyson.

'*Yeh Bombay sheher haadason ka sheher hai*' drifted through the speakers. Rita lazily stripped off her shirt and panty, and walked into the bathroom. A cold shower was mandatory before bed.

Dinner, she had no plans for. Jim had filled her up with liquid alone.

She tried calling Ash again from the shower, but his phone went straight to voicemail. She had left a message for him earlier, and he had left one for her in turn. They hadn't been able to speak to each other directly. Well, just two days to go and Ash Mattel would be in town again. She slipped into bed thinking about it, a smile on her lips. The smile all but vanished when she noticed a premature grey hair in her mane: a rogue gene from her father who had inherited it from someone up the ancestral chain. Her father never dyed his hair, but she was self-conscious. The vanity of a woman dictated that hair defined age. Being older was nothing to be ashamed of; if anything, it proved you've lived longer than the younger person eyeing your silver. But still.

She abandoned her bed thirty minutes after the first morning alarm, wolfed down two half-boiled eggs and sluiced it down with an extra-large mug of dairy-free coffee before setting out for work.

INTERLUDE
1998

I had appeared for Class XII final exams when my parents decided they'd had enough of each other. It wasn't the wrong thing, if you asked me. These past few years had gotten quite claustrophobic living under the same roof with them. The jibes, the taunts, the acerbic remarks, the caustic undertones; the two had started sleeping in different bedrooms and using separate bathrooms. The dinners that were a pain earlier had become unbearable over time.

Perhaps they had waited for me to finish school so as to protect my young mind from the trauma of the divorce, but I don't think that was the reason, although my mother, more than my father, may have convinced herself that she had done the right thing by waiting for this moment.

She announced that she wanted to move out.

Not move out to live on her own.

Not move out to live in a different location in Delhi.

No.

She admitted she had been seeing this Australian guy, her colleague, and she had decided to move to Australia with him. I had met the guy twice; he had come for dinner to our place as a work-colleague. He was at least a decade younger than my mother.

'*Shameful*,' disparaged Nutty-me. And he wasn't off the mark this time.

To add insult to injury, my mother did not even ask me whether I wanted to accompany her to Australia and live with her. She was quite clear in her mind on this front, as she told me, Dad could take care of me or, if he didn't want to, she was happy to have me put me into a hostel and the two would share the fees and expenses. End of discussion.

My disgust was further compounded by the fact that my father didn't bring the roof down. He didn't, even once, show any anger or loathing. He didn't even ask any questions or threaten to take her to court for planning to live with another man when she hadn't been legally divorced.

'*Told you, he's a pussy*,' Nutty-me didn't mince words, did he?

Perhaps my father understood that taking my mother to court would be futile. She wasn't asking for custody of her only child – who was eighteen, anyway – she wasn't asking for alimony or any money or even a share in the apartment that we lived in. What would the court say? How would a judge stop her? If anything, my father would look like a cuckolded old fart.

Nevertheless, I loathed him. As much as I hated my mother for doing what she did, I hated my father for playing a doormat.

My mother moved out within days of announcing she had a younger lover.

'*The over-sexed cougar can't wait to be with her new boy-toy, don't you think?*' Nutty-me sneered. How was I supposed to respond to that? Every time I closed my eyes, the rerun of Tina bound and spread-eagled on her stomach, the fat-old man taking her from behind, ran like a film in front of me. Intermittently, Tina changed to my mother and the old man turned into my mother's Australian boyfriend.

With mother moving out, my father took to the bottle like a godforsaken *Majnu*, when I knew he was anything but. He had let his wife walk away with her lover, hadn't attempted to reason with her, to stop her even. Pretender!

Did you ever, ever, ever-ever even in your deepest nightmare, think that your life would turn out to be what you had never imagined. Or intended? Welcome to my world!

I decided I didn't want to live with my father either. He invariably got maudlin every night after he got drunk. Was *I* supposed to comfort him? Assure him that his wife, my mother, was fine with someone else in Australia, while he smooched the whisky bottle day and night? As a matter of principle, I did not apply to any college in Delhi. I wanted to get out of the place, and I got admission into St Xavier's, Mumbai. That was it. I left in June that year. I sent my address and bank account details to my father so he could send me money. But he sent me the money just twice. Then, all of a sudden, he stopped, and I was left scrounging for money. I felt let down, but I wasn't going to beg or belittle myself before someone who, in my mind, was gutless and spineless. We stopped corresponding. I got myself a part-time job in a music store, and then in a restaurant, waiting tables. I managed the fees and living expenses, albeit on a shoestring budget, but it was still better than begging.

Even Nutty-me was proud of me.

2001

Technology had been witnessing exponential growth in usage and adaptation at the time I completed my first college degree. Every company was rapidly expanding; everyone wanted to grow more quickly than their competitors. Spending was lavish and salaries were being pelted out like money grew on the proverbial trees. I got my first job in a software technology firm that offered me stock options. All my co-workers held on to the stock, but I was fortunate since my misfortune helped me. As I was cash-strapped, I sold half of my stock options exactly on the day they matured after one year, not a day later. I had nine lakhs and loose change in my bank account three weeks before the historic collapse of the dot-com bubble. Nine lakhs was a lot of money in 2001.

The internet saved my life, to be honest.

Nutty-me was ecstatic when we first dialled up and connected to the web and watched porn in the early college days. I realized I wasn't alone in my proclivities. There were enough people in the world who liked super-sex, which the boring people labelled as aberrant. BDSM – Bondage, Discipline, Sadism and Masochism – was more than an acceptable form of release. There were enough people participating in it for it not to be termed 'deviant' anymore. The frenzied release I had when I was with Tina years ago was now accessible to watch whenever I wanted. I didn't need to re-enact it to myself to feed my fantasies, which eliminated the high risk involved.

MSN and Yahoo! chat rooms were a blessing. As someone said: if you asked to have sex with a goat, people no longer thought you were weird; instead they asked, what kind of goat? This was a whole other world, a world of absolute anonymity with people holding each other's hands to find bliss, satiating the mind's darkest cravings, without a fear in the world.

TEN

Commissioner Sanjay Saxena kept his word. It could be argued that it wasn't so much to keep his word to Joshi and Rita, but to satisfy his own curiosity, but the end result was the same. He made the call to Rajat Khanna the very next morning.

'Mr Khanna, this is Saxena from Mumbai Police.' He knew very well that the secretary would have already told Khanna or his assistant – whoever picked up the call – that it was the Police Commissioner of Mumbai on the line. He didn't have to reiterate his position.

'I like your sense of humour, Commissioner *sahib*. You aren't just another officer from Mumbai Police. You are Mumbai Police, sir. How may I be of assistance?'

'Is your company in the process of issuing an IPO?'

'The news isn't public yet, but yes, sir, we are planning to offer one. I won't ask how you came to know our little secret … I am sure you have your informers everywhere. We've been meaning to expand our operations into smaller cities but, as you know, capital from banks and other lenders is always expensive, so we decided to go straight to public. I didn't know you were an investor. We have some preference shares in case you—'

'I apologize if it came across as that; that wasn't the reason for my call.'

'Oh, I'm sorry I misunderstood. How can I help?'

Sexy wondered whether this corroboration was sufficient. Isha had said she had been asked to get Ranbeer off because his obnoxious hobby would have become an embarrassment to the forthcoming IPO, and Khanna had just affirmed that. Khanna was the chairman of PMC; he may or may not be involved in the day-to-day activities.

'Do you know Isha Thapar?'

'Of course, sir, she is one of our external legal consultants.'

'Ah, I see. Isha and I spoke a little while ago and she had mentioned she was handling something for PMC.'

'Is anything the matter, sir?'

'Why do you ask?'

'Don't get me wrong, but you didn't make this call to check on our IPO or Isha Thapar, so it makes me wonder if there's something I'm not aware of ...'

'Would you know someone by the name of Ranbeer Kumar, Mr Khanna?'

'Who? Ranbeer Kumar? No, not off the top of my head. Who is he?'

'He's someone we caught with his pants down, so to speak, and Isha Thapar was brought in to get him off the hook by someone in your organization?'

'Is Ranbeer an employee of ours?'

'He's certainly a member of your esteemed organization – either a full-time employee or a contractor, I wouldn't know.'

'That's strange. We have our own legal department for employee-related issues, so why would someone hire Isha – she's one of the most expensive lawyers in town? Beats me. Do you want me to check and come back to you?'

'No, it's not imperative, and I'd appreciate it if you don't mention this conversation to anyone, especially Isha.'

'I'm curious now, sir. What is this about?'

'Do you know anything about the recent serial murders in Mumbai, the media has given him the moniker of "Lipstick Killer"?'

'Yes, now it makes sense to me. I know who you're talking about, sir. I'm sorry I didn't know the name of the guy – we have a staff of over a thousand people, plus the contractors, so it's impossible to know everyone by name, but I remember my head of finance, who is responsible for the IPO, mentioning some guy had been taken into custody, and he needed to be bailed out and then fired. I wasn't aware he had retained Isha for this.'

So Isha was not being mendacious. PMC was going for public funding, and someone at the company had hired Isha to save their ass by getting Ranbeer out of their hair. The commissioner saw no reason to probe further, especially because he did not want to involve too many people, least of all the finance head who might have hired Isha. Rita could arrest Ranbeer on other charges if the techies could break into his hard drive and gather evidence.

'Thanks, Mr Khanna, you've been a tremendous help in providing corroboration to what was conveyed to us.'

'I can't say it's a pleasure, but it's certainly my duty. As I'm told, we'll be distancing ourselves from this person, so if he is actually involved in any crime, I'll ask my head of finance to not obstruct the investigation.'

'Oh, don't do anything I request you. The miscreant will be arrested soon on other charges, which I cannot divulge for now due to the ongoing investigation. Mr Khanna, I wish you all the best for the coming IPO.'

'Thank you, sir.'

Sexy then called Rita to inform her that Isha Thapar had been honest, and that Rita should continue investigating Ranbeer. He may not be the Lipstick Killer, but it was vital that a guy like him not be wandering around at large in Mumbai.

'Given the situation, there was a definite link between two of the three homicides. I understand it was crucial for you to check out Ranbeer Kumar; but the bust did mean that you jumped the gun.' As per his itinerary, Ash Mattel was in Mumbai two days later. As he didn't have any other business to attend to and didn't need to check into a hotel, Rita had arranged for a police car to pick him up at the airport and brought directly to Crawford Market precinct. Harry quickly brought him up to speed on the events of the past few days, filling in the gaps after the information faxed to him in Delhi. Rita decided to keep him at an arm's length in the office and she had only now come into the conference room after he had been briefed and was ready to analyse their investigation so far and provide any help in profiling the Lipstick Killer.

Rita, Vikram, Jatin and Harry looked askance at this opening remark.

'With all due respect, Ranbeer hardly fits the profile of the killer you're looking for in this case.' Ash explained. 'If you had only had Gina and Radha as homicide victims, maybe yes, but the murder of Anu Singh was a game changer for me.'

Rita and company exchanged glances, wholly at sea. What had they missed?

'First of all, your unsub is not a teen or a youngster so yes, Ranbeer does slot into the profile by age, I give you that. I reckon he is between twenty-five and forty max ...'

'How can you say that?' Harry wanted to know.

'Remember, this isn't an exact science, but he would neither have the confidence nor the wherewithal if he were any younger. It takes money to hire hookers and he needs some experience to impress Anu in the sexual foreplay. She wouldn't let a college guy tie her up, no way. And he can't be older than forty, because if he were, where has he been until now? He couldn't have suddenly decided to go on a killing spree on his fortieth birthday.'

'But if he were thirty, you could ask the same question: where had he been until now?

'My analysis is that Gina wasn't his first murder—'

'I need a coffee,' Rita cut in.

Harry volunteered to fetch some. Rita smiled; she knew he needed a smoke break too. They swore the analysis wouldn't continue in his absence. He returned with a decent brew in styrofoam cups.

'The first murder may not have been planned, but it predates the murder of Gina. It must have given him a high, a release that led to further murders. There was a considerable gap between the first murder and Gina's. The unsub has resisted the temptation for a long time for reasons we don't know yet. Then more quickly ... he has gone from a five-month gap to three months between the second and third kills. A clear sign that he's unable to fight his pent-up frenzy any longer.'

'Do you mean the unsub could have been okay for the last decade or so and then suddenly went postal because something tripped? What may have set him off again, if he managed to resist the urge all these years?' Rita asked.

'Some event triggered the heretofore latent or controlled desire, or something reminded him of his past that never really got buried, and now he's finally gone berserk like he has been set on fire. The wanton lust must have been driving him crazy all along, but he still seemed to be in control. Someone or something has taken the lid off his crazy jar.'

'But serial killers are identified by their MOs,' argued Vikram, 'so, if he killed someone before Gina, it should be on record. We've gone back as far as the records go, but found nothing with the same MO.'

'The MOs are similar if not exactly the same in most cases, you're right Vikram, but the MO could evolve and change over time. However, the craving that compels the psychopaths to commit those crimes seldom diminishes. It only grows. It's sparked by something initially. There has to be a pattern in the victims – Gina, Radha and Anu were more similar than dissimilar, and in situations like these, it's not a superficial desire, it's almost a pathological need. He would only kill the ones that fit the mould – both physically and mentally because merely killing doesn't fulfil the need, killing a certain kind satiates him.'

'For a moment, if we overlook Gina and Radha, it tells me that the unsub is definitely from a well-to-do background,' Rita surmised. She had always felt that Ash unleashed the best in her. He was like the ignition for her brain. 'Anu Singh was hardly the kind who would go with just anyone. The guy would need to have a reasonable social standing, minimum. She wasn't slumming, she was looking for something that was deficient in her marriage. The spice, so to speak.'

'Correct. Your unsub would be a normal man and a killer at the same time. Two personas. But he's smart enough not to let the two overlap. He wouldn't fluidly switch from one persona to the other in full public view. He has total control.'

'Team,' Rita took over, and Vikram started jotting down each word in his own shorthand. 'I think the subject here has a real life of some kind ... he doesn't take trophies from his victims like some psychopaths. He doesn't want anything that could link him to the crimes. Perhaps he lives with someone. He doesn't want anyone to chance upon his trophies, which could make them suspicious and serve as evidence. He may not be taking pictures or videos for the same reason, because however discreet one may be, there's always a chance that someone could inadvertently stumble upon such footage. He's meticulous, we know that, and therefore he won't be easy to figure out.

'He blends in. He leads a normal life as far as anyone who knows him or interacts with him is concerned. But that normal life is an illusion. He lives that life to get by. He actually thrives on enacting his fantasy and he cannot stop himself even if he tried, for whatever reasons,' Rita looked at Ash who nodded.

'You've got it. Some hurt must have led to hatred of some kind towards someone. I'm guessing it's hatred for his mother or sister, some female in his life, or a combination of them when he was younger, and the warped mind is taking revenge, not necessarily targeted at the people who hurt him, but at the people who unwittingly kindle similar feelings.'

'And the angst that he had been suppressing all along has got ignited again.'

It was almost evening when Vikram stood up and bulleted all the points on the whiteboard in the Ops Room that could define the profile. Of course, they would need to tidy up and add details as they went along, but this was a good start.

Everyone thanked Ash. Vikram offered to drop him wherever he needed to go, but Ash made an excuse, saying that he was staying with on old friend, who would pick him up later.

'With all this nasty business going on around you, I can feel the hair at the back of my neck fairly bristles,' Ash said when they were alone in Rita's office later.

'Not for me, mate. I get my back waxed.'

'Ooh-la-la.'

'And who is this old college friend who's coming to pick you up?'

'I'm already with her, aren't I?'

INTERLUDE
Present

Some people may think that I'm unemotional and insensitive. When I'm gone, some people may tell you that I was evil, perhaps even call me a psychopath. Don't believe them. I am not. I am anything but irrational and impractical; perhaps only slightly more detached than your average guy on the street. I've lied. Not harmless, innocent lies, but lies, which, when uncovered, will question the very façade that I live behind. But there's nothing to worry about. When the time comes – and it will, someday – I'll be gone. I have fake papers, forged by one of the best counterfeiters in the world: passport, ID, driving licence. I have even travelled to New York on the counterfeit passport, and neither the officials at Mumbai airport nor in New York caught on. I have stashed money in banks abroad, and I have no attachments here in Mumbai that I cannot leave behind. I have no interest in childish, self-indulgent things like other human beings have – no stamp collections or heirlooms to carry with me. And putting on a disguise is child's play for me. So, you see, when the time comes and the heat gets too much to bear, I'll be gone like I never existed.

Not even once have I thought of my parents in all these years after college, when I made my fortune hand over fist. What was there to remember anyway? She had emigrated with her lover, leaving me with her weak ex-husband. Was I supposed to cry for her, or for my father who spinelessly watched his wife waltz out of his life like he was a spectator at Wimbledon and the referee had asked him to keep silent?

'*A wimp*,' Nutty-me called him.

I continued with my passion for solitude, the me-time, and never made any close friends. Business associates yes, since I couldn't survive in a vacuum. One needed people to work with. Whenever someone asked about my parents, I told them that they had passed away in a tragic accident when I was eighteen. In a way it was the truth. Death did not necessarily mean leaving the planet. My relationship with them was deceased around that time, so it wasn't strictly untrue.

Nutty-me never fails to incite me. Every time I'm in the company of a female who remotely resembles Tina Aggarwal – petite, powerful, conceited, adulteress – he starts jumping with ecstasy. I would be lying if I said the prospect of having them at my mercy doesn't excite me, but the risk is simply too great. I have come too far from Tina to return to that. That was a part of me that I despise, but I have moved on, I think.

I've read all about *Retaliatory Fantasies*. Such fantasies are subconsciously sired by the evil in early life, like memories of my own mother. Back then if I had wanted to retaliate, to take revenge, I couldn't because she was way more powerful than me; physically, mentally, financially. But I abhorred her. Then Tina Aggarwal, who was in the same mould as my mother, came along – the physical semblance, the sexual deviance. I wasn't the only one who drew a parallel; Nutty-me approved too. In my darkest hours I've read about someone called Bobby Long whose mother, like mine, had crossed sexual boundaries and he, too, believed that any woman who reminded him of her was deviant and he had to take care of them, in his own way. Another one called Ed Kemper was like me as well. He killed ten women similar to his mother before he could work up the courage to kill his mother and then turned himself in. Nutty-me urged me, now and again, to follow Long and Kemper, to seek revenge. I told him off firmly.

Similarities aside, I know none of this applies to me. Tina had been a one-off. An adolescent mistake, however gratifying it might have been. Moreover, I could never accomplish the grand finale that Kemper achieved. It's never going to happen for I know my mother is somewhere in Australia. Where? I don't know and I don't care.

Like I said, I've moved on.

But.

This world has been wicked right from the start. One day, in the office, I received a phone call from someone that wrecked my resolve. Turned out to be someone who knew my father since he lived in the same neighbourhood.

He said that my father was dying of liver cancer. It had metastasized and he had a few weeks left. The caller identified himself as a 'good neighbour' but I blocked him out. Who cared for the neighbour when I had no interest in all that I had left behind? I heard the neighbour out, thanked him for the information and decided to give the news a pass. I didn't care for my father when he was alive, why would I bother now? What had changed? Nothing.

Nutty-me turned chicken on that occasion. Which was very unlike him. He had always shown more resilience than me, but he insisted that we must visit my father, if only to have closure.

That night in February, I couldn't sleep at all; morning, I called the office and made an excuse – I couldn't tell them that my already deceased father was dying once again, could I? – and took the midday flight to New Delhi.

He still lived in that godforsaken apartment in Vasant Kunj where his wife had left him, only the apartment now resembled a dump. It was the same furniture, the upholstery stained and in tatters, the curtains yellowed and torn, the paint peeling. My father, too, was a fraction of what I remembered. Just skin and bone, like a skeleton that could barely walk. I wondered what had kept him alive so long. Perhaps death hadn't found a reason to get to him earlier.

A faint smile broke out on his lips when he saw me. I didn't even pretend to be happy. My mother didn't make an appearance at his deathbed. What was the point anyway? Was she even alive? And where? I couldn't care less. Honestly if you asked me, they were both full of lies and full of shit.

The neighbour who had called me was the only happy soul in the room. I wanted to throttle him for calling me, for finding out about me, and passing on the information. To his credit, he kept quiet. I didn't encourage him one bit. The only thing worse than being sad is pretending to be happy. I know because I had spent my entire childhood doing that, and I wasn't doing it anymore for anyone.

The doctor said my father had weeks to live, but he died in his sleep on the very night that I got there.

'Won't you perform his last rites?' My neighbour was shocked when I told him I was leaving the next morning.

'No, I'm not his real son,' I told him, 'and never ever call me again.'

'What about the property?'

'That's none of your business.'

I walked out and went to the airport. All the memories that I had put a lid on erupted. Tina … my adolescent days … my pretend-happy childhood …

But my umbilical cord was finally cut. Like the wind takes control of a kite after its string is cut, I sensed Nutty-me taking over. This time around I let him.

ELEVEN

'I've got something for you,' Ash said, when they entered Rita's apartment. They had had to wait in the office for everyone to leave while they apparently waited for Ash's 'friend' to come pick him up. Rita gave her chauffeur, Kuldeep, the evening off. It wasn't that Kuldeep would tell anyone that Ash stayed with Rita, but she didn't want tongues wagging, just in case.

Rita turned around and kissed him. It was long and passionate, tongues tangoing in the dark.

'Was that kiss to shut me up?' he asked when it culminated.

'There was no other way.' She kissed him again with equal fervour.

'I miss you, but I can't ask you to quit your job and accompany me when I know that that was exactly why you broke up with your previous boyfriend.'

'So, what have you got for me?'

'Jack. I thought I'd get you someone other than Jim so you can have a threesome sometimes. And a new record.'

He had visited her enough times to know where everything in the apartment was. He opened a bottle of Jack Daniel's and poured a large one for each of them, walked to the kitchen and topped it up with ice. When he came out Rita was sans jeans and boots, squatting in her shirt tails in front of her turntable, the new LP in her hands. It was the original soundtrack of the film *Searching for Sugar Man*. As she gently extracted the record to put it on the gramophone, Ash told her the film was based on the true story of a 70's rocker, Rodriguez, who, after two albums that did not do too well in the US, had resigned himself to a life of obscurity. What he didn't know was that a bootleg recording of his had made it to South Africa and he had become quite a sensation there for two decades before some fans travelled to the States looking for him.

Two drinks down, they ordered pizza.

Three drinks down, the pizzas were finished and the boxes discarded into the trash.

Four drinks down the clothes started coming off.

Rita wound her arms around Ash's neck and pulled herself closer to him, their bodies almost clinging. He didn't resist, giving in to her embrace. She liked him wanting and providing at the same time, both strong and tender. His lips hungrily tasting the skin on her neck, his body odour mixed with the aftershave filling her nostrils with the spicy tang of his manly fragrance, as the embrace grew fiercer with every passing second. He picked her up and carried her to bed.

Her head fell back, her climax long and fulfilling and a simple '*Ash*' escaped her lips. But Ash kept moving, sweat building and moving down his back where she held him in her encircling arms. Then acrobatically he rolled her over, their bodies still fused at the centre. He thrust harder until he climaxed with a loud gasp and let his seed rush into her.

'You were a man possessed,' Rita spoke when he had withdrawn from her.

'You're trembling, sweetie? I'll go easy next time ...'

'Are you this funny with all women in bed?'

'That's a trick question, isn't it?'

'You're smart, I'll give you that.'

'A smart stallion with a sense of humour. Anything else I should put on my résumé, DCP?

'Before I give you any endorsement to apply for a position of international gigolo, I'd like to try you out a bit more.'

'Now?'

'Yes, any problem, Mr Stallion?'

Rita mounted him the second time around. Their lovemaking was passionate but delicate, not primal like the first time. They moved in tandem to a high crescendo until both lay panting.

'Once more?' Rita asked.

'Are you crazy?'

'It's Sunday, why not?'

The telephone rang at three in the morning. It was Ash's. It would be ten-thirty at night in the UK, he calculated. He slipped out of the bed and took the call.

'What's up?' Rita asked, when he returned to bed.

'I've been called back.'

'What?! You said you could stay here as long as you wanted.'

'I'm needed. There has been a series of murders back in the UK and they need me to come in asap to build a profile.'

'But you're doing the same here, how is that more important than this?'

'I'm a free, freelance consultant here; I'm employed there.'

'So, it's all about money?' Rita joked.

'Yes, honey. Let's not waste precious moments bickering about my return journey.'

'Is the stallion ready again?'

'At your service, ma'am.'

Before Ash left, he reiterated: 'something has to link the victims. That's how the game is played. Something in all his victims had to resonate with the women he goes after. The physical similarity is obvious, but how does he choose these similar-looking women in Mumbai?'

The link between the three women wouldn't be easy to establish, Rita knew, but they had to keep trying. Had the women known each other, however tenuously? If Ranbeer wasn't the common link, what else did these three women share? Where they shopped? Worked? Travelled? Ate? You find the connection, you've found the guy.

'I'll drop you at the airport,' Rita said.

Since receiving the call from his work, Ash had spent the morning contacting various airlines to get a ticket. He booked an early afternoon flight and was all set to go.

'Don't be ridiculous, just call me a cab.'

Ash left her around 9.30 a.m. and Rita's mind almost immediately switched back to the case. It was Sunday; the entire team had worked late into the night the previous day and hence, everyone decided to take the day off, unless of course there was an emergency.

With Ash's abrupt departure from Mumbai, Rita decided to fill the void with research. She had studied all about serial killers and psychopaths several times before, but it never ceased to amaze her how much new content was available every time she went online. It was a published statistic that at least a hundred serial killers were in operation at any time in America alone – each one working to fulfil their fantasies and devising new MOs all the time. But the real gen came from those who were nabbed and interviewed. The FBI was full of profilers at Quantico who analysed that data to come up with various motivations that drove these people. All of the published papers agreed on the definition of a textbook psychopath. They were devoid of any emotions, with a high enough IQ and a supernatural ability to plan. Much like Mumbai's own Lipstick Killer who made the notorious Dawood Ibrahim look like a novice. Killing, to this kind, was no different from a sportsperson pushing the boundaries and striving to jump higher with each attempt. Each time a psychopath got away with a risky manoeuvre, he'd attempt a riskier move. However, most serial killers stuck to their pattern. The known path. Venturing into the unknown was inviting trouble and prone to the possibility of making mistakes. Nevertheless, the Lipstick Killer had switched from hookers to a married woman. It would have given him that much more satisfaction to take a higher risk. Immaculate planning, from spotting the victim to the getaway. Only amateurs planned just the act. Anyone with even a half-decent IQ would choreograph the act and the getaway. Entry and exit. It was crucial to every plan.

Having had her first fill of literature on psychopaths, Rita looked out of the window. The sun was up there somewhere in the azure, cloudless sky although she could not see it. She glanced at the clock. It was lunchtime, and she hadn't even had breakfast.

After taking a shower, she put on a faded Pink Floyd T-shirt – XL – that ended just past her shapely derrière. Like a short skirt or a short dress. The old knitted material was soft and clung to her body. If she wasn't stepping out, she had to at least be comfortable. She wandered into the kitchen to forage and discovered two packets of Maggi masala noodles. She added some frozen peas to this and made herself a meal, as her mind continued to cogitate on the material she had read on the web.

While the published papers screamed that when a psychopath veered off his planned course, it could well be an early sign of him decompensating, the murder of Anu Singh was anything but. All their unsub had done was to alter the demographic profile of his victim. The physical profile and the MO hadn't altered at all. The Lipstick Killer was nowhere near losing control. He was still in control of his frenzy, not letting the compulsion control him. There would be much more gore if he lost control. Or if his need became more frequent.

There was never a single version of the truth. Some said that was fortuitous too, but you couldn't get people to agree on that statement either. One's upbringing coloured one's perceptions and hence one's version hinged on one's point of view. How was their unsub looking at the world? She failed to see any logic in his actions, but one couldn't see logic in everything. Not because there wasn't any; but because she couldn't apply rational logic to a twisted mind that lacked empathy. What was rational or right to her might be illogical to a delusional mind that had its own interpretation of the situation's logic – however warped. The unsub's motivation was outside her frames of reference. She couldn't think like him even if she tried because she would inadvertently empathize and rationalize things. He didn't. From an emotional standpoint he was more robot than human. How was Rita supposed to think like the rabid robot? In any case, she knew, her validation of his reasoning meant shit to him.

Dr Harold Shipman, considered one of the most prolific serial killers in the world, had killed over 250 of his patients in the UK before he forged a patient's will that outed him. One of the theories advanced was that he had done that deliberately because he was tired and wanted to be caught. Perhaps, one of these days, Rita mused, the Lipstick Killer could have a change of heart and walk into a police station and confess. A theoretical possibility, but she wouldn't hold her breath, nor could she let another victim die if she could help it.

Rita finished her lunch and fixed herself another coffee. This was the sixth since this morning. She didn't know what people meant when they said 'too much' caffeine. She could have coffee any time of the day, as many times as she could get one. She equated coffee with fear. Coffee woke her up, and it made her sleep. Fear galvanized her into action; fear also made her freeze.

Back at the computer with her large mug of coffee she read all about *Paraphilia*: psychopaths were enthralled by power. It gratified them sexually to have power over their victims, power over life and death. It was all about control.

With nothing else to do, Rita read until late in the evening. A waxing one-quarter moon had made an appearance; it would be a dark night. She fixed herself her first glass of Jim and put on the Sugar Man LP again. Music always gave her hope. So did Jim, although Jim added a splash of colour as well. She decided to alternate between Jack and Jim tonight. A threesome, as Ash called it.

Sixto Rodriguez's voice boomed out of speakers: '*'cause the sweetest kiss I ever got is the one I've never tasted.*' She smiled. She had planned her entire weekend around Ash, and he wasn't around now.

Back at the computer, something grabbed her attention. She froze. She read the paragraph twice. Then again:

'If there is an unexpected interruption midway through his ritual of enacting the fantasy OR if the police get too close soon after a murder, during his cooling off period OR if the police break his fantasy by making a wrong arrest and hijack the credit for his work, the psychopath would be compelled to seek his next victim sooner rather than later because the high wears off with such unplanned abortions.'

Fuck!

Psychopaths were perverts who were known to avidly follow the news. They got off on the part where their misdeeds were the talk-of-the-town. That was what they thrived on, an essential part of their game. Whoever the Lipstick Killer was he would have known that the Mumbai Police had arrested Ranbeer Kumar.

Had she and her team unwittingly rained on his parade? It certainly seemed possible and that should drive him into a frenzy. They might have inadvertently reduced his cooling-off cycle.

He was going to strike, and soon.

Fuck! Oh, it was so much more than 'fuck' and she could feel her pulse racing.

Fortunately, Jim and Jack helped tranquillize Rita and restore her equilibrium. She began to wonder if Homo sapiens were aliens who had shanghaied earth of its original inhabitants; whether Darwin's theory was just that: a theory. Perhaps she had imbibed too much Jim and Jack, and too quickly. The threesome wasn't for her, she noted.

TWELVE

Ranbeer Kumar was tired and famished. It had been more than a week since he had been set free by that godsent lady lawyer who had then promptly forsaken him on the pavement outside the Andheri precinct. At the time of his arrest he had been frogmarched out of his apartment without getting a chance to take any of his possessions with him. After his release he had steered clear of his home because it was still swarming with cops. When he eventually broke into the place in the dead of night, he found to his dismay that it had been turned upside down and inside out. They had confiscated his computer, his papers, his mobile phone, his wallet. Although the wallet didn't have much cash in it, it contained his only credit card. He lived a hand-to-mouth existence on the meagre earnings from his contract work with PMC. His credit card was used in advance before he paid off the dues at month-end. How was he supposed to live now?

Conscious that if the police had taken his computer, his hard drive might've revealed his under-the-radar activities, he decided it wasn't worth the risk to contact the police to ask for his credit card.

He begged a shopkeeper to let him make one call, but when he made the call to PMC for new work orders, panic shook him right down to the soles of his feet. He was emphatically told that he had been taken off the register of contractors and that he shouldn't contact them anymore. His question *why* was met with a stony silence. The HR manager at the other end of the phone had hung up. Strange!

With nowhere to go, no money to buy food, no place to sleep, he decided he would go to some railway station and find himself a place on the platform to weather the storm. This situation couldn't last forever.

What Ranbeer Kumar wasn't aware of was that the technical wizards of the Mumbai Police had recovered incriminating data from his hard drive. An arrest warrant for Mr Ranbeer Kumar had been issued and circulated, along with his photograph, to all the police stations across the state of Maharashtra.

They hadn't found him at his residence, as expected, and a citywide hunt had commenced.

What the Mumbai Police wasn't aware of was that someone else was looking for Ranbeer Kumar too. They had no reason to even imagine that anybody else might be interested in hunting down a scumbag who was wanted by the police for cybercrimes.

INTERLUDE
Present

As time progressed, my disgust changed to rage upon my return from Delhi. The memories that I had kept locked in the bottom drawer for decades had slipped out like an apparition to haunt me, twenty-four by seven. There was no barrier I could erect to keep these ghosts of my past at bay. The emotional turmoil was killing me. Nutty-me told me that the only way to find release was to find someone like Tina and … '*let your instincts take over*,' he advised. '*That's the only way you'll ever find peace*.'

But I was not an impressionable kid anymore. If I risked this course of action, I would have to be careful. Extremely systematic, which was hardly a chore for me as I've always been meticulous to a fault, bordering on obsessive-compulsive disorder (OCD).

I bought books on police investigations. All purchased in cash from various stores in different cities. I read all the literature available on forensics. I had no intention of getting caught, ever. I had no desire to be another substandard, boilerplate murderer who got nabbed after their first crime.

Every piece of information I read said: there was always some evidence left behind somewhere – hair, body fluid, prints, DNA; it was just a question of *when* and not *if* the police got to it; and what it could and would reveal. I wasn't going to give the police anything. I started waxing my body, and I liked it hairless like Tina's, every inch of it. That was to prevent any stray hair falling off my body when I started meeting other women.

The only hairs on my body are my eyebrows and eyelashes, which would be difficult to remove without getting noticed. I bought fake ones online, but they were a dead giveaway from five feet away. So, the eyebrows survived. And so did the eyelashes.

If you checked the traits on the Hare Psychopathy checklist I might come up as a psychopath, which I positively am not. Some guy in Canada called Robert Hare came up with a loony list. He should have been called Robert Hare-Brained if you ask me. Ha! One of the traits listed is that a psychopath is incapable of loving anyone but themselves. If that was something that the police believed, then I had to move away from that profile, didn't I? And I did.

I am not a narcissist, but I am an extremely handsome man – given that some of my genes came from my mother's pool. I keep my head shaved, wear John Lennon glasses and dress up well. Dapper. You don't expect women to trust you if you're unkempt and smell like goat's cheese that has passed its expiry date.

Hence, I asked a girl out on a date. She is a powerful woman in her own right; not someone in my office, but we've interacted a few times on occasion. I had to shed the persona of being a loner first of all. A man is but a creature of habit, they said. Wrong. Nutty-me and I are different. The girl I am courting is nothing like Tina or her type, either physically or psychologically. My girl is much taller, good looking – not the slutty good-looks – speaks well, and has curly hair, not straight. See, I am pragmatic, not some hopeless romantic. When I read up the literature and realized I couldn't remain a recluse, I needed a cover. There have been times when I've had to force myself to kiss her. She has hinted at staying over, and I've made excuses. I've used all sorts of ruses to keep her at a distance. If she were to get up close and personal, it could blow the lid off my most closely-guarded secret: I'm sexually different. I don't like what other men like. I know the situation will last only as long as it takes for her to figure out why I avoid her advances. Perhaps, I'll find a reason to break up with her before then. She could think I'm gay. Who cares? For now, she feels I'm the last of a dying breed, from the old school, that believes in marriage before sex; but it works for me and I keep up the pretence. Soon, I'll be expected to pop the question, and the status quo will change. Until then, we're apparently a couple, at least as far as the world is concerned. We've been seen in public, I've made sure of that. Perception is reality after all. Once the relationship culminates, I plan to publicly vow not to fall in love again and carry on that façade for a long, long time.

I simply cannot afford to leave anything to chance.

My next task was to find the sluts.

'*A hooker would be good to start,*' Nutty-me suggested. I started looking for someone that physically resembled Tina. In any event, hookers are promiscuous, so they neatly slotted into the sort I was looking for. But somehow, I felt let down. My interaction with two of them didn't provide the release I had anticipated.

Nutty-me recommended that I needed to find women who, in their daily lives, were respectable wives or girlfriends, but turned into sluts behind their husbands' backs. The real villains: the adulteresses.

You wouldn't agree I was sent to this earth for a reason, but that's your perspective and prerogative, because you work with limited knowledge. On some level I don't consider myself human. I'm suspended somewhere between God and humans. My gender is irrelevant; gender is pertinent for humans. I even had to undergo plastic surgery. No, I'm not a narcissist, it wasn't for vanity; it was more a corrective surgery. I travelled to Thailand to get my navel removed because it was an anatomical error. Adam and Eve did not have parents because they were not humans; neither am I. So, the navel was a mistake in my case.

Rarely, but yes, I've had this desire to give the police a call. Nutty-me wants to do that real bad. But I don't. I don't because if I make that one call, Nutty-me will make me call them every now and again. And every contact I make with them will provide them with an opportunity. They can analyse the voice, figure out the geographical position from where the call is made, if not by triangulating my mobile phone from the towers, then by the background noise. If I were to post a letter, they'll look for a postmark, fingerprints, DNA from saliva … I'm not saying I'm stupid enough to leave any evidence, but even someone with my level of intelligence can slip. So why make the police's task easier? Why do their jobs for them?

As I see it, that train has left the station with Nutty-me and I on board and neither of us is in any mood to pull the chain. We're having fun. We never started with an exit plan and I'm certain that we cannot stop now. Something inexplicable happens, forcing me to seek out these women. Subsequently, when I get these women to meet me, it's like all the blood in my veins pushes against a dam. The pressure goes all the way north until the dam bursts. The release is not human. The sensations travel to every fibre in my body. It's like a live electric jolt administered on an exposed nerve. The scale of pleasure is something like human ejaculation; I end up creaming my waterproof underwear every time. Add the thrill and the excitement to the cocktail and it's an incredibly potent high.

Once I'm done, I'm back to focussing on my work with renewed vigour. I'm successful in more ways than one: a polymath with an infinite variety of skillsets.

But the hunger strikes again after a while. I find something missing from my life. Sometimes you can only describe something because of its absence. I know when that occurs, I know I have to find someone to play with and I go hunting for the lucky candidate.

THIRTEEN

Profiling was once sneered at by most police forces around the world. Most detectives, in the absence of witnesses, relied solely on their deductive powers to investigate heinous crimes by looking for motives and opportunities and tying them together with the physical evidence that they unearthed. That's how Sherlock Holmes detected. That was how Hercule Poirot used his grey cells. And for the most part the pieces of the puzzle did fall into place. However, it has always been a challenge if the police find no known connection between the predator and the prey. Lack of any connection eliminated the motive. The ability to assign guilt rested solely on physical evidence; evidence which wasn't always traceable. As science progressed with various ways of collecting bodily evidence, the criminals too got savvier and found novel methods to avoid leaving their mark at the scene of the crime. Serial killers were the most notorious. By definition, no serial killer ever got apprehended during or soon after his first kill. Theirs was an incredibly sharp brain put to the wrong use.

Nevertheless, however careful they were in eliminating physical traces – blood, bodily fluids, DNA – there were indelible psychological traces that they left behind at the scene. Of course, these were subtle and open to misinterpretations. It wasn't an exact science; it was based on tell-tale patterns upon which the experts started to build a personality. It was a bit like looking at a moving shadow in dim light to paint a portrait. One of the reasons cited for the police failing to apprehend Jack the Ripper was that they never had a profile to work with. And with no physical evidence it was destined to become a cold case.

Primarily a lot of profiling worked on the premise that every serial killer had a subtext: a past, a reason – however twisted – for doing what they did. The trick was to reverse the clock. The *why*, the catalyst – what did the psychological traces left behind say about the experience, and therefore age – of the subject? Did the behaviours he exhibited suggest something about his education or social status?

Nobody ever had all the answers; not Jesus, not Buddha, not Krishna. But they asked the right questions. The right questions generated information, but even that didn't necessarily provide the answers – sometimes it was junk – but they were all building blocks. Like profiling.

Rita knew that such profiling went hopelessly wrong every now and then and, at times, came back to bite the investigators in the ass; then again, failure was always one of the many possibilities in every task. Even the best could make a mistake sometime. Nevertheless, she had drawn up a list:

Unsub Profile

1. Male
2. Age: 23–35 years, maybe 40, but no more

3. Sadist
4. In a reasonably good social and financial position
5. Holds himself in high esteem – he thinks he cannot be caught. False sense of pride
6. Arrogant … *She stopped to think: his arrogance would get him in the end, but the police couldn't wait for it*
7. Charming, persuasive … *She knew he had to be. Like Ted Bundy had been persuasive enough to let a married woman take him into her bedroom. The Lipstick Killer had done the same.*
8. Strong enough to strangle victims
9. Intelligent to plan, execute, get away, without leaving any clues
10. Works days, maybe weeks, rigorously planning his exploits. There was no way the rendezvous was put into Anu's diary on the day of her murder after her husband had travelled out of country that same morning.
11. Doesn't take trophies from victims – perhaps a family man?
12. Doesn't sexually penetrate the victims – compensating for some inadequacy?
13. Spends a minimum of 2 to 3 hours with victims – considering the damage to the bodies

The profile was sketched on feedback from Ash Mattel, the crime scene investigators and Mr Syed Khan, the morbid pathologist. Rita went through it numerous times. Forwards, backwards, sideways, diagonally, but nothing jumped out. She could have added that the psycho wetted his bed as a child and there was a high probability that she would be right. It was a common symptom displayed by such individuals, but it didn't help solve the case, so she left it out. The unsub spent upwards of two hours with the victim and left no footprint. It was like he didn't exist.

How did he establish contact? Nothing so far had been dug out from the two computers that the IT teams had been analysing. The victim's smartphone seemed a viable medium. But records from the mobile phone company showed no calls to or from an unknown number on Anu Singh's mobile on the day or for two weeks before the murder. She seemed to talk to people in her contact list and no one else. The mobile phone records of Gina and Radha were a different story. Most numbers weren't in their contact lists, but that was hardly surprising considering their profession. Tricks didn't usually give their numbers to be put into hookers' contact lists. The whole industry worked on discretion. Nevertheless, the numbers were taken. Local police personnel were asked to check them out discreetly. Ironically, prostitution is a crime, but the rich men who used the prostitutes couldn't be charged. Nothing new came to light. None of those contacted fitted the profile.

As Rita made her mental notes, she reckoned the mystery broadly hinged on two questions: *who* and *where*. If they knew who the next target would be, or where, it would be simple enough to set up surveillance. The unsub would be flushed out with a little patience and effort. Unlike other homicides, the *why* wasn't critical to this enquiry. Whereas most murders happened for a motive – money, inheritance, jealousy, animus, rage – these rubrics didn't apply to psychopaths. These people killed without set and standard motives. The wirings of their brains were different. They thought and planned differently. If one saw them, one wouldn't know what was in their minds. They would play poker with both God and the Devil and win. No, the *why* didn't matter.

The same logic applied to *when*. There was no precise date. The madman's frenzy knew no timelines except a reducing timescale. But, as Rita knew, he didn't have a turn-on-turn-off switch. If the news of Ranbeer's arrest served as a trigger, the unsub was certainly out of control, although he may not realize that. He might want out, once he knew, but he wouldn't admit that. Admitting was tantamount to accepting defeat, a huge blow to the ego, and ego was everything to a psychopath.

She added three more points to the profile:

- He's unhinged.
- He's dangerous.
- And now, he could be desperate.

Enough theory for a day. Rita had woken up early and been on the computer for a couple of hours now. It was still only 6.30 a.m. She switched it off, shed her clothes on the way to the shower. It was only while she was drying her hair that she noticed the lone white hair once again. Should she colour or not? Perhaps she should wait for a few more to surface. She remembered her father with the snow-white head and a sad smile flitted across her lips. The ability to be a child passed away when one's parents passed away. The memory of her mum and dad still lingered like the fragrance of an incense stick after it has been snuffed out.

She donned her jeans and white fitted shirt; pulled on her shoulder holster, checked the Smith and Wesson before slipping it in, pulled on a light khaki jacket and switched on the TV to catch some news on *Mumbai24* before she left.

Ranbeer Kumar was born in a remote village called Amaithi in the Darbhanga district of Bihar. Life hadn't been easy from the start. His mother had passed away early and his father had remarried. The stepmother was as vicious as they come. When he was eighteen, his stepmother accused him of inappropriately touching his younger stepsister and demanded that his father chose between her innocent daughter and his wayward son. There were no surprises which side his father took. Nevertheless, he gave his son some of his savings and advised him to leave the village, go to some big city and learn some skills. That is how Ranbeer ended up in Mumbai.

His life had never been well and truly comfortable, but it had been a lot better than what it was now. After been locked out of his own residence with no money and nowhere to go, he had parked himself at Dadar station, but this arrangement wouldn't do for the long-term. He couldn't survive like this for long. As travellers ate their food at the stalls on the platform, he hung around waiting for them to finish and then asked them for their leftovers. He scavenged for half-smoked cigarettes that people had discarded before entering the station. He hadn't had a drop of alcohol since the night he had been pulled out of his apartment. He begged people for money, but it was nowhere near what he needed to buy even the cheapest drink. He hadn't had a shower in over a week, his clothes stank, his hair had grown matted and his stubble had grown into an unkempt beard with each passing day. To add to his misery, he had to stay alert because loitering and sleeping on railway platforms was a strict no-no. The police could haul your ass away or throw you out; if found a second time, it could either mean a fine, that he had no way of paying, or get arrested. He understood the ramifications of his arrest; it was unlikely that he would ever be able to secure gainful employment with a criminal record.

He was always paid for his services after the job, and he suddenly remembered that he hadn't been paid for the last assignment. With the little money he had managed to scrape together by begging, he called PMC to settle his account. The HR manager was reluctant at first, but eventually softened. He said he would check and get back to Ranbeer. Ranbeer didn't want to tell him that he was now a hobo with no home and no phone to receive calls. He called back the next day. And then again the next, until the HR manager, having checked with the powers-that-be at PMC, relented and agreed to settle Ranbeer's meagre account.

'Into which bank should we transfer the money?'

'I'd prefer cash,' Ranbeer replied. They had always paid in cash. Why did they imagine that he would suddenly decide to open a bank account now? Stupid!

'Then you'll have to come to the office to collect the money and sign the receipt.'

As risky and difficult as it sounded, Ranbeer didn't have much of a choice in the matter. It was that or nothing. *That policewoman, bitch, Rita,* he cursed. For the life of him he couldn't recollect her surname, but who gave a fuck! All he could think of was, if he had his way, he would tie her to her bed, face down and screw her senseless as he simultaneously throttled her for what she had done. In one fell swoop he had been rendered homeless, a starving penniless beggar; something less than human.

'Could I come this evening please? I'm a bit tied up, at the moment.' Ranbeer knew the police were looking for him. His life had been reduced to a single imperative: survival, and as such he planned to slip out in the dark, collect his money and then take a train out of Mumbai forever.

The HR guy told him to collect the cash from the security guard, who would be there, twenty-four by seven, and not forget to sign the receipt.

At 8.30 that evening, Ranbeer took the local train. He knew he could get away without a ticket on the Mumbai Local. Millions of people boarded the trains without a ticket. He had heard that there was an insurance you could buy for that. You paid a certain premium per annum to this company and boarded the Local without any worries. If you were ever caught you could claim back the fine you paid to the ticket collector. He had no insurance, but the odds of being pulled over by the TC at this hour were minimal.

He collected his cash at 10.20 p.m. – INR 1,110.50.

He resisted the urge to buy himself a drink at Churchgate. He needed the cash to run.

He returned to Dadar at around midnight and decided to treat himself to a packet of smokes.

It was almost deserted when he walked out of the station.

'Mr Ranbeer Kumar?' He stopped when he heard someone mention his name from behind. But before he could turn around, a gloved hand covered his mouth and a knife slit his jugular vein, the vein that carries deoxygenated blood from the head to the heart. Blood spurted out. He heard footsteps receding as he crumpled to the ground. He tried to shout for help but his voice let him down and he could only gurgle. He put his hands on the slit in a vain attempt to stem the flow. Scenes that he had seen on his computer screen of women being snuffed out flashed before his eyes before they closed forever.

In an otherwise capitalist society, the death of one Ranbeer Kumar, a straggler on a railway platform, begging and foraging for food, wouldn't have made it to the back pages of the least circulated news rag there was. But the fact that he had been arrested, albeit erroneously, as the notorious Lipstick Killer and then went missing when an arrest warrant had been issued in his name for smutty cybercrimes that closely resembled the same genre as the serial killings in Mumbai, generated interest amongst the media bodies. The media interest that had all but petered out after the last murder, got reignited. What with the two deaths in quick succession, both being attributed to the same perpetrator. Headlines. Front-page news. Articles doubled, quadrupled. The news went national, publishing one meaningless conjecture after another.

Wrong Arrest, Wrongful Death! It was an eye-catching scroll on the *Mumbai24* channel. It was run by a group that had made its mark in the last few years when a group of newsreaders and news analysts had broken away from the various Rupert Murdoch corporates they'd been working for and set up their own shop. The news channel broke news, always.

Rita watched one of *Mumbai24*'s star reporters, investigative journalist Chavi Nair, on the screen. She was a respected face and name. Scathing, truthful and brash, she had made a name for herself. Chavi was asking pertinent questions.

If the Mumbai Police had been looking for Ranbeer Kumar in connection with a heinous crime, how did someone else find him first?

If Ranbeer Kumar had been arrested, why had the Mumbai Police let him walk away?

Was the Mumbai Police certain that Ranbeer Kumar wasn't the Lipstick Killer who had been murdered by some vigilante?

Was the slaying of Ranbeer Kumar an offensive by the real Lipstick Killer?

What was the police doing about the safety of Mumbai citizens?

Rita looked at the clock. It was only seven in the morning, but she knew she had to get to the office ASAP.

Only Harry was in the Operations Room when Rita arrived. He gave her a wry smile and looked at the coffee in her hand that she had picked up on the way.

'Sorry Harry, I didn't know you'd be here, or I'd have picked up one for you as well.'

'No need to apologize ma'am, I had one on the way up here too.' He pointed to the wastepaper basket. A discarded styrofoam cup lay there. As Rita settled into a chair, he said: 'Small mouth, big talk' – Harry's literally translated version of *chota munh, badi baat* – 'but this Mr Ash Mattel, I think he likes you.'

Rita wondered if her face had flushed and whether Harry could read her thoughts as she pondered on the best way to respond to his statement.

'What makes you say that?'

'The way he looked at you when he was here the other day ...'

'We studied together for a year in college, maybe he felt comfortable talking to me more than the others. There's nothing romantic there, he's married—'

'Divorced.'

'What?'

'He was married. He's divorced now,' Harry told her confidentially.

'How do you know that?'

'I Googled him. He seems to be quite a big shot. He consults for Scotland Yard in the UK, FBI in the US and *Police Nationale* in France.'

'True that, that's why we consult him.'

'Must be part-time.'

Rita's heart pumped like it was about to explode. She had used the term naïvely in another context … '*I have a part-time boyfriend.*' Had Harry put two and two together? If yes, should she be worried?

Harry must have guessed her confusion. 'I mean he has to be working part-time if he works with so many agencies, isn't it?'

'Yes, yesssssss …' She deftly changed the topic and segued into the news of the hour, 'Did you hear the news this morning?'

'Ranbeer Kumar got killed,' Vikram Patil had just come into the Ops Room.

'Yes, ma'am,' Harry acknowledged. 'Who'd have wanted to kill him?'

'Our unsub.'

Vikram and Harry looked at Rita with their eyebrows raised.

Vikram and Jatin were at Dadar later that morning to take charge of the homicide of Ranbeer Kumar. His murder appertained to the Lipstick Killer case and ergo, the local police were told to provide all assistance, as this homicide would be treated as a consequence of an ongoing inquiry already being overseen by Crime Branch. There was no resistance from the local Station Head Officer, DSP Anmol Kale; although his people were the first at the scene of crime, it was one less headache for his team, and the orders were from way above his pay grade.

A murder outside a local train station was as open a site as could be. The body had long been removed when Vikram and Jatin got to the scene. The police had placed barriers. A throng of curious onlookers had gathered. This would be a first-hand viewing of something that they would see on television later. Perhaps one of the media cameras might catch them. A moment of fame at the cost of a homicide. Everyone in the crowd, ranging from the barely legal to the one-foot-in-the-grave, had an opinion. An old man was expounding on the theory that television, and all the sleazy channels, had precipitated *Kalyug* a couple of generations earlier than expected.

The rain that had been elusive for a while had now returned with a vengeance and had washed the pavement clean, obliterating any prints the perpetrator may have left, although given how the Lipstick Killer had operated in the past – if it was the same killer – there wasn't much optimism on that front. The only hope had been that, as he had changed his MO, changed his target, and also acted in a haste, he may have made an error. Ranbeer's blood had also been washed off the concrete where he had fallen. There must have been a lot of blood because there was still a mild tinge of red in the rainwater that had penetrated between the tiles. Some of this would eventually get washed away when the next rain fell, although some part of Ranbeer could become a permanent speck in the tiles. Vikram and Jatin, working with the local uniformed police, spent close to four hours scrutinizing the area. The police spoke to scores of people residing beneath an underpass close by – they ate and slept there, surely they would have seen someone knifing another man – but that was a dead end. When it came to violent crimes, no one ever saw anything. Mumbai, the city that never slept, took a catnap at the most inopportune times.

With not much to go on at the scene of crime, they had put in a request to expedite the autopsy. As Jatin had some court hearing for another case, Vikram alone travelled to Byculla from Dadar to attend the postmortem. He donned the white cotton overalls over his clothes and the bootees over his shoes and entered the theatre where Dr Syed Khan prepared to slice open Ranbeer.

'Do you guys think I don't have enough on my plate already that you keep sending bodies my way?' he quipped when he saw Vikram.

'It's a nightmare, these psychos.'

'I spoke to Rita earlier. She suspects it could be related to the same Lipstick Killer but, purely based on physiology, it seems a totally different killer to me. Psychologically too.' Dr Khan's knife dug into the cut already made by the killer and sliced open the front of the cadaver to reveal the innards. 'The killer appears to know his biology well. He slit the jugular vein.' He looked up at Vikram and continued, 'the vein carries deoxygenated blood from the head to the heart, and reputed to be an extremely vulnerable part of the body – it has even inspired an idiom: to go for the jugular – and looking at the size of the laceration, death was almost guaranteed, unless help arrived within seconds.'

Vikram took it all in, jotting down his notes as usual.

'Death would have been almost instantaneous. The subject might have been foggily mindful of his end approaching fast, and had it been a tiny slit, he could have squeezed the cut and staunched the blood flow but, in this particular case, he had as much chance of survival as a snowball in hell. He would have gone down almost instantaneously.'

'Anything else you can tell me?' Vikram asked when the doctor had been silent for a while.

'We'll send samples to toxicology, but I wouldn't get my hopes up on anything. This seems a straightforward case of knife attack. What difference does it make whether the subject consumed alcohol prior to being murdered? If that had been the case, it would only prove that he had been a little slow in perceiving or reacting to the threat.'

Nothing. Not a witness, not a clue. The murder of Ranbeer Kumar provided no new information to the investigating team. It was coming up to twenty-four hours since the murder, but they still had nothing to go on. It was a generally accepted maxim that if the police didn't find some leads or crack the case in the first seventy-two hours, the trail went cold. However, this did not necessarily apply to serial killers. Considering the psychopath wasn't done with his killing spree and was probably back to planning his next target, there was always a chance that he would make that first fatal error. Rita, Vikram, Jatin and Harry understood that it was highly unlikely that Ranbeer Kumar had been the victim of a random killing. He had over a thousand rupees in cash, which hadn't been taken. The motive was certainly not theft. He hadn't been physically or sexually assaulted. Moreover, Dr Syed Khan had established that all it took the killer was just one slick slash. Too neat to be an amateur.

'What baffles me is how the killer ferreted out Ranbeer Kumar when the entire Mumbai Police force couldn't track him down,' Rita voiced when all four of them reassembled in the operations room.

'And why?' asked Jatin.

'Deliberating on the reason is pointless, Jatin. The killer is psychotic. It could be because we dented his ego by wrongly ascribing his work to a lesser being. Poor Ranbeer would have been safer in our lock up ...'

'I'm not trivializing his death, ma'am, but such screw-ups go with the territory. In any case, Ranbeer was no *sadhu*. I mean, sooner or later he would have come by his just desserts and either spent the rest of his life behind bars or come to a grisly end. Hopefully, our unsub's lust and frenzy has been satiated for the time being, and he won't attack for a while.'

'Hmm … I'm not so sure about that.'

There had been no answers, only conjectures and deliberations.

'He's anything but spontaneous. He plans meticulously; but this time, he seems to have gone berserk and committed this murder in haste. He's more disturbed than he knows or admits. Monumentally fucked-up, if you'll pardon my French, which makes me think he may have inadvertently left some pointers for us.'

Vikram, Jatin and Harry nodded, but had nothing to add.

'We need to find out how our unsub found Ranbeer? Perhaps take a step back – how did Ranbeer have over a thousand rupees in his pocket? Did he go to a bank to withdraw money where he was spotted or borrowed money from a friend who gave him away? It's possible that the killer followed him from there, although he had no interest in stealing the money.'

'Makes sense,' Vikram noted and got up. The other two men rose as well. The meeting was over.

Rita returned to her office, still deep in thought. Phones had been ringing non-stop since the morning. Having seen Vikram and Jatin take charge of the Crime scene at Dadar, the media had been quick to do the math. This had to be related to some other case, some big case, and what was the biggest investigation into homicides by the Crime Branch currently? The Lipstick Killer. Rita knew that they couldn't ignore the media forever. In the absence of real info, the media was known to extrapolate, exaggerate and pad their articles with the wrong kind of information, which would only raise the anxiety levels of the Mumbai citizens. The police had a job to do; similarly the media also had a job to do.

'So, someone knew Ranbeer worked at PMC, and more importantly that someone also knew he would be travelling to and from the PMC office at Nariman Point ...' Rita summarized for the benefit of all. The local police had checked with the PMC office and traced Ranbeer's final journey. Ranbeer had gone to Nariman Point on the fateful day to settle his account. 'It's possible that the unsub chanced to see him when he returned and it's equally possible that the unsub had prior information that Ranbeer would be in Nariman Point and followed him back to Dadar.'

'If it's the latter, why would the unsub follow Ranbeer? There was a chance he would lose Ranbeer on the way. It would have been far simpler to eliminate him as soon as an opportunity arose on the way.' It was a valid argument from Harry.

'Perhaps that was the plan, but the opportunity didn't present itself until they got to Dadar?' Vikram offered.

'Hmm ...' Jatin didn't sound convinced.

'I doubt that it was at all a fluke. The killer couldn't have been cruising around Mumbai with a knife in his pocket, looking for Ranbeer. What were the odds he would: one, find Ranbeer and two, locate him at an isolated place?' Rita mused. 'There had to be a leak at PMC. We need to know how many people at PMC knew about Ranbeer's visit and who, if any, did they convey it to. If someone was interested in Ranbeer's movements, we must know.'

The team debated for an hour before they split again. The media had splashed Ranbeer's murder, linking it to the Lipstick

Killer, all over the front pages and also on television. Rita's boss, Vinay Joshi, had received an invite for a live interview on *Mumbai24*. Joshi, despite his seniority, was camera shy. The stark difference between Commissioner Sexy and ACP Joshi was often the topic of conversation around the water cooler. Sexy loved being the poster boy while Joshi would only make a public appearance at gunpoint. The rank and file often wondered how Joshi would head Mumbai Police when Sexy retired.

Joshi had deflected the media interview to Rita who sat wondering whether this was an opportunity. Psychopaths loved to hear about their exploits, their victories, and if she played her cards correctly, this could help draw out the unsub into doing something rash. Although it could be just another nonstarter, it was a new tide of hope. Not be a rainbow, but a sundog perhaps. Who could say that a shot in the dark would never find the target?

INTERLUDE
Present

I hate it when anyone denigrates me as rash or irrational or impulsive, but the very idea of someone else getting credit for my craftsmanship was annoying. Accusing and arresting Ranbeer was an insult to my intelligence. I am the artist, me, and you ascribe my work to a half-brained cretin who is so stupid that he gets caught watching pornography. Seriously? How dare they impugn my reputation? Oh, someone had to pay for this.

Nutty-me was going nuts. Even if it was someone else who had attributed Ranbeer Kumar with my expertise, it was Ranbeer's fault that he had shown some tendencies to make them believe that. He had to go. He had to go as soon as possible and all I needed was one clue about where to find him. A dip into his background revealed who he was. I knew he was on the run, and I could calculate who he would possibly approach for money. Then it was simply a wait. That day, I lay in wait for him outside the office building when he collected the cash and trailed him back to Dadar. Following someone from Churchgate to Dadar in the same compartment of a Local, I was apprehensive:

what if the loser caught sight of me and recognized me? It was late, the crowd had thinned. Although I stood at the opposite end of the compartment, seemingly absorbed in a newspaper, my eyes never lost sight of him. He didn't notice me. When he disembarked at Dadar, I waited until the train hissed and moved again and leapt out at the very last minute. He was blissfully unaware of my antics. I had initially planned to wait for a while until he fell asleep, but he walked out of the station and the opportunity presented itself to me just then. Bam! I slipped on my gloves and slit his throat.

I had a premonition that the police would immediately connect the murder of Ranbeer to the other serial homicides, and they did. No big deal; even Don Quixote would have accomplished that. And as soon as the police acknowledged the link, the media wouldn't be too far behind. Oh, Nutty-me so wanted to be there when the police arrived, but one thing – I am not is stupid. He chewed my brains for being an old stick-in-the-mud and missing out on a lot of fun by prudently steering clear of the scene of crime. But I know that the police would expect me to hover around, gloating, as they ran around ineptly like headless chickens. That is their theory about 'psychopaths', as which they have wrongfully termed me. They would be scouring through the curious crowds of onlookers that gathered there to see if they could place a face at more than two scenes of crimes, a common factor. And that theory let them down; you see, postulations point towards predictability, and why on earth would I return to watch the circus? What is the television for?

So, I sit in my living room in my boxers, feet up on the settee, a tall glass of Smirnoff and ice in my hand, and the big television screen on the wall. Not to watch the highlights of some cricket match, but a special live telecast on *Mumbai24* on yours truly – The Lipstick Killer. It was none other than Chavi Nair talking to

DCP Rita Ferreira about me. How could I miss this? Nutty-me is always super thrilled at watching us being discussed by media. He loves attention no end. He makes me read every news item, every story, every op-ed, every article. Even snippets and mere mentions. His id is insatiable. He often murmurs that we are celebrities now.

'*Good evening, DCP Ferreira, and welcome to this special telecast.*' Chavi Nair introduces the lead detective on air. I've read all there is about DCP Rita Ferreira. She's the crème de la crème. I know she's after me. And the stakes are high, but so is the fun …

Hmm … this Rita Ferreira isn't bad to look at. I had seen some pictures of her earlier, but it is different to watch her on television. She looks rather like the kind of women that I like, except that she is tad tall for my taste. Then her face morphs into Tina's. Nutty-me gets on my case right away. '*She'd be as slutty and horny and yummy as Tina*,' he whispers to me. Then begins to hum some imaginary tune. To be honest, the thought of having the DCP tied up in bed and at my mercy occurs to me too, but I let it pass because being a policewoman she'd be that much more cautious if anyone approached her. I cannot afford to get caught. Too much at stake. Going after Rita Ferreira, however exciting, is a full basket of risk, and I don't need to take the game to the highest level of risk. Not yet anyway. It's too much fun to stop.

The DCP's gaze is fixed on the lens: she seems to be looking directly at an audience of one: me. She appears a bit miffed like a sulky child who hasn't been able to decode a puzzle, but she also looks determined to solve it. From what I've read about her, she isn't someone you wanted to mess with. Not directly at least, but then you can't make an omelette without breaking a few eggs; in any case, her cage needs rattling.

I hear her narrating my exploits to Chavi, requesting members of public to come forward if they suspect anyone. It makes me chuckle – this DCP is so close to someone I know, and yet so far. Doesn't she know that the long-legged, gorgeous, curly-haired woman in the short, pencil skirt beside her is my girlfriend? Yes, I'm dating Chavi Nair. If an investigative reporter who knows me better than most doesn't suspect a thing, what chance does anyone else have? And as I watch her now, the ferocity in her eyes reveals to me that Chavi is damn good at her job. She is talented. But it's one thing to be talented and another to actually put one's skills to use. Chavi is successful because she knows the difference and works on it. You don't become the nation's darling journalist if you don't work at it. Especially when a lot of peeps hate the press. Chavi is made for the camera. Her face, her body language, the poise, the style, the faint yet visible cleft in the chin …

'*DCP Ferreira, could you confirm that the homicide of Ranbeer Kumar is associated with the recent serial murders of women by the Lipstick Killer, when the MO, the victim and the location are starkly different?*'

I'm all ears now.

'*We* suspect,' *DCP Ferreira, says,* '*I can't confirm anything while the enquiry is still open—*'

'*Why not? After all, the more information you provide to the public, the higher the probability for someone to notice an anomaly and report it to the police, isn't it?*'

'*It's a double-edged sword, Chavi. We're quite certain that the killer is watching this interview. He might even record it, so the more we disclose the more he knows what we know.*'

I know more than you anyway, you stupid policewoman, I want to say. I take a sip of chilled vodka and let the burn descend down my throat. This telecast isn't turning out to be as interesting as I had anticipated.

'*… so, do you think this serial killer otherwise leads a normal life?*'

'Oh, psychopaths are human chameleons. They hide in plain sight, Chavi. There have been cases where wives, married to men for twenty-thirty years didn't know that their husbands were killers until the police was at their doorstep with evidence. These men don't do anything in half-measures, their Obsessive-Compulsive Disorder aids them in keeping the two identities airtight ... nothing seeps from one role to the other.'

I let the television run in the background but stop being attentive. I get up, fix myself another drink and return.

Does DCP Ferreira want me to think she can predict my behaviour, my next move? That she knows me? That the police are cleverer than I am?

Even if I were to believe that the police expect me to react – the way DCP Ferreira is making it sound so banal – howbeit they still failed to protect Ranbeer? Forget saving him, they had been unsuccessful in locating him.

'*... I request the members of the public to remain vigilant and be patient.*' Thereupon she adds something that makes me chuckle. '*We also urge and request the person to hand himself over to the police. He might not realize that he needs help, and we will try and provide all the help that we can ...*'

Oh, is she offering some kind of clemency to me? Does she think I need her charity? Don't I know that if I walk into the police station, help would be the last thing extended to me? DCP Rita Ferreira might be smart, not giving away anything about the investigation, but as smart as she thinks she is, she cannot change the past. And she cannot – and won't – decide my future.

And then I hear her say the words that really get my goat, '*... we will get him, and get him soon, I promise you.*'

This DCP Ferreira is infuriating. Catch *me*? Soon? Good luck with that!

Sometimes one should make a move that one's opponent doesn't anticipate. Something that throws them off their game. If nothing else, it's fun to watch. And that is only possible if I play unscripted.

So.

I decide to do something that wasn't even in their peripheral vision. I shrink the timeline.

I have a strong craving to call DCP Ferreira and tell her that the most dangerous dog is the one that doesn't bark; it only bites. But I don't make that call. I don't want to bark. She has no clue what she is up against. Don't you just love it when people pretend that they're ahead of the curve when instead they're actually plain stupid? Perhaps that's just to compensate for their shortcomings, methinks.

FOURTEEN

The next murder was completely out of the blue.

While Rita Ferreira and the team grappled with the aftermath of Ranbeer Kumar's homicide, which they were convinced – considering the timing and circumstances – was the work of the same maniac, another dead body was the last thing they needed. The killer seemed to have abandoned his meticulous pattern of observing timelines and had condensed the intervals of months between murders to days. A rather acute cut. With two murders in a span of four days, Rita wondered if he had completely lost control of his psychosis and was rapidly decompensating. Or was this his way of punishing them?

'For a moment, if we hypothetically accept that eliminating Ranbeer Kumar was the unsub's way of retaliating to our wrongfully giving credit for his contemptible actions to the deceased, how does one explain this homicide?' Rita asked aloud.

At 2.30 a.m. on the said morning, an anonymous source had called to inform the police control room about a murder in Bandra West. The anonymous Samaritan did not end the tip there. Calling from an unlisted, untraceable phone, the man went on to provide details that only someone who had witnessed the murder could have known. Listening to the recording even for the nth time, everyone in the Operations Room strained their skilled ears to catch anything in the background …

Police Control Room: '*Police, state your emergency.*'

Anonymous Caller: '*I want to report a murder.*'

The male voice sounded extremely calm and composed like he had just completed his meditation after a full body massage.

PCR: '*Where are you calling from?*'

AC: '*That doesn't matter. What matters is where the body is, isn't it?*'

PCR: '*Where's the body?*'

AC: '*Pali Mala Road, Bandra West. I'll give you the address …*'

The anonymous caller gave the name of the building and then: '*Apartment four hundred and six. Fourth floor, got it?*'

PCR: '*What's your name?*'

AC: '*I'm not obliged to tell you anything about myself.*'

PCR: '*Do you know who's been murdered?*'

AC: '*Sapna Patel. Missus. She was married.*'

PCR: '*How do you know she was murdered?*'

AC: '*I was there when she breathed her last.*'

PCR: '*What do you mean?*'

AC: '*What does it sound like to you when I say "I was there"?*'

PCR: '*Did you kill her? Have you called in to confess?*'

AC: '*Nope.*'

PCR: '*What's your name?*'

AC: '*You're wasting your time now. You should be rushing your teams to the address I provided you. Call up DCP Rita Ferreira; she's not very far from the murder scene. Less than two kilometres, five minutes tops at this hour, right?*'

PCR: '*How did you know the deceased?*'

AC: '*Who said I knew her? Then again, who knows who all knew her and how intimately they knew her?*'

PCR: '*Are you her estranged husband or boyfriend?*'

AC: '*Oh no, her husband is out of town. Okay, enough questions … send your troops there.*'

PCR: '*Hold on a second sir … please give me your name and address, and I promise the police won't bother you. We will only contact you if we need any info.*'

AC: '*Isn't the mystery better than an answer?*'

PCR: '*Sir, please—*'

But the caller had already hung up.

Rita, Vikram, Jatin and Harry sat silent and still, the words reverberating in their ears. It was eight in the evening now. A little over sixteen hours had passed. The team had attended the scene of crime and found the tableau identical to the previous homicides. Mrs Sapna Patel had been found face-down, naked, spread-eagled with her hands and feet tethered to the four bedposts; abrasions on both wrists and ankles proved that she had struggled while the unsub tortured her. The welts on the skin on her back and thighs indicated that she had been whipped with a belt; products from her own dressing table had been inserted into both the orifices between her legs. And the crimson lipstick had been bitten off her lips before her wounded mouth had been doused with bleach.

The autopsy had been prioritized and the results were duly noted:

Sapna Patel was victim A-721/5.

The lipstick was Maybelline Jewels Refined Wine.

The sharp, pungent smell of bleach: ammonia. The sanitization.

A blue nylon cord had been used as fetters.

The cause of death was asphyxiation by strangulation.

There were too many similarities. No one needed any more proof that it was the Lipstick Killer.

Sapna's husband, Anil Patel had travelled to New Delhi only that morning for a short three-day trip. He had promptly returned, been questioned and let off.

The apartment had been thoroughly checked. There had been no break-in, which indicated that the victim had known her assailant and had let him into her apartment and her bedroom willingly. *Why?* No one knew. The autopsy didn't reveal any signs of excessive alcohol in Sapna Patel's blood.

'Sonofabitch,' Rita swore. It was good to let off steam sometimes.

'Ma'am, should I get some coffee?' Harry asked. He was certainly due for a nicotine fix. Rita couldn't remember how many coffees she had had since she had returned from the scene of the crime. Nevertheless, another one was welcome.

'A whiskey would be better,' she thought in dark humour, but nodded to Harry.

'Camel will come soon under the mountain, ma'am,' as if on cue, Harry came up with the anglicized idiom and everybody burst out laughing.

'We've been locked in this room for several hours and we're getting nowhere,' said Rita. 'We need to get out for some fresh air.'

The four investigators trooped out.

'He's getting malicious … informing the police after a kill,' Rita said as they sat sipping on steaming mugs of coffee in a café across the office.

It was fairly obvious that the anonymous tip-off on the night of the murder of Mrs Patel had been from none other than the Lipstick Killer himself. Although no one had any evidence to substantiate this, it was clear that it couldn't possibly have been anyone else. How did the caller know about the murder? All the neighbours had been canvassed, checked and ruled out. No one blinked an eyelid when asked to provide an alibi. Every man in the building and adjacent buildings prioritized a clean chit over privacy. How had the caller known that the victim had been Sapna Patel? And the fact that her husband was not in town?

The call logs confirmed that the call was approximately at the same time as murder. Which meant that the killer was still in the vicinity when he had made the call. This brashness reflected his growing insolence, his confidence in his own invincibility and that he could get away long before the police responded. He was not merely escalating the violence; he was taunting them too. Why? Every killer in the world knew that the colder the case, the more difficult the trail. Why was he galvanizing the police into action? Was he actually smarter than the police gave him credit for?

'He wanted us to know about the murder. He wanted to emphasize the fact that the killer hadn't been the person we had erroneously arrested earlier. Ranbeer is dead; but the murders continue. This gloating behaviour is as primitive as a primate beating its chest in triumph. He is no longer satisfied with violating the victims; he has upped the ante and is playing a warped cat-and-mouse game with us now. He's now being driven by his overinflated ego.'

There was silence around the table as everyone absorbed Rita's assessment.

'And?' Harry prompted.

'I'm worried; we need intelligence to understand this severe cut down in his cooling-off time.'

'We should speak to Mr Mattel.'

You know I will, she wanted to say but she nodded. 'Yes. I'll call him and get his opinion.'

'How's the most gorgeous commissioner of police in the world doing?' That was Ash's response to Rita's *good-afternoon*. She had gotten home a little after half-seven that morning, taken a quick shower and she calculated it would be around 2.30 p.m. UK time.

Ash didn't reserve his cheesy lines for late evenings. Initially, Rita had detested them, but she later realized that he, too, having to deal with the macabre and grotesque on a daily basis, perhaps used this method to buffer himself from a harsh reality. This was the same technique that she and her team used every so often, so that the repugnance that they dealt with everyday didn't get to them. Self-preservation underpinned all their childish banter and jests.

'Is this a good time to talk?' she disregarded his wisecrack and carried on. With Ash, retorting was never a good idea. Ignoring his questions was.

'It's always a good time to talk to you. What are you wearing?'

'Nothing.'

'Oh-my-my—'

'Ash,' Rita came back sternly.

'You sound serious now.'

'And time for you to get serious, too.'

'I'm listening.'

Rita took about twenty minutes bringing Ash up to speed. Ranbeer Kumar's murder, her interview and then the recent homicide of Sapna Patel, and what her and the team's view was. 'He would have been a class-topper at school with a high IQ and all that, but his mind is now out of control.'

'You're assuming that your unsub reducing his cooling period is a sign of psychotic decompensating, that he's losing control. However, it could be an eruption of *narcissistic rage* ...'

'What in the world is that now?'

'Narcissistic rage is a late-coined term, but it is a result of *narcissistic injury*, which has been around since Sigmund Freud. There is ample evidence that if a person, known to be delusional or paranoid, feels threatened or distressed – if their motive or importance or some such is questioned – they react. And the reaction is never pretty. From what you've told me, I think his ire got the better of him because of two factors: (a) the wrongful arrest and (b) your interview challenging him that you will *arrest* him.'

'Which he should know anyway, he cannot escape forever—'

'Wrong. You will never arrest him.' Ash went quiet for a few seconds. 'Most serial killers don't want to be arrested. Ever. Their entire game is about control. Arrest takes away that control from them ... imagine them living in a cell, controlled by the police, watched twenty-four by seven. They would rather commit hara-kiri or get killed by the arresting cop.'

'How is getting killed being in control?'

'You're forgetting it's a twisted mind. For such minds, they dictate the terms, even deciding their own execution.'

'So, what, will he commit suicide after some time?'

'No. Understand his psychology. Suicide would be cowardice to him; he's a narcissist, someone with a huge ego. My money would be on suicide-by-cop.'

'You mean ...'

'Yes, when you get to him, he'll ensure you or someone at the scene shoots him, which in his warped mind would be the way he wants it. Remember he believes implicitly in his façade and in his version of distorted reality, it is he who is compelling you to kill him. He's taking that decision because he alone has the power over life and death, not you.'

'Oh God!'

'But the fact that he's carried out these two homicides in quick succession, and even altered his MO and target victim for one murder, I'd have thought he would have made some mistake.'

'That's the thing, we haven't found anything yet.'

'Hmm ...'

They discussed the subject a little more and then Ash told her that he had been summoned back urgently because of a similar case in the UK, where it was not one, but two killers operating in tandem. And then Ash being Ash, he, once again, slipped into the sweet-sleazy-steamy lines before they disconnected.

Time for Jim Beam, Rita thought. She had been up since three that morning when she had attended the scene of crime at Sapna Patel's residence. A drink, or two, would be a brilliant way to relax, she convinced herself. No threesome tonight.

FIFTEEN

Rita woke up sweating. Then she heard something. Footsteps? A furtive scratching? She quietly slid open the drawer in the bedside table that housed her Smith and Wesson. As she lived alone, she always kept it loaded because there was no danger of it accidentally going off. She decided not to switch on the light because, having just woken up, her eyes quickly adjusted to the darkness. She remained motionless, concentrating on the sound. It didn't seem to be getting any closer, but it didn't stop either. The drumming of the rain outside made it a challenge to figure out the direction from where the sound originated. Although she was awakened by a strange noise, her auditory receptors weren't fully awake and functioning yet. She gradually tuned out the background noises; now it sounded more like a pitter-patter than footsteps. She tensed as she realized the sound came from somewhere closer than she had initially thought. It wasn't in the next room. It was in her room. Or just outside it.

She took a quick peek at the balcony door in her bedroom, which she had shut before getting into bed. There, in the pouring rain, stood a drenched black cat, scratching frantically at the door. Rita was ambivalent towards cats. Dogs she knew well because her parents had a German shepherd when she was growing up. But this poor feline was in dire need as the torrential rain lashed relentlessly against the glass pane. Rita sighed, and switched on the light. Ever cautious, she glanced at the cat and got up, still with gun in hand. She shrugged into her dressing robe, drawing it over the long T-shirt that served as her nightgown. Switching on all the lights as she walked through her apartment, she checked the main door and living room windows first. All still securely locked. Safe. Only then did she return to her bedroom and unbolt the balcony door to let the bedraggled kitten in. The sweet smell of jasmine or mogra was in the air. Mild but lingering. The moment the cat came in, it shook itself violently to get the water off her fur, stretched languidly, stalked under Rita's bed and disappeared. Rita peered down and saw that the exhausted creature had curled up into a damp black ball, fast asleep.

It was only 3 a.m., but the night's adventure had left her wide awake; she determinedly switched off the light, lay in bed and did her best to catch a few hours' sleep. She may have dozed off, but it was fitful and she kept jerking awake every fifteen minutes. A thought at the back of her brain wouldn't stop niggling. There had to be something they had missed, something that could lead to the maniac. She finally gave up after an hour and decided to get her matutinal caffeine fix a little earlier than usual. She peeped under the bed, but the cat slumbered on peacefully.

As Ash had pointed out, the unsub couldn't have carried out two murders in quick succession without making any mistake. The guy was all about planning, not spontaneity. It was evident that the killer didn't accidentally stumble upon a particular kind of woman. There was something she had surely missed, but she couldn't put her finger on it. Anu Singh and Sapna Patel had been murdered less than three weeks apart. And that wasn't all. There had been another murder in between. Did this guy spend all his time scouting and stalking his victims? Didn't he have anything else to do?

But that didn't fit with the profile.

She switched on the lights and booted up her computer. On the profile that they had compiled of the Lipstick Killer, two of the characteristics seemed to contradict each other. One of them highlighted that the unsub was in a reasonably good social and financial position, which on its own was understandable if women of equally good social backgrounds were willing to entertain him. The other one pointed out that the unsub planned in advance, that he worked days, maybe weeks, rigorously planning his exploits, which again, in and by itself, wasn't incorrect. But put the two together and one had to wonder how much time the unsub devoted to feeding his frenzies. Even when she put aside the murder of Ranbeer Kumar for a minute, Rita couldn't fathom how this fiend found the type of females that he favoured, set up some kind of surveillance to stalk them, established contact, wooed them, gained their confidence so much so that even the married women allowed him into their bedrooms and let him tie them up without a murmur. Unless he had already started the hunt for Sapna before he attacked Anu, it seemed a little implausible. And if he was concurrently hunting and grooming both Anu and Sapna, it must be his only day job. Hence, either he wasn't devoting much time on each subject – at least not as much as the investigators assumed – or he wasn't employed. If you added Ranbeer's assassination to the mix, it got more bewildering. The murders of four innocent women had been an encore of each other. Ranbeer, unfortunately, stuck in the web, had been offed and his death, ironically, had taken on a life of its own. It was best not to be linked as far as the investigation into the women's murders went. Ranbeer had been an unwanted wrinkle in the unsub's pattern. The biggest difference between killing the women versus Ranbeer was that the process of killing the women was more important to the unsub than the killing itself. In Ranbeer's case it was the opposite. He did it out of compulsion and made it quick.

Rita's thoughts were derailed when she felt something soft and furry rubbing against her bare legs. The kitten had woken up and demanded to be let out now that the rain had stopped. It was dawn when Rita opened the door to the balcony. The sun wasn't visible yet, but its brightness had started spreading across the horizon despite the clouds adamantly covering the sky. As rain was forecast, the cumulonimbi were only doing their part. As sleep was out of the question now, she decided to get herself another caffeine fix; the strong black brew could grease the cogs of her cogitation.

And she had thought correctly. Although the answer didn't spring up like a sunflower in her mind, she quickly got back to where she had left off.

Maybe, just maybe, Ranbeer Kumar wasn't even killed by the Lipstick Killer himself. And while the motive was there, perhaps he had hired a henchman to slit Ranbeer's throat. The MO was different anyway. She decided to return to Ranbeer later and parked that thought. Ranbeer's murder was no more than a red herring. It may not have been in the unsub's plan originally. It appeared more of a knee-jerk, narcissistic reaction.

Back to Anu and Sapna.

Did the unsub have an accomplice who scouted vulnerable women for him?

Doubtful. Unless the person finding women for the unsub was a psychopath himself. But the coincidence of two psychopaths in Mumbai, who revelled in annihilating women in exactly the same fashion, in cahoots, was beyond the scope of possible. Even if one took all other things into account, that they regularly shared info, possibly organized the entire event together, maybe even partook in the exploits, what were the odds that both men got their rocks off without penetrating their victims? Subzero.

Considering the less-than-three-week timeframe window to kill two women, there were just two options: if he had gone for Sapna without his customary due diligence, some mistake or oversight was inevitable and they should restart the investigation. However, Rita was confident that the police had done a comprehensive job the first time around. Still it never hurt to be more thorough.

Or.

As everyone before him, he had overplayed his hand as well. People often misinterpreted familiarity as safety. The first time on a route, one was generally hyper-alert, eyes on the road, checking the traffic, taking in the surroundings, focussed. When one had travelled the same route for the hundredth time, everything around became a blur. The terrain was familiar, one didn't concentrate … and made that one fatal mistake. Maybe, the Lipstick Killer, in his zeal to overachieve, fuelled by his narcissistic rage had unwittingly exposed a chink in his heretofore impenetrable armour. That small sliver of surmise combined with the inventories taken at the crime scenes started a fresh conjecture in Rita's caffeinated brain. Her neurones had sparked into life.

All puzzles, by definition, came with missing pieces or they wouldn't be called puzzles. They appeared unsolvable and intimidating in the beginning, but the similarity didn't end there: all puzzles also had a solution. *I will get you sooner than you think*, she murmured. It was five minutes to seven now. Before she went into the shower, she sent an email to Vikram, Jatin and Harry to get to Crawford Market as quickly as they could. She was in a brown study as she showered and dried herself before buttoning her white shirt and pulling on her blue jeans; she knew she could be way off the mark, but like the proverbial drowning man clutching at the proverbial straw, what other choice did she have? For now, she was going with the old maxim of '*Hear hooves, think horses, not zebras.*'

Rita was buzzing on her fourth coffee when she arrived at the Operations Room. The other team members had already warmed their seats by then, their eyes wide and expectant. What was it that had made her send them a meeting invitation so early in the morning? Good mornings, nods, smiles and then Rita described how two of the characteristics in the profile of the unsub were contradictory. Either he had all the time in the world, or he didn't. He either had a flourishing career to impress the women who invited him home, or he didn't. He couldn't be both. The juxtaposition didn't work.

The three wise men immediately cottoned on to her logic.

'Perhaps he doesn't need to earn and is living on inherited wealth,' Harry volunteered after a few minutes.

'So, you're basically saying that he flaunts his wealth to impress the women.'

'It's possible that he feeds them some story about how wonderful—'

'Hold that thought,' Rita interrupted. 'You could be right, but he could actually have a successful career. Why didn't that strike us before – he doesn't need to target and stalk his victims physically until the first date is fixed?'

'That's why the victims' phones are taken away from the crime scene, because the rendezvous isn't arranged through voice calls, but they meet on some social network,' Vikram contributed his two-penny worth.

'And, because this social network also has an app that's downloaded on the victims' phone, it's signed in,' added Jatin.

'People generally sign out from websites on their home computer, but the app stays logged on permanently ...' said Harry.

'Bingo. I thought as much, but I didn't want to influence your trains of thought. And I like the way you have connected the dots and completed the logic here. What a team!'

The new strategy was to dig into more than the better-known social networks. It could well be some not-so-eminent one, if sleazy assignations were planned on it. The technical team needed to be briefed to scout for all local and international online social networks of all kinds, but in the first phase mainly restrict their search to the ones where the first interaction was possible. For example, WhatsApp only came into play after two people had already made their acquaintance, interacted somewhere and exchanged telephone numbers. That initial intersection point needed to be identified first. The investigators could then snuffle around for anything fishy. They might need extra heads and hands at that juncture, but the team unanimously decided to cross that bridge when they came to it.

'What should we be looking for?' Harry asked. It was a genuine question. India had the largest number of Facebook accounts in the world: over 150 million active Facebook users of which, over 145 million accessed FB through their mobile phones. And that was just one social network. How does one look for the proverbial needle in 150 million stacks?

'Behind the filters of the internet, people create a different persona; but here's the interesting thing: they don't just pick any persona for themselves; most often, they make themselves appear to be what they would like to be. Like an unfulfilled fantasy. Or a dream gone sour. People pretend to be models, racing-car drivers, cricketers. Of course, they can't lie about being the stars that the world knows about. But they can pretend to be the almost-there variety. "I'm shortlisted for the next Vogue shoot" or "I was in the final seventeen in the IPL team. I'll make it next time", see? My money would be on that's how he must be projecting himself to his prey.'

Nods.

'Also, pathologically we know he suffers from satyriasis, which is the male form of nymphomania. He needs extreme sexual gratification that doesn't come to him in the form of normal sex. I guess he'll be disguising his violent desires in the first few interactions – appearing to be the exact opposite – but he can keep his desires latent only for so long ...' Rita stopped. She knew this was purely a hypothesis and, even if it was correct, it wasn't going to help. How was one supposed to start? The unsub wasn't going to be advertising BDSM on a social network.

Nevertheless, twenty minutes later, the answer was staring her in the face.

SIXTEEN

Cookies were something that our dear old grandmothers used to bake, using a batter of sugar, flour and butter. That skill is now lost in the mists of time, like knitting and needlepoint lace. Cookies, in the digital world, were initially described as microcosms of data from a website, stored on the computer by the user's web browser. In the early days, most cookies disappeared as soon as the surfing session was concluded and the browser was shut down. Then some smart alec argued that, if the person returned to browse some more on the same computer, why not let the cookies remain in the browser unless the user explicitly clears them? It would aid the user and help the businesses target the user better and as a result, sell more. A win-win. Then came logins. Google wanted you to sign in. YouTube wanted you to sign in. So did Facebook and Twitter. All on the pretext of providing the user with a seamless experience across devices, which it did. As soon as one logged in, the cookies began to build up on the server, so no matter which computer one used, one's history remained etched somewhere in the digital universe.

DCP Rita Ferreira hadn't logged into her Facebook account for a few weeks. Being an officer of the law and a public figure, Rita maintained a low profile on social media. She received friend requests from whoever had heard of her. Some she accepted without knowing them; others she didn't respond to. There was little point in either, because she didn't do anything with her account – she logged in from time to time only to check if some old school or college friend had sent her an invite. But that had never happened in all the years she had signed up to this account.

A few weeks ago – more than a month, actually – she had sat at her laptop at home, almost twenty kilometres away from office, and researched asphyxiation and choking as parts of BDSM and sexual gratification, to better understand what Dr Syed Khan had explained to her after the autopsy of Mrs Anu Singh. And, true to the cookie inventor's dream, she ended up being served targeted advertisements on FB, filtered by location: Mumbai.

Right in the middle of her home page, a Facebook page set up by someone unknown to her was now suggested by the Facebook algorithm for Rita to like and join. She noted the name of the group: 'Erotica – Play Beyond the Boundaries'. Obviously, based on her searches, which must have been picked up somehow from her Google browsing history and fed to Facebook, her interest in BDSM had triggered the ad. Serendipity? Or another dead end? She didn't know yet. Had they caught a break at long last? It could be a solid lead or just a coincidence that ended up wasting her time. Well, every now and then people did get lucky … isn't that how lotteries worked?

The club was a members-only affair. She clicked, but one had to apply to be a member before any content was displayed. '*Join this group to see the discussion, post and comment*,' it stated.

Should she, shouldn't she? Requesting for membership to this group would set off jangling alarm bells to whoever was the administrator. A policewoman would be a strict no-no if this were something illegal or immoral. If it wasn't, she would just be wasting her time and needlessly risking her reputation.

The cover was a photo in silhouette that seemed to suggest Bondage and Discipline with a shadowy figure tied up and the other, brandishing a whip. The profile logo was a pair of handcuffs. It proclaimed: members (371) and three admins – Rockman, King&Queen and Lovely. Aliases, obviously. No information on other members was accessible. Reasonable. Which member would want to let non-members know of their predilections? Rita clicked on the profiles of the admins. All three accounts were set to private and revealed zilch. They were trying hard to be discreet and cautious, which got her even more suspicious. And interested. She was reminded of Occam's razor: the simplest explanation is the best one: it is what meets the eye. Or the law of averages: future events turn out so that they balance any past deviation out? The unsub had been winning for so long; maybe it was high time that he lost. Rita's heart pumped harder, thumping within her ribcage.

In the annals of investigations across the world, a lot of mysteries that had baffled the long arm of the law for years were solved by examining aspects other than the investigation into the case per se. Dennis Radar, a serial killer, got caught because of his sheer arrogance: he sent taunting messages to the police on floppy discs. One of the biggest serial killers of them all, Ted Bundy, who broke out of prison twice and was on FBI's Ten Most Wanted list, wasn't apprehended for the crimes he was being hunted for; he was caught driving a stolen car. And David Berkowitz aka Son of Sam was nabbed because of a parking ticket. Translation: a lot of them let their guards down and got sloppy when it was an offence that wasn't their regular stock-in-trade.

The same club, Erotica – Play Beyond the Boundaries, had its footprints on Twitter, Instagram and a dozen other social networks, but while the other social networks had a presence, the subscription to this group was sketchy. Perhaps the privacy settings weren't as trustworthy or perhaps the club had enough members and didn't need to focus on fresh pastures.

'Do they shepherd everyone who contacts them through other networks to FB?' Jatin had a valid point. It made sense to have all the activity in one place. More manageable, more security. A tight-knit group?

Rita didn't deter the tech teams from digging further for a couple of days more. This was just one group that they had chanced upon. It fitted the bill, but who was to say whether several others, yet undiscovered, might also? However, logic dictated that if the qualified police technicians couldn't find something in the given category and geography, how would someone like Anu Singh or Sapna Patel? Whoever ran the group had no intention of hiding their presence – it had after all been suggested to Rita, albeit by an algorithm, by FB – the restrictions were on accessing the content. And contacts.

'I'm pretty sure someone validates members when they ask to be allowed to join the group,' Rita said.

'You mean physically?'

'I don't know, but I'm fairly sure that, if I applied, first my FB profile would be checked out, and then maybe someone would ask for my address under the pretence that membership was only given to certain kinds of people – based on geography, social status, gender and whatnot. I can't imagine everyone who applies getting through.'

The foursome sat in front of the computer screens with strict orders from Rita that no one should even accidentally click the *Join* button. If they were on the correct trail – *if* being the operative word – the unsub would smell a rat the moment anyone from the police got anywhere near that online group.

'None of us can join this forum,' Rita sounded frustrated.

'It took us so long to find a single crumb on this trail …' said Jatin mournfully.

'There has to be a way ma'am, otherwise *the buffalo will go into the water.*'

Rita, Vikram and Jatin looked wide-eyed at Harry in wild surmise; after a few seconds of dead silence, they directly translated the idiom into Hindi in their minds. The gales of laughter brought tears to their eyes. The entire precinct reverberated with their mirth.

'Everything must invariably come full circle. Everyone's luck runs out at some point,' Rita gasped, clutching the stitch in her side.

No information on the three administrators, Rockman, King&Queen and Lovely was found on any other social network – perhaps under different aliases.

It was agreed the four would keep this discovery to themselves until they figured out more details. The unsub, they knew, must listen to the news and if this leaked to the press, they would have lost another opportunity.

'What if this is a red herring,' Harry questioned, 'and we burn time and resources?'

'We won't focus solely on this until we come across something concrete. We should lay the trap and go on with the investigation, which, to be honest, isn't going anywhere.'

'So, do we make a fictitious FB account, ask for membership to the club and wait?' Harry asked.

'We can't just "make an account". He's too sharp to fall for that. If someone made a Facebook account today and asked for membership tomorrow, I'm sure the admin or admins will scrutinize it cautiously. And if they do an actual check of the person, we would be caught out. We cannot make it obvious. We need to find a Facebook account that already exists, is old enough with enough activity to show it's a genuine woman seeking membership. We need to make him join the dots, feed his ego by making him feel that he is cleverly profiling a prospective victim.'

'Why don't we change the name on your account ma'am?'

'That's a dead giveaway, even if we change the name and other details. How do we backdate the posts, and photographs? We need to find a someone that's similar to Anu and Sapna … let's make a list of what we know about them.'

The four victims of the Lipstick Killer had a string of commonalities.

The physical description of all matched. Five feet two or three, fifty to fifty-five kilograms, medium-to-light skin tone – a complexion that made the crimson lipstick stand out – and short-layered hairstyles that ended between the bottom edge of the neck to upper shoulders. The unsub hungered to annihilate petite women. Perhaps this was an obsession because the catalyst of his sick fantasy had been a woman of similar build. Perhaps, this dainty kind of woman required less effort to overpower.

The target age-group ranged between twenty-two and thirty-five, although this was just a guess.

The other commonality was the women's liberal attitude towards relationships. Although the first two were in the trade, it didn't merit Rita & Co. setting up a Facebook profile as a hooker to seek membership to Play Beyond the Boundaries. Anu Singh and Sapna Patel were both married and seeking an unusual relationship outside marriage. Whether or not they had done it before with someone else was difficult to establish. In any case, a married woman with a similar physique, who was a libertine seeking a kinky relationship when her husband was out of town, was unanimously agreed as the best fit to entrap the unsub. Provided, they were on the right track. But then again, it wasn't like any other leads were racing towards them at this juncture. Rita knew it was time to close the science book; it was time to go with her instincts. Even the best scientist in the world needed to take that risk. Most puzzles got solved with that one solitary clue that miraculously made it all come together.

'I'm sure you and the team have been through a thorough ratiocination before bringing this to me for approval, DCP Ferreira,' Commissioner Saxena, the public-school educated wordsmith, asked Rita but looked at ACP Joshi who sat beside her. Joshi had the incredible talent of sitting on the fence until the very last minute possible; probably, until his arse went numb. He warily watched from the sidelines, well aware of Rita's rationale that underpinned this proposal.

Rita and team had reasoned and debated – *ratiocinated* – long and hard on how to set the trap.

The plan to contact Facebook offices to intervene was almost immediately voided. Facebook as an organization valued the privacy of its patrons and couldn't be constrained to squeal on its subscribers. In any event, it did provide the police with an email address. However, the police had no evidence at this point; not even circumstantial. An erotic, members-only FB page was not proof of anything unlawful. It could well be an online forum where people enacted their fantasies in a virtual world. It would have been immensely useful if the police had been provided access to at least the administrators' profiles – there was always a chance to spot something if there were pictures – but, given the fact that the admins were using aliases, Facebook knew an information leak wasn't worth the risk. If the powers-that-be at Facebook got wind of the fact that the police were snooping around a particular group, they would instantly clam up tighter than Fort Knox.

Setting up a new account had been ruled out earlier.

The next task was to find a willing participant to take up the challenge. Then they had got lucky. As they zeroed in on profiles of women in Mumbai, they found one that fitted the picture to a T. A serial killer's primal desire was to kill the same person over and over again and hence, the women he preyed upon looked like clones of each other. Although a lot of women fitted the description, this was a face Jatin recognized. She had mentioned her profession as an 'entertainer'. Jatin had been posted in Marine Drive police station some years ago, and he told Rita and the team that the girl was an escort. Bingo. The plan was to convince her to work as a decoy. She would be housed in a secure house or apartment, provided with a fake ID and a businessman husband who travelled a lot, before she sought membership to the Facebook club to draw out the unsub. The background around this profile would establish that the couple had recently moved to Mumbai, so no history would be found should the administrators get antsy over the new arrival into the group and run a series of rigorous checks. However, the whole plan pivoted on getting the seal of approval from Sexy. Planting a decoy to lure a killer wasn't an everyday event. And despite the plan appearing foolproof and safe on paper, things could go disastrously wrong. All it took was one rogue variable to capsize the whole plan. There was no guarantee that the unsub wouldn't be armed when and if he turned up for his rendezvous with the police plant. The fact that the police had no record of any weapon, except for a knife, being used did not mean that the unsub didn't carry one. And who knew whether Rita & Co. were even on the right track? And that the unsub would take the bait? It was just one of the theories. But the police had so far only been reactive. This would be their first gamble at being proactive. Kill the mosquito before it caused malaria.

'Have you ever tried such a tactic before? Anywhere?' Sexy asked after a long silence.

'No, sir. But every case is different, and we have to try new approaches.'

'And there is no assurance that this *is* the online group where the Lipstick Killer hunts for his prey?'

'No, sir.'

Sexy looked at her for a full minute, then looked at Joshi. Then he smiled a genuine smile. 'What's the worst possible outcome?'

'For starters, it could be a total waste of time—'

'Worst only, DCP Ferreira,' he reiterated.

'It could turn violent, if we are on the right track.'

Sexy nodded, looked at Joshi and continued. 'Will this … this girl who will play the role … will she be in the apartment when the killer arrives?'

'Yes, sir, but we'll try to get her out as soon as we can. We'll secure the place like a fortress.'

'I want to see the plan in its entirety, DCP Ferreira. Especially, the security detail, they need to be impermeable, airtight. All the i's dotted and the t's crossed.' Sexy's voice didn't sound like a vote of confidence but half a loaf was better than no bread. He concluded the meeting like he had handed a one-time special offer and Rita could either take it or leave it.

'Yes, sir.'

Sexy wasn't wrong in asking for additional info. The mission was a calculated risk, akin to walking a tightrope over a very deep ravine. Just one slip and … Rita didn't even want to think about the fallout.

Rita had put in a requisition for more officers for their investigation and Sexy signed off the request without blinking. Inspectors Akhil Mathur and Ravi Mathur were released from other non-urgent duties and immediately reassigned to their little task force. While the two had the same family names, they were not even remotely related to each other. If anything, they were stark antipodes. Akhil, who was bald, bore the moniker *Takla* Mathur; Ravi had been rechristened *Chota* Mathur on account of his lack of inches. Political correctness had taken a walk. Rita had specifically asked for them as they had worked with her and the rest of the team on a prior case, and being inspectors, they wouldn't have any issues about playing second fiddle to Vikram, who was a senior inspector. Furthermore, the newbie, Harry, wouldn't have to struggle with his enormous workload of single-handedly organizing the presentations and meetings, liaising with the other departments, generating reports … the list went on and on. The two new recruits effortlessly slipped into harness and set out to expedite the tech teams; this effort paid off almost immediately.

The tech squad came back to confirm that both Anu Singh and Sapna Patel had visited the stygian site on FB. It had been difficult to trace so far, but now that the page ID was known, it was fairly simple to establish that the computers collected from the two victims' homes had surfed that page. This couldn't possibly be a mere coincidence. Now, if only Rita could convince the escort to buy into the arrangement to entrap the unsub, they would be able to confirm whether or not the two vics had been members. If they were, that would be a hundred per cent confirmation that this was the killer's hunting ground. Also, if the unsub didn't fancy their bait, they could discover other existing female members who did fit the profile and perhaps locate them somehow – pick up hints of the area they lived in, the car they drove, etc., with the help of the backdrops in their photographs. In any event, it would be the police's duty to warn all those who they perceived as likely targets of the psycho.

SEVENTEEN

Ruby wasn't her real name. While the police knew about her – she had once, and only once, been picked up for soliciting – they hadn't been able to process the charge, so her real name wasn't on their records. No sooner had she been brought in for questioning than the son of a state minister burst into the Marine Drive precinct and bore her away. He had been emphatic that it was all a stupid misunderstanding because she was his girlfriend. So, although Ruby had only been taken into custody, she was not even questioned, leave alone being charged nor convicted. Long story short: her picture and contact details had remained in the police files in case she was ever brought in again. When Rita saw Ruby's mug shot and then her FB profile, she seemed like the right candidate for their masterplan. Also, convincing someone the police did not already have some leverage on, Rita knew, would require far more effort.

When Rita made contact with Ruby, she politely declined to see Rita. Why would someone engaged in any illegal activity be interested in talking to police, even if it were only for a friendly chat about a proposal; a proposal that the police were reluctant to spell out over the telephone? That too with a woman who claimed she wasn't interested in free sex. Ruby had learnt through bitter experience that freeloader cops often turned up for a jolly; and she didn't fancy a roll in the hay with any woman, whatever the price. Rita, understanding the poor girl's contempt for the long arm of the law, strived to make it abundantly clear that, having no lesbian leanings, she had no interest in Ruby sexually. However, when Ruby dug her heels in and refused to meet Rita, she was left with no choice but to arm-twist the unfortunate girl. It was either *help us or we'll find a way to book you.* With Commissioner Sexy having bought into their strategy, exerting pressure came instinctively.

Rita had chosen to drive alone to meet Ruby. Taking a male police officer along could be an overkill and there was no reason for things to get nasty this early in the game. At the end of the day – escort or not, legal or dirty – it was the police that needed a favour, and they didn't want to antagonize Ruby.

The throb in her temples had become a full-blown headache; Rita dry-swallowed two aspirins as she drove out of Crawford Market. Her mind was still engrossed in the case. After five murders, the police had failed to find even a molecule of evidence of this misogynistic and meticulous predator. He killed and vanished into thin air, like he didn't even exist. His only gratification seemed to be the violence of torturing and flagellating his victims. She was now certain that Gina wasn't the first murder. The epicentre lay elsewhere. The first, the very first murder that had started him on this path, would be the catalyst. It might not even have happened in Mumbai. Certainly not in the timescale she was looking at, otherwise someone, nationwide, would have contacted her. Every serial killer had a subtext. A past, a reason, however twisted, for doing what they did, but how could one reverse the clock to see that? It seemed like an old wound had recently opened up. Something happened that had triggered the killing spree. A switch had been flipped in his mis-wired brain.

The car barrelled along until she turned right from G Road to Chowpatty Seaface. The traffic was crawling with bumper-to-bumper vehicles, but this suited Rita just fine because she was scanning the area to locate the building indicated in the address. To Rita's right was the azure expanse of the Arabian Sea, and to her left were some of the most spectacular art deco buildings in Mumbai. If one had a sea-facing balcony, it would be a view to die for.

Ruby lived in an apartment on the third floor of a building which boasted of having such spectacular views. However, the structure exhibited the ravages of time on the outer walls, like the cracks on an octogenarian's face. Despite its dilapidated exterior, a two-bed apartment in the building would be worth a small fortune and Rita couldn't help wondering how Ruby could afford this luxury. However, it was possible that Ruby was merely a lodger and shared a room with someone or perhaps the minister's son, who had claimed to be her boyfriend, had gifted it to her in exchange for her favours. Rita reined in the thoughts. She wasn't here to assess Ruby's income-tax returns. She was here for a purpose, and it was best if she focussed on that.

The guard at the gate didn't challenge Rita when she drove into the parking lot of the building although he did come over to her as she alighted from her vehicle. Rita told him that she was looking for number 3C and he helpfully directed her to the lift before returning to his post to continue his contemplation of the ocean.

Ruby answered the door almost instantly, like she was just waiting for the bell to ring. Perhaps it was part of the portfolio of the gateman to communicate the imminent arrival of their guests to the residents.

Ruby was in her early thirties, about the same age as Rita, which meant that she had been in her mid-twenties when she had been picked up for soliciting. Given her profession, she wore her years well. She had a lean face, a body like an athlete, vibrant and voluminous coffee-brown, shoulder-length hair. Her eyes were beautiful and expressive although they seem to have permanently settled into an expression of sadness and mistrust. Hardly a surprise given the life she lived. She could have been a model used in advertising on billboards and in catalogues to sell upmarket fashion brands. She could give some priest a moral hiccup. Gorgeous, without being arrogant.

Contrary to her angst on the telephone, she actually welcomed Rita into her apartment with a smile. In the cream-coloured cotton shirt above denim shorts, she looked like a perfect pocket Venus.

'How can I help you, DCP Ferreira?' Ruby sat down on a plush sofa, her slim legs folded under her and motioned to Rita to sit beside her.

Rita didn't want to divulge all the details until Ruby agreed to helping the police. If for any reason she couldn't convince or coerce Ruby into cooperating, it made little sense to take her into her confidence. If nothing else, the more the number of people who knew about the covert entrapment, the higher the chances of a leak. Ruby was a wildcard at the moment and one wasn't sure whether she would become mercenary and sell this insider information to the highest bidder, or gossip about it with her group on FB.

'What is this about? You have to tell me something … some indication of what it is that I'm agreeing to,' protested Ruby when Rita's preamble was to ask her to blindly agree to cooperate with the police's game plan and swear her to secrecy.

It was a logical and perfectly reasonable request. Rita realized that this was a catch-22 situation and could go round in circles forever. Rita decided to take a calculated risk.

'You must have heard of the Lipstick Killer on the news?'

'Yes. What's that got to do with me?'

'Nothing, nothing at all. We need your help to nail him.'

'How?'

'You're the only one outside of our investigation team who is in on this plan,' said Rita, 'so if it leaks out, we'll know it came from you, and you could be charged with obstruction of an investigation. Do you understand?'

'Oh alright, I won't do anything stupid.'

Rita summarized what the police suspected about the Facebook group, the killer's hunting ground, and how, if Ruby assisted, they might be able to save lives and bring the pervert to book.

'Why do you need me? You could set up an account yourself and do it yourself, couldn't you?'

'Anyone looking keenly would immediately notice that it's a new user account and be sceptical. It might make it conspicuous if someone joins Facebook and immediately asks for membership into a closed group. If that happens, we might lose the guy.'

'How would he know?'

'Most of the information is displayed on Facebook if someone digs into a user account. For example, the date that you first joined Facebook cannot be changed; also, the uploaded photographs have a date stamp. What one can change is one's name and relationship status. We need to take control of your Facebook account and ask to become a member of the closed group.'

'Is that it?'

'Nope; we need to provide you with a new residential address and provide a security—'

'Whoa! ... Whoa! Why?'

'Because we're reasonably certain that he'll scout around to see if you are who you say you are. He'll definitely recce the place. Our plain-clothes policemen and cameras should be able to pick out anyone who looks suspicious, but we'll have to play it by ear since we don't know a lot about the guy and how he operates.'

'Why do you think he'll pick on me?'

'You fit the physical profile of the women that he goes for. We'll have to set you up as a married woman looking for a liaison.'

Ruby grinned, 'so I get a husband too?'

'We have to come up with some story to make it sound convincing,' Rita shrugged, 'so, we'll work on all of that as soon as you agree.'

'What's in it for me?'

'What do you want, Ruby?'

'I want a ticket out of my current line of work ... you know what I do, right?'

Rita nodded. She always believed that no woman ever sold herself voluntarily. It was always extenuating circumstances or having been pressured into the sordid profession by an unscrupulous individual.

'Several years ago, you were brought into the police station for questioning; why didn't you tell the police you were being forced to sell yourself?'

'Who could I trust? And to be honest who would the policeman have believed anyway? Me, a hooker? Or the powerful man who had come to bail me out ...?'

'Fair point.'

'But—'

'But?'

'There are people who would never let me go free,' although tears shimmered in her eyes, Ruby smiled wryly to deflect the sombreness of the moment.

'Leave that to me.'

'You don't know them. You don't mess with that sort unless you want to end up as fish food in the ocean.'

'Like I said, I'll take care of it. As soon as you agree to help us, we'll see to it that you're protected until the end of this mission. And after that, I promise to provide you with a new identity in a new city of your choosing and you will never be found.'

'Can you do that?'

'We have done so in the past, so it isn't something new. It's mostly reserved for witnesses in high-profile cases where we fear that the life of the witness could be at stake.'

Ruby's eyes brimmed over. 'You've no idea how many times I've vowed to get myself out of this disgusting life and vanish into a dimension where no one would ever be able to find me,' she impatiently wiped away the tears and blew her nose. 'At times, I even believed myself. But I'm aware that that's not possible … not without help, anyway. And what help could I hope for when I know that there are bent cops hand-in-glove with my pimps? However, you seem convinced that you can get me out of this wretched life … I'd risk anything for a way out, so thank you, thank you.'

'Don't thank me just yet. Let's do this; it'll be several birds with one stone.'

Ruby sniffed but smiled.

Rita leaned forward and patted her hand. 'I'll personally see to it that you're provided for so you can pick up some vocational skill. Is that acceptable?'

'Yes, DCP Ferreira, I'm in.'

'Good. Then start by calling me Rita.'

'Thank you,' Ruby spontaneously hugged Rita.

Rita accepted the generous offer of a cup of coffee and the two girls sat chatting desultorily. Ruby was worried about her seedy clientele discovering their ruse because they were in cahoots with the local gendarme.

'Pack up the essentials. We'll get you out of here as soon as we can,' Rita said encouragingly as she walked out.

As she headed home, Rita's mind was preoccupied with thoughts of Ruby and the unfairness of the young woman's life. It hardly required any profound Freudian analysis to see why Ruby had, almost instantaneously, complied to fall in with their game plan. Even if both reality and the past are absolutes, the future is not. This offer was a get-out-of-jail-free card for a young woman who had been exploited by rich and powerful men. A litany of trivial and philosophical thoughts followed, until she gave herself a mental shake and gunned the engine.

The sun was setting somewhere beyond the Arabian Sea reddening the cobalt with its final simmering glow. Rita, connected to the Bluetooth in the car, called the Ops Room and told the men about her successful meeting with Ruby. They were to make the necessary arrangements to transfer Ruby the next day from her current residence.

'Would a hotel be safe, ma'am?' Jatin had a valid point. Ruby's pimps or clients could get wind of the fact that the girl was attempting to escape from their clutches. This could turn nasty. However, it wouldn't be right to temporarily put her up with Jatin or one of the other guys.

'Let me sleep on it. Let's discuss this first thing tomorrow. In any event, one of you please get to her residence asap and bring her along with her baggage to Crawford Market. We cannot afford to let her be on her own.'

As she hung up, Rita knew that if Ruby didn't work as a bait for the unsub, nothing would. The only thing that bothered Rita was, what if their unsub, the Lipstick Killer, was already on Ruby's client list. If he knew Ruby somehow, their master plan would be rendered null and void.

The next few days were hectic for Rita and the team. Although Jatin offered to let Ruby stay with him, given that he was a bachelor and had been injudicious once during the time they were pursuing the killer in *Bhendi Bazaar*, Rita wasn't particularly keen on this idea. From Jatin's perspective, perhaps he wanted to prove he was older and wiser now. However, neither Rita nor Vikram – without explicitly saying so – were comfortable with the notion. Why tempt fate? Ruby was, after all, drop-dead gorgeous.

Ruby was already packed and set to go when Jatin and Harry picked her up the next morning before sunrise. To whomsoever it may concern, she had vanished into the blue. She was to be placed in police custody for a short period of time.

In the interest of the mission, Ruby was to be Rita's house guest until such time that the rest of the details of their elaborate scheme had been worked out. Rita's reclusive lifestyle would serve as the perfect hideout. Ruby's bank account was cleared out. The police didn't want the villains in Ruby's life to follow the money trail if Ruby operated her account. Her mobile was switched off. Ruby had eradicated her digital footprint. The police would monitor her accounts and if someone were to look for her frantically, they would handle the situation. It was best to shred her history, ditch her identity – the sooner the better.

The wheels were set in motion. Every step needed second and third thoughts, and the team didn't hesitate to put forward their suggestions as they second-guessed the killer's thinking.

Ruby's Facebook profile settings were reduced to the bare minimum at the outset. Only the profile pic and a couple of others would be displayed to non-friends. They let them stay – with the dates of the uploads visible. Her date of birth would remain accessible to everyone. For the benefit of the unsub, her marital status was changed from *complicated* to *married*, and then the feed deleted from her timeline. There was no point in the status change to be reflected too prominently on the profile. Her name was changed from Ruby Diamond – which sounded more like a porn star than an entertainer of sorts – to Alka Dixit, and her husband was christened Sameer Dixit. Sameer, obviously, had no Facebook account. Althouth they thought about creating an account, they decided not to bother with it. Not existing on Facebook was a better option than creating a fresh account. In case someone pulled a Sherlock and probed Sameer, it would be better to not find him at all rather than finding a suspiciously fresh profile. Lots of people didn't have Facebook or LinkedIn accounts and preferred to live in the real world. Best to leave the unsub guessing.

With a bit of freethinking, the backstory was: Mrs Alka Dixit had recently moved to Mumbai from Singapore – she had once been to the country and had pictures from there and that added to the authencity – and since her husband Sameer was yet to move back, she was looking for some adventure. Sameer was a recruitment consultant, if someone asked. As he was still in transition from Singapore to Mumbai, he would be travelling back and forth a lot. Hence, Alka Dixit desired company. And more.

The next big question was where?

Bandra was debated and ruled out for two reasons. One: the last murder had occurred in Bandra, and the unsub had even boasted about it by making a call to the police. What if he already knew Bandra well and didn't need to scout afresh? That would be a serious handicap to the mission because they wanted to pick up anyone staking out Mrs Alka Dixit's residence. Secondly, and although there was nothing on file that could be interpreted as the pervert being wary of the police, perhaps the unsub might decline picking up another target in the same vicinity suspecting a high probability of police vigil in the locality. Why jeopardize an operation that they were going to such lengths to set up? If it didn't work first time, the probability of getting another approval from the powers-that-be was as remote as sighting a unicorn.

Versova seemed a good locality. Posh, not too far from Bandra, but not too close to set off any alarm bells either. The unsub had already killed in Andheri so this locale wouldn't be too alien for him. Mrs Alka Dixit would be put in a first-floor apartment in a building called Rajdoot, that had a similar non-existent 'security' like the other buildings in the vicinity. The last thing they needed was to deter the killer from approaching their decoy. The apartment was rented in the name of Sameer Dixit. To reinforce the charade, the move was orchestrated like a genuine one. Household stuff – furniture and furnishings – arrived like someone had moved residence from abroad. Who knew who was watching? What if the unsub knew someone in the area and asked around? Why take any chances? It was best for the mission that everyone sang from the same song sheet and there were no inconsistencies.

Sexy was furnished with the details of Rita's audacious plan, with all the i's dotted and the t's crossed. Plan A was to provide the tightest security they could in plainclothes, without being conspicuous, like an invisible Z security. Sexy had been clear – he wouldn't risk the life of an innocent to catch the unsub, however terrible the crimes that he had perpetrated. Rita nearly fell in love with Sexy as he revealed this humane side. She had always considered him a politician in uniform, but now realized that despite everything his heart was in the right place.

Plan B was submitted to him too. If things went belly up, they would abandon the entire plan and walk away, taking Ruby with them. The apartment would be empty if they suspected that the unsub had any inkling that it was a set-up. Bottom line: Ruby would be safe, no matter what.

After a series of questions, couched in his signature style vocabulary, Sexy signed off on the blueprint. Vikram, Jatin, Harry, and even *Chota* and *Takla* Mathur understood what was at stake here: Sexy's reputation. If it all went south, he would be heading traffic constabulary – provided the media let him. And the team also knew that, but for Rita, there was no way on God's earth that Sexy would have approved a scheme as outrageous as this.

'Go, get this spawn of the devil,' Sexy had said and the plan was put into action.

The truck rolled into the apartment block to offload the consignment. Mrs Alka Dixit was moving in from Singapore.

INTERLUDE
Present

I sometimes wonder what if I decided to quit. I've had enough fun. I have, up until this point, been fortunate. The blood of six, seven women on my hands – I don't keep a count, I can't; I'm not a bean counter – and not a clue to the police. This is the best time to walk away. Did you know that they never caught the Zodiac Killer in America? He operated in California in the '60s and '70s, even sent cryptic messages to the media and police; but then, abruptly stopped. The case could still be open in California. He just disappeared. Vanished without a trace. I could do the same. And the Mumbai Police would stay baffled. But as Nutty-me always reminded me: '*You do know that the more you try to stop yourself, your rage builds up along with the compulsion and urgency to find someone, don't you?*'

Nutty-me knows me better than I do. Although I'm the better-looking of the two, he's the brainier one.

You'd think the passing of time would make life easier for me. No. Time passed but the memories wouldn't fade. If anything, the images seared into my brain only grew more vivid. Violence was the only true release. The fermenting fury fulminated as I choked the life out of an adulteress, giving her the ultimate orgasm. Why? I didn't know and might never know. Perhaps it was something that only Nutty-me knew, but withheld from me.

I had intermittent thoughts of calling it all off and getting together with my girlfriend, Chavi Nair. Settle down. Get married. In time, like the film *Mr Brooks* – that I've seen more times than I care to remember – where Kevin Costner leads a double life and his wife, played by Demi Moore, is completely in the dark about his homicidal alter ego. I could be a loving husband to Chavi and carry on with my passion on the side. However, I am sceptical. I am sceptical because the very thought of copulation with a woman disgusts me. I can't bear to even think of how it would be if Chavi came on to me sexually, irrespective of how much I love her. Or care for her. I'd be instantaneously exposed and she would know that there was something fundamentally wrong with me. Plus, I'd have to return to being hirsute, which would make me susceptible and vulnerable and increase the risk of being caught if a hair follicle was inadvertently dropped at the scene of my escapades. It is a strict no-no. I can't afford emotional involvement: it is a weakness. Attachments find a way to control one; once controlled, one is prone to making mistakes. Even fatal mistakes. My affair with Chavi is an imitation of life. I am above suspicion at the moment. And I intend being invisible forever. Chavi is the perfect disguise.

I know my deficiencies. I know I'm incapable of love. Something's broken. It broke all those years ago when I was in the discovery phase. Small talk isn't my strong suit. Or inclination. Or interest. I come across as taciturn to some and it doesn't bother me if people don't look beyond the surface. Privacy isn't about hiding. It's about not letting people look into your soul. I aim to keep my brain occupied all the time. An empty mind is not my thing.

Every time I wonder how long I can carry on like this, Nutty-me reminds me that the obstacles are actually inspirations. Risk, besides everything else, attracts me and draws me in. So why worry? I had envisioned and put into place a perfect way of finding my marks – isn't that what they called the people one conned: marks? – and it was foolproof.

If, and it's a big if, someday I'm caught or my identity is revealed, I know what people will say: *Oh, he was such a nice, friendly man. So handsome. Impeccable manners. I can't believe he could murder anyone.*

Enough said. I repeat my mantra several times a day: stay focused, stay sharp, avoid attention.

Social media is a brilliant tool to fool. That's how I began. I spent time on the profiles of women who hadn't a clue about privacy settings. The kind of personal information people inadvertently give away is astonishing. Their everyday schedules, their friends and family, their holiday pictures, their dreams and desires. But I wasn't merely a voyeur. If anything, some of the pictures I saw turned me on enough to go looking for the women. Then the idea hit me to form an online club on Facebook. It took me a while to find a suitable name: Erotica – Play Beyond the Boundaries. I wanted the club profile to be a teaser. It needed to tempt people to dig deeper to find out more. I'm anything but stupid. Using separate computers, separate locations through VPNs, I set up three profiles through different email accounts and made them admins for the club: two males, Rockman and King&Queen; and one female, Lovely. A single admin would come across like a pervert scouting for women. Three admins, however, seemed like a proper club of sorts, didn't it? Then I made some more profiles, ten in all – some male, some female – to join as members. Anybody probing into my newly formed club would find it a legitimate mingling of erotic minds. The first few people seeking membership were men who were obviously looking for females. I know that because the phoney female profiles I had made kept getting hit by messages. I responded to some only for vicarious pleasure to understand other men's psyche. What were their expectations? Then the first woman asked for membership. Most people created avatars, but this woman didn't. She was in her thirties and single and looking for a date. Not my type at all, so I let her play with other men. She even sent Rockman a 'thank-you' message when her membership was approved.

Over the next few months, scores of people applied for membership and I stopped handing it out without insisting on for further details. I declined people if they weren't from Mumbai. I declined men with aggressive-looking profiles. I declined escorts seeking business. Out of the three-fifty-plus members, over three hundred were men and therefore, I was liberal with female applicants.

Then Anu Singh walked in like a sequel to Tina. Petite, gorgeous, married and looking for kinky fun, and my synapses fluttered. I had to have her. I confirmed that she was in Mumbai before Rockman approved her membership. Then I gave it a few days and approached her using one of my member profiles by sending her a message on FB Messenger. Most of the conversations I had with Anu, using member profile number five, were on her mobile she told me. To prove my theory, most women I interacted with on Messenger confided to me that they used their mobiles to chat. That their home computer belonged to both husband and wife, and the mobile was personal. Even the pick-up that I hooked up with initially told me that she only chatted with me on her mobile. It was easy enough for me to take away their mobiles when I met them. I didn't want the police or anyone to see that they had been chatting with someone in the FB club that I had created before their last rendezvous, although even if the police found their computers I was protected, because the police would never get as far as decoding whatever profile I was using with that particular tart – but why leave a trace? If nothing else, they would have spoken about my group and then my unfortunate Facebook group of Erotica would have met its untimely end. Best to erase evidence. I always, always, always took my victims' mobile phones; our chats were ours, so why should the world have access to them? It also eliminated our little interaction by deleting the chat logs. As I said, I'm anything but imprudent. And never rash. I know what I'm doing.

Most people don't accept that they're wrong. Without acknowledgement there can be no guilt. Without guilt there can be no remorse, no absolution. Someone has to bear the cross for them. Yours truly and Nutty-me. You see, I don't kill at random. It may appear as such; it is anything but. We only help relieve a certain kind of women.

Unbelievable.

Un-fucking-believable! Tina incarnated yet again. A new one has applied for membership. Alka Dixit. A newbie recently arrived in town from somewhere abroad. She's looking for company. Really?

I saw some pictures. Amazing. Amazing because she is so befitting Tina. Same height, similar weight, matching interests. Looking for company while her husband is away in Singapore burning the midnight oil to keep the lights going in the Versova apartment into which she has just moved. How horny is she? She's barely moved to Mumbai and already seeking 'companionship' until her husband joins her? Just my type. Oh God – or devil – save my soul, for here I come.

I waited ten minutes before granting her membership.

I'll wait weeks before approaching her. It won't do to come across as overenthusiastic. I've been extremely careful and fortunate so far. Why tempt fate by rushing into anything? I'll give her some time to settle down and view whatever other profiles she wants to see. Perhaps, I'll hit on her using one or two of my profiles for fun before I make my real move. I'll charm her socks off when I want to.

'*She needs it badly …*' Nutty-me started humming again.

EIGHTEEN

Setting up surveillance is easy if one were in one of the television shows like CSI where every department and every investigator seems to be bankrolled by the likes of Warren Buffett or Mukesh Ambani. But when it came to real police in Mumbai or any other city, for that matter, resources were less than scarce. Manpower and equipment were provided by State. Budgets were forever getting cut and overruled by other priorities or inanities, like providing security to vacuous VIPs.

Rita and her team had never set up anything like this before: an apartment that was staked out twenty-four/seven. While the cameras on the TV shows could record HD and showed faces even in dim lighting, Mumbai Police had none of those gizmos in their arsenal. Bureaucracy was just a bunch of old women, afraid of their own shadow. After much persuasion, threats and wheedles, the team collected cash to secure dime store, third-hand cameras that would record and relay black-and-white images. One could see shadows moving, but capturing a face would be wishful thinking. But they would have to do.

Two cameras were installed on the outside. A passer-by would probably not notice these cameras, but the installation of the one on the community wall of the apartment block would be conspicuous, so the installations were carried out at night. One, high up on a tall tree that grew outside the building, with branches spreading over the boundary wall, and the second one, on the lamp-post by the building's gate. Rita was dead against the interior of the apartment being placed under surveillance. Cameras inside an apartment was an invasion of privacy. You didn't want someone spying on Ruby aka Mrs Alka Dixit lounging around in a negligee or changing. Instead, panic buttons were placed in all the rooms, including the two bathrooms and the kitchen. They procured alarms that worked on SIM cards and would relay the signal directly to the police control room.

The plan was that Ruby would let the police change the password of her FB account and transfer control to Rita's team. At no point did Rita want Ruby to access any information, in case the perp tried to make contact. They also restricted the settings so no one could write on Alka Dixit's wall. The last thing they wanted was Ruby's friends giving the game away by demanding to know why she had changed her name. It would be an amateur mistake. Ruby's old friends, colleagues or clients would have to send private messages to communicate with her. Private messages could be ignored or blocked. At least no one else could see them. In any event, if Ruby wanted to escape the murky world of high-class escorts, it was in her own interest that all communication was suspended with the people in her present life. As soon as this was over, they would delete the account and advise Ruby to maintain a low profile in the online world. She would be instantly recognized if she posted her pictures online even if she changed her name.

Alka Dixit's membership to the closed group Erotica – Play Beyond the Boundaries was approved by the administrator. It was doubtful whether anyone probed deeper into her past. Perhaps the administrators did check out her profile; there was nothing in it to indicate her home address.

The instant she was accepted as a member, Rita and the team agreed that they would always use one dedicated computer and one mobile number to log into the account. It was not so much as discipline as making consistent the ruse of a bored housewife. If the unsub was some sort of a geek, he would probably smell a rat if he realized that various devices were being used.

Rita, Vikram, Jatin, Harry and the Mathurs spent hours going through the profiles of the other 371 members and three administrators. Most of the profiles were obscure. Random names like the administrators' Rockman, King&Queen, Lovely seemed to be the mainstay. Batman, Superman, Catwoman, Mermaid, Phantom and Tarzan all appeared to be rutting like sheep in mating season. Almost eighty per cent of the pictures on member profiles were animations or of celebrities taken from the web: fake. Anu Singh's membership may have been deleted; she wasn't there. Sapna Patel was still a member, but with an animated pic on her profile. That was enough to tell the police they were on the right track. Of the seventy-plus profiles with photographs of ordinary people, twelve were women. Some looked honest, but there was no way to tell if it was the member's own picture. The sixty-five male profiles were downloaded, printed and analysed to get some clue as to the actual individual. Zilch.

It was disheartening to be so close and yet unable to find the spoor.

'Fingers crossed, I hope it isn't *digging-the-mountain-finding-a-dead-mouse*,' Harry quipped. It was one of the less complicated idioms to translate and smiles ensued.

It was deemed pointless to approach any member. Who could they start a dialogue with?

Ergo, they waited. Something had to give.

The first message dropped into Facebook Messenger three days later.

Mumbai Superman: Hello ...

As agreed, they decided not to respond immediately. Nothing should give the impression that they were waiting.

Two hours later, Rita responded.

Mumbai Superman: Hello ...

Alka Dixit: Hi, sorry I was busy. We just moved in

MS: From where?

AD: Singapore

MS: All alone?

AD: Husband had 2 go 2 NY for a meeting

MS: Oh, missing him?

AD: Kind of ... but I'm used to being on my own. He travels a lot for work

MS: What does he do?

AD: He's a recruitment consultant

MS: Why have you moved back from Singapore?

The guy was being thorough. Trying to smoke out whether Alka was genuinc.

AD: He will shuttle between Singapore and Mumbai. R U one of the admins of this group?

MS: No. Are you?

AD: No, I just joined a few days ago

MS: So, were you part of some network in Singapore?

AD: No, out there I knew some ppl who organized parties, but Mumbai's a bit conservative so I need to be discreet. Plus, I don't know anyone around here

MS: Where are you from, originally?

AD: Rajasthan

MS: I'm probably not the first to say this, but you're very beautiful

AD: TY ☺

MS: I feel I've seen you somewhere. Have we met?

Shit! The whole plan could fall apart at this point. Of all the scenarios they had plotted this was the last one they had anticipated.

AD: U hv no pic on ur profile so I can't say. BTW, y haven't you put your pic up?

MS: Touché. I'm in a job where I cannot afford to be seen on social media

AD: Lol. Y?

MS: Company policy. And could I make a request please?

AD: Yeah

MS: Please don't use SMS shorthand with me

It had been consciously decided to use SMS lingo. They wanted Alka to be young and mobile-text savvy, but it hadn't struck the right chord with Mumbai Superman.

AD: y?

MS: I find it intensely irritating

AD: OK

MS: So, what's the plan?

AD: Nothing

MS: Want to meet up?

AD: Yes, I'm free later this week, but where?

MS: Didn't think of that. Maybe coffee?

AD: Sounds like a plan. I have to go now ... I have an electrician working in the apartment. How do I get in touch with u later?

MS: You not 'u' please

AD: Sorry

MS: Send me a message here. If I'm busy I'll respond later

AD: OK

MS: Don't you have a smartphone?

AD: I do, why?

MS: It's more secure. I'm sure your husband and you share a computer, and he might see our private conversations

AD: No, I have my personal Macbook. We don't share laptops

MS: OK

AD: Bye then. I'll ping you

Mumbai Superman went offline. So did Alka Dixit.

'That was good stuff, ma'am,' Vikram applauded.

'Notice something unusual?' Rita asked.

'He doesn't like SMS lingo.'

'Yes, which sort of tells me that Mumbai Superman might be in the age bracket that we hypothesized for our unsub. The younger generation is well-versed with SMS shorthand and uses it effortlessly.'

'Unless you're Harry ...' Jatin quipped and looked around. 'Where's Harry?'

'His mother isn't well, so he has taken a couple of days off. He didn't want to, considering we are so close, but I told him to go,' replied Rita.

'I hope she feels better soon. We're missing his idioms.'

'However, there's nothing to indicate that Mumbai Superman is our unsub. He could be any of the random male members,' Rita shrugged ruefully.

'Especially because he's suggesting a coffee date which, I assume, would be at some café.'

'Let's wait and see. Perhaps someone else will contact her as well.'

'Give it a few days.'

'What next?' Jatin.

'We don't make any contact with him. Let's see if he messages again.'

For the next two days, Mumbai Superman left short benign messages for Alka Dixit: *How goes your day? Hope you're enjoying Mumbai*, but nothing else. The little questions came in sporadically as the time stamp showed, but each time Alka responded to his question, he had logged off without waiting for a chat. In none of the messages did he mention the coffee date that they had discussed earlier.

Alka sent a few messages about catching up, but he claimed he was travelling.

The plan seemed to be crumbling. Mumbai Superman didn't seem overly keen about meeting Alka. At least, not in the near future. He almost seemed wary about something. Had he realized that she was a lure? How could he? The police had planned the whole arrangement to a T. Perhaps he was just biding his time and didn't want to come on too strong at this stage.

Two of Alka/Ruby's friends messaged to ask why she had changed her name and locked down her profile. Ruby told Rita that those girls were escorts too. After a brief brainstorming, the friends were told that a client had wanted her to play his wife for a reason and hence she wasn't allowed to disclose anything. However, this was just a short-term assignment and she would return in a while. One friend responded with a thumbs up, the other told Ruby to keep in touch and let her know how it went. If either of these girls had been asked by Ruby's handler to ferret out where she was, this reason would have mollified him. As for someone aspiring to flush out Ruby's coordinates, it was impossible. The servers used by Mumbai Police were strongly masked and would require someone with the skillset level of Julian Assange to penetrate.

Rohit Sharma was the second man who approached Alka Dixit. The profile pic was a white Mahindra Armada, photographed from the side with no identifiable marks or stickers. The background had been cropped to the bare minimum, some foliage but nothing discernible, not even giving away an area of Mumbai. He could have been anywhere. Perhaps not even in Mumbai. The administrators of the group couldn't physically check for Mumbai residency in all cases. A similar conversation ensued enquiring about her, her move to Mumbai, her husband, and the fact that she was gorgeous. He didn't seem interested in meeting her even when she proposed it. He was more eager with an online relationship, asking her about some of the sexcapades she had had so far. How kinky was she? What were her limits?

Limits?

While nothing in his behaviour suggested that Rohit Sharma was the unsub they sought, he was a goldmine in erotic vocabulary. The police had looked up Wikipedia and other forums for the jargon, but there was nothing like having a first-hand conversation with someone who practised it. Even if only for online fun. *A/S/L?* had been his first sentence after *Hi*. Age. Sex. Location. Even though the profile picture clearly showed

Alka Dixit and her age could have been guessed, he had asked. Rohit also wanted to know whether she was a DOM or a SUB. *Dominatrix* or *Submissive*.

The first time they chatted was late evening and there was a long exchange of messages; he was lucid and moved from erotic to downright lecherous. Rita felt a bit embarrassed responding to some of the questions – *Do you shave there?* – with her colleagues glued to the screen beside her. But this was something she had brought upon herself. This had to work. The tell-tale signs of the Lipstick Killer were all over the computers of the victims, she remembered. Each one – where they could check – had been on these pages of Facebook. He had to be here, lurking somewhere in the background.

The next morning when Rohit Sharma came online, he wasn't as fervid. His passion had cooled off. It was either that, or he had been sloshed the previous night and letting his libido do the chat. However, his prurience seemed to have waned. Perhaps that was how he got his rocks off – chatting with women. Perhaps he would try again another day when his urges got the better of him. Or when he was plastered again.

Net result: this experiment was going nowhere.

Frustrating as it was, Rita was cognizant that it also meant the clock was ticking. Before they knew it, another murder could take place, while their team sat around the computer watching Rita make scintillating and titillating conversation about the grooming of her pubes.

The press, as always, was rife with conjectures and possibilities. Even if Virat Kohli was having a hard time at the crease or Shah Rukh Khan's latest box-office release had bombed, the Lipstick Killer was still going strong as front-page news. Despite the classified status awarded to the operation, there was always the worry that information could be leaked to the media and then the whole operation would be in vain. Although she knew that none of the men working directly for her would talk to the press or anyone, there were others involved in the plan, albeit indirectly: the technicians, the secretaries, and other lower level staff who managed the room or computers or telephones. Although no one outside of their coterie was given the entire scenario, it was definitely possible for someone to do the math. All it required was one leak. And the police department was known to have more leaks than a recycled condom.

'What can we do?' Rita asked.

'Are we abandoning this project?' Vikram.

'I mean what *more* can we do? This seems like a wild goose chase. We were naïve to imagine we would be able to identify our unsub if the target were reduced to 371 people within a defined group, but what we hadn't accounted for was that most members in the group would be as secretive as we've made Alka Dixit. Their profiles restricted, with not many of them having their own pictures on their profiles. Even the names are aliases. Mumbai Superman,' she smiled mirthlessly, 'If the Superman is here I wonder which building is Mumbai Spiderman scaling at the moment ...'

It was infuriating. To come so close and still not find anything. Aborting the project would be rash. It had only been ten days since Alka Dixit got her membership.

'It could be that our unsub is travelling,' *Chota* Mathur suggested.

'But he would surely have access to a computer or a smartphone ...'

'Perhaps he's already romancing someone else at the moment?'

That was a point. Perhaps the unsub already had a target whom he was grooming at this very minute. The posit wasn't comforting.

'Is there any way that we could hack into all 371 of these member profiles to check?' Rita knew the answer would be negative. Facebook servers weren't bought second-hand from dime stores in Chor Bazaar and glued together with sticky tape.

'We can check,' Vikram jotted down the suggestion like he jotted down everything. He picked up the phone and called IT. Two minutes later, he was shaking his head like a morose pendulum on a clock that was winding down. 'Doesn't seem possible ma'am.'

'Okay, let's look afresh at the last murder: Sapna Patel at Bandra. Let's see if we missed anything. I think two of you should go back to Bandra and start a fresh investigation besides delving deeper into the notes and files here. I think we should assign this to the ones who weren't on the site then.'

'I'll go,' Harry volunteered.

'I'll go with him,' said *Takla* Mathur. This announcement generated a burst of laughter in the room because *Chota* Mathur looked crestfallen ... almost as if *Takla*, who had always been his partner, had publicly divorced him. *Chota* realized the joke was on him, but sensing it was all good-humoured mirth, joined in.

For the next three days various short conversations were initiated by a number of the male members of the Erotica group. Veiled behind the anonymity of the internet, the members seemed more interested in lewd and kinky chats using X-rated language, desirous to know more about Alka Dixit's anatomy rather than engineer an actual encounter or meeting. Alka, on her part, didn't want to request a meeting, for fear that her overeagerness might render the ploy useless. For one, it might alert the unsub if he was the online chatter, and second, what they were looking for was primarily predatory; he could be put off if the prey came across as aggressive. The fine line had to be maintained.

Mathur and Harry were out for three days digging up new information, but it turned out to be another dead end.

INTERLUDE
Present

'Hello, Mrs Dixit.'

I log-in as Gautam. No last name. A name like Gautam gives confidence to the person you're chatting with. In this faceless world – my profile pic is a bold question mark in gold within an ornate picture frame – most people receiving a message from a stranger inadvertently visualize its sender. With no last name if you closed your eyes and uttered Gautam, invariably the face of the founder of the religion begins to materialize. The question mark is a gentle push towards the same. Gautam Buddha questioned the status quo, sought answers … it all comes together to exclude the unsavoury, even though a conversation between strangers of the opposite sex within a closed erotica group would be anything but.

'Hi,'

… comes the response after fifteen seconds. I can see the message being typed on a computer.

'*Ask her when she wants to meet up*' – Nutty-me is on my case straightaway. '*She wants you …*' Nutty-me is like a dog with a bone. He has to charge in. What he does not understand is that the prey should never sense that it is being approached with evil intent.

I ignore him. Take a large glug of vodka and carry on.

The second mantra I use to put my quarry at ease after the preliminary pleasantries is to tell her my side of things. Ergo, after the little introduction, I give my age as thirty-one to which she responds as being thirty. Then I tell her I was born in Mumbai – harmless lie – and run my own small business enterprise – doesn't matter whether that's true or not. I also tell her that two years ago I was rated by some organization as the fourth best small business – how would she ever confirm that? – and live in Worli. I say I have recently broken off with my long-term girlfriend and am in no mood to get into another relationship so soon and hence, am looking for some fun.

She tells me her husband is some consultant. Even tells me his name without my asking: Sameer Dixit. I look up Facebook, but he doesn't have an account. Perhaps he leaves the social butterflying to his rakish wife. They have moved from Singapore, and the husband travels a lot. Perfect.

'Have you met someone from the online world?' I ask.

'Never needed to. In Singapore, a few of us had a close-knit circle ☺.'

'*Awww, look at the smiley … she's missing it already. She's horny … come on …*' Sometimes, Nutty-me annoys me no end. He has had a damaged psyche from the word go, I know, but lately he seems to be plummeting into a bottomless pit. It's scary because he could pull me down with him as well. I have to be careful, as I'm a bit drunk, and Nutty-me has an obsessive personality. Not an ideal combination.

Without warning, I log out of Facebook, shut my computer, finish my drink in a generous swallow, and get up to make another.

Pretension is part of the game. Let the target wonder what happened. Did she say something wrong? Would I come back? Keep her on tenterhooks. Cat-and-mouse. Generally, if one is dealt a bum hand, one is in a rush to play the next round. And if my opponent were to rush into a hasty decision, it's all the better for me.

NINETEEN

The only new information that Mathur and Harry gleaned from the fresh search into Sapna Patel's murder at Pali Mala Road, Bandra, was that one of the persons interviewed – a dhobi who had a small cart three buildings down the road and ironed the clothes of the apartment-dwellers for a living – recollected having seen a large, dark-coloured car parked in the neighbourhood that looked conspicuously out of place. By that he meant it didn't belong to anyone whose clothes he ironed.

Bandra, once a tiny fishing village back in the twelfth century, was now home to the rich and powerful like Shah Rukh Khan, Salman Khan and Sachin Tendulkar. To be able to afford a flat in Bandra – whether owned or rented – meant that one was well-heeled enough for an opulent lifestyle in Mumbai. The dhobi insisted that the car was the 'three-box' kind, meaning a saloon or a limousine. But even that description was too general. The second qualifier – dark colour – could mean anything from navy blue, brown to bottle green to black and all the darker shades of grey in between. It was like looking for a black cat in a coal cellar. The dhobi hadn't noted the make and model of the vehicle; nor did he manage to catch a glimpse of the driver or taken down the registration details. However, with this nugget to jog the memory of other neighbours, the team interviewed a lot of people once again. They also canvassed the other hawkers in the area – the corner cigarette seller, the bicycle repair shop – but it seemed like another dead end. With the thousands of large, dark-coloured cars that passed through the area, they had no recollection of one particular vehicle. Furthermore, the small-time traders didn't want to get dragooned into a police dragnet. The luxury automobile could be the key; it could be a red herring; but there was no way to know anything for certain at this juncture.

It had been over thirty days since Ruby aka Alka Dixit's Facebook account had been approved as a member of Erotica – Play Beyond the Boundaries, but nothing of consequence had been achieved. There had been random conversations with various men, some more than once, but none of them had shown any real interest in a face-to-face meeting. Mumbai Superman had occasionally come online to ask when her husband was due in town, but nothing more. He hadn't even mentioned the coffee date that he had initially proposed. Rohit Sharma, the lascivious one, had other insalubrious, late-night outbursts, but it was obvious that he was merely an online player. In fact, Rita, masquerading as Alka, asked if he was interested in meeting up, and he declined to answer. Gautam, the one who had abruptly abandoned their first conversation midway, didn't resurface for the rest of the day, which made the police wonder if he was a one-timer. But then, he soon became a regular feature. He'd talk about sex, bondage, limits and even asked for more pictures; the request was politely declined or rather postponed until such time as he revealed his face. He hadn't asked for pictures again, but he came online to chat on and off. His appearances were random and sporadic – sometimes during the day, sometimes late at night, but there was a common theme: he would suddenly go offline. When subsequently asked *why*, he always evaded the question. Perhaps he lived with someone and disconnected when that someone was around.

Rita and the team were learning the hard way that *it could happen* did not exactly translate into *it was probable* or that *it would happen*. Perhaps the unsub was shrewder than they assumed and smelled the proverbial rat. Maybe. The police may have been totally off the mark and this wasn't his hunting ground.

One point of view was that Alka should try and make conversation with some of the other female members of the group to ascertain if any one of them had been approached for a date by another member. But that idea was dropped almost immediately. How does one draw a picture of the invisible, those hidden behind the murky curtains of the dark web? Who was to know if the unsub operated behind some of the female identities? It wasn't worth the risk.

Meanwhile, the rocketing expenses were burning a hole in the purse. The rental rates for an apartment in Versova weren't as exorbitant as the ones in Bandra, but it was still expensive. Add to that managing the security arrangements and monitoring and running the equipment and it wasn't difficult to grasp that this arrangement couldn't last forever. Three to four months tops, and then the powers-that-be would pull the plug. Ruby would still have to be reallocated as per their promise and the police would be none the wiser. But it would merit a slap on the wrist for their department, adding insult to injury.

'Hi …' said Gautam.

Of all the members yet to communicate with Alka, Gautam seemed the most persistent so far. This time he had come around after a gap of four days.

AD: How have you been?

G: Busy. How about you?

AD: The other day, you disconnected abruptly again. You have to tell me why you do this every single time

G: Okay. It's because of my wife. She keeps tabs on me. So, if I sense her coming, I disconnect totally. Happy now?

AD: That explains it. I didn't know you're married

G: Yes, but that shouldn't matter. You're married too, so that makes two of us

AD: Of course

G: Nature of this game. I mean most people here, who are members, might be married, I would imagine. Or at least in a relationship, don't you think?

AD: You have a point

G: Is your husband in town?

AD: No, he's back next week. How about your wife?

G: She's out of the country at the moment, so it seems we are both at loose ends. And when the cat is away …

AD: You mean?

G: I thought you said you've met other men before, didn't you?

AD: I've never met anyone in Mumbai

G: How is Mumbai different?

AD: It isn't

G: Where do you live?

Rita stopped. This was the first time any of the members had asked for the address. But if they had to entice the rabbit out of the burrow they had to respond. AD: Versova. Where are you located?

G: Bandra. Want to meet up?

AD: Discreet?

G: Of course

AD: Let me think

G: What's there to think? This is what this place is for … to hook up. I guarantee more fun per second than you can think of

AD: You sure know how to pull a girl's strings

G: Oh, wait till I have you in bed

Rita's heart thumped. Gautam was pushing the line. He hadn't mentioned a coffee or a dinner. He had jumped straight into bed.

AD: What's your full name?

G: Don't worry, you'll only need to scream my first name

Rita looked at Vikram, then Jatin and then *Chota* Mathur who were in the room. Gautam seemed to have morphed from the civilized chatter that he had started with to a whole different line.

AD: Have you met anyone from this Facebook club?

G: Yes

AD: Who?

G: Why? Do you want to check my references to confirm that I can give you more pleasure than your husband or whoever you've been with yet?

AD: No, I just wanted to know

G: So where in Versova?

Gautam seemed persistent.

AD: Rajdoot Apartments, off Yari Road …

G: Okay

Rita looked up. The guys were watching. Yes. She had given him the building name.

AD: But, don't just come around, unannounced.

G: Why? D'you want your husband to be there so he can watch me tie you up? LOL

Then, in his usual manner, he abruptly disconnected.

'What do you think?' Rita asked as she closed the browser.

'It could be him,' Vikram said slowly. 'There's no way to confirm that until he actually pays a visit. Considering that most people in this online club are kinky, bondage doesn't necessarily mean it's the guy we're looking for.'

'Beef up the security. He is the only person who has asked for the address so far. There was no reason to know where Alka lived unless he has plans to visit. We cannot take a risk.'

INTERLUDE
Present

The raindrops are heavy, sounding like erratic heartbeats on the roof of my car, as I sit in the car parked inside the gates of Alka Dixit's building, Rajdoot. It was built by the Rahejas, so her husband must be doing okay, financially. Not too well, but not bad either. I keep the engine running just in case a neighbour passes by or parks next to me. Always be prepared for the worst. If someone cares to note down the registration number of the car, there is none. I put black stickers on both front and rear plates, which I will remove as soon as I get away from here. The wipers, at their fastest speed, are struggling to keep up with the pelting rain. Visibility is low, and the rain has kept the neighbours indoors. Both of which suit me.

The apartment block looks like all the other buildings in the dark. A tall concrete structure with incandescent squares and rectangles; lights that the windows let out. The rest is completely invisible. Most of the windows are clear glass except the ones on the ground and first floors. Some do not have occupants or perhaps the people aren't in the rooms that face this parking area.

'*Go in now, go in now,*' Nutty-me screams in my ears hysterically. '*Go fuck her, it won't take long; you know you want to …*'

Then: '*At least, talk to her. Become friends. Fix a date. Then let's go take her together.*' Don't you just love Nutty-me sometimes?

Which apartment is she in, I wonder. If her profile picture on Facebook is genuine, then I shouldn't have any problem recognizing her if she comes out. Anyway, why wouldn't it be a real one if she wants to meet up? You would think people would be more wary of exchanging information online, but there are so many who think they are too smart to fall into a trap. Anu Singh thought she was safe. So did Sapna Patel and so many others. So does Alka Dixit.

I have a copy of her picture in the car now. I pull it out of the glove compartment and admire her. A stirring begins between my legs. Not in the least because she looks glamorous, but more due to what I'd do to her in a few days.

Nutty-me wasn't entirely wrong. I have to set up a date with her without coming across as too aggressive. And it needs to be done as soon as possible. It has been quite some time.

I pulled out my smartphone – it's VPN enabled – and open my Facebook App.

'Hi,' I type.

'Hello Gautam,' she types in, two minutes later.

'So, have you decided when and where?'

'When and where what?'

'When and where we're meeting up.'

'How about meeting for dinner?'

'Why waste time eating dinner. Tell you what – I'll bring along a bottle of Chianti and some great Thai food,' I type.

'So, you've already decided to come over to my place?'

'Let's inaugurate your bedroom.'

'What makes you think it's yet to be inaugurated?'

'Not in the way we will. We'll set the room on fire. I cannot wait to take you.'

'Why don't we meet next week?'

'What's wrong with tomorrow night?'

It isn't just Nutty-me; now I'm going crazy too. It has been a while since my last adventure and if I don't get a release soon it might spell disaster. I want it now as a matter of fact, but I don't want to spook her by telling her I'm already at her threshold.

'I can't do tomorrow.'

'How about the night after tomorrow?'

'Could I come back to you on the date, please?'

'Okay.'

I end the session.

Is she playing hard-to-get or is she having second thoughts?

I reverse the car out of the parking slot, do a quick three-point turn and drive off. I'll be back soon, I know, but not in the same car ... just in case someone has noticed the vehicle. I need to figure out which apartment Alka Dixit lives in.

TWENTY

'A big, black car just backed out from the queue of cars parked in the building,' one of the guys monitoring the surveillance cameras called the Operations Room just as Rita saw Gautam go offline. 'He was parked inside the block for the last twenty minutes with his engine running.'

Rita gathered that a car parked with the motor running for twenty minutes did seem suspicious.

'Registration?'

'Was blacked out, ma'am.'

'What was he doing parked there?'

'The cameras aren't the best ma'am, and they're positioned to look down so it's hard to tell ...'

The cameras had been positioned at discreet angles so as to avoid the neighbours getting antsy. Ergo, what they captured was compromised.

'What make was it?'

'A Volkswagen, ma'am.'

Everyone looked around the room. The unsub – if it was indeed he – seemed to be doing rather well financially.

'Send us the footage.'

'I'll transfer the files straightaway, ma'am. Give me ten minutes.'

The car was dark-coloured and big just as the dhobi at Bandra had claimed. It was a Volkswagen Passat in a dark colour. The windows were tinted and to say that the view of the inside was limited would be an understatement. But there was a blue light that came on ten minutes after the car parked there. Like the driver had pulled out his smartphone ...

'Oh my God,' Rita exclaimed. 'He was chatting with us sitting outside Alka's building.'

If this assumption was correct it was a chilling discovery. Not only had they found the unsub, but he had had the nerve to drive to her apartment building to chat with his quarry, seated right on her doorstep.

As the initial adrenaline settled, and rational minds cogitated over the episode, a feeling of accomplishment enveloped the room. For several weeks now, they had had tirelessly looked for clues that could lead them to the insidious Lipstick Killer. Through all the ups and downs, gruelling week after gruelling week, following the setting up Alka Dixit's account, they had wondered whether they were on the right track. There had been times where frustration had got the better of all of them cumulatively. Sitting in front of the computer, watching as perverts and weirdos relayed obscene messages seemed a huge waste of time, effort and energy. They just gritted their teeth and stuck to the plan, and their patience had finally paid off. At long last they had made a breakthrough.

Had they indeed caught a break or was it coincidence playing a cruel joke on them?

'He has taken the bait, ma'am,' Jatin heaved a huge sigh.

'And it's about time he was looking for a prey; it ties in,' agreed Vikram. 'He has been chatting up Alka for more than a month – let's check the date logs on Messenger. I think he cannot keep a lid on his fantasies anymore.'

'Should we move Ruby out of the apartment?' asked Jatin.

'No way,' Rita looked surprised. 'Why would we do that? We don't know if this is the first time the guy has been here. What if he has planted some kind of surveillance to watch her or any activity around the place? We need to be extra vigilant. No one in uniform should be seen in the vicinity. Even we shouldn't be seen there, at least not together. However, a single police officer can be mistaken for a social visitor to someone in the building, but a few of us together would set off his alarm bells.'

The group pondered the situation, parsed Rita's narrative. They understood the gravity of the challenge that they now faced. It had been on their agenda to give out Alka Dixit's address when asked by any member of this exclusive Facebook club, but they hadn't expected the unsub – if the man in the black saloon were in fact the unsub – to rise to their bait so fast.

'We shouldn't agree to the date that he's pushing for,' Harry said firmly. He had a point. It would be wise to upset him by delaying their meeting for as long as possible. Stretched to breaking point by his fantasies and desires, he would make that long-awaited mistake. Equally, it was very possible that he had been grooming some other innocent wife simultaneously and if Alka couldn't make time for the rendezvous, he could be compelled to turn to someone else. They would be completely blindsided if that were to happen and they would have inadvertently triggered another murder.

'We'll need to agree to a date, but not so quickly,' said Rita. 'Let's arrange for the best security around the apartment block. Now that we know it *could* be him – this man in the VW – why don't we change tack and talk to him differently.'

'How?'

'Maybe push him to share his photograph for one? Although I think it's highly doubtful that he would comply, and even if he does, it might not be his ...' even as she spoke the words, Rita realized it would be a futile tactic at best. At worst, if by pushing him too hard, they ended up turning him away from Alka forever. Then they would be groping in the dark and back to square number one. 'A non-starter,' she sighed.

'There can't be an infinite number of black Passats in Mumbai,' Harry volunteered.

'There will still be too many to check. Plus, if the car isn't his—'

'You mean he could be using a friend's car?'

'He could well be a chauffeur who uses his boss's car when the boss travels.'

Far from convinced nods. Rita's clarification, her words and her demeanour conveyed that she didn't believe in the chauffeur-theory herself. It was too far-fetched to think a chauffeur could have successfully wooed women like Anu Singh and Sapna Patel. And the person who chatted to the fictitious Alka Dixit hardly came across like a minion.

'What I was saying is, whoever drives a VW Passat has to be reasonably well-off, and if we poke the wrong man, before we know it, he'll kick up one hell of a fuss, and Sexy—' she hadn't meant to call him that, but it had slipped out, making the five men in the room grin in juvenile amusement, 'I mean

Commissioner Saxena will whip our sorry asses, so the short answer is, *no*, we cannot run a check on every man who owns a black Passat in Mumbai. In any event, merely knowing who owned that car won't be of much help unless we can watch every one of them for the next seven days to see where they travel.'

The recordings from the surveillance cameras were checked again the next day. There were no signs of the same car. It was evident that the dark VW had driven into the parking lot of the apartment block, and just stayed there for twenty minutes before driving away. No one had alighted from the car. Two plain-clothes policemen were dispatched separately to all the apartments in the building to check if anyone had expected a guest the night before in a VW. There was a possibility that someone had come to visit a resident but had changed his mind due to the heavy downpour. He had probably made an innocent call to apologize to his hosts and then left. Two seven-storeyed blocks with two apartments on each floor – it took two men under two hours to confirm that no one had been expecting any friend who drove a black VW the previous night.

The circle of suspicion was tightening. The questionable black car hadn't appeared in any recordings in the entire month since the cameras had been installed. It had only made an appearance after Alka Dixit had given Gautam her address. Which suggested that Gautam hadn't recognized that Alka as a decoy. Which was the only good news at the moment.

'Five days, max …' Rita told the group. 'We cannot make him wait more than five days before setting up the date. He might not be able to control himself and we definitely do not want another murder.'

G: Hi
AD: Hi, Gautam

G: Hi, gorgeous

AD: I'll take that as a compliment, so thanks

G: I sit here and wonder how much better you would look sans clothes

Hmm ... Rita looked unimpressed. She realized she was growing immune to unsavoury chats with strangers. But this may be the last time, she thought. A smile escaped her. She decided to try something as vulgar on Ash.

AD: You embarrass me

G: This is only the beginning. When are we meeting?

AD: Soon

G: Soon isn't good enough. Give me a date, so I know you're serious.

AD: It's Tuesday today, 08 December, why don't we meet Saturday night?

G: Can't you do it any earlier?

AD: I've got a friend coming over for a few days ...

G: Oh, okay

London.

Ash walked out of his one-bedroom apartment in Kensington. There had been a forecast of snow, but none had fallen yet. However, it was bitterly cold, and the wind was chilling to the marrow. His iPhone buzzed in his pocket and he swore softly. He would have to remove his nice warm gloves to take the call. Rita's beautiful smiling face was displayed on the screen as he withdrew the phone from his pocket. God! He loved this woman. He was one lucky sod!

'Hi, gorgeous, I was just thinking of calling you.'

'When?

'I'm booked to be with you this Saturday.'

'Shit.'

'Whoa, whoa, whoa! That's not a very nice way to welcome someone.'

'I'm sorry, I meant—'

'Do you mean it's some new and kinky act that involves faeces then?'

'You're disgusting.'

'Am I now? I was trying to picture—'

'Stop it,' Rita said and told him that she would be on red alert on Saturday and, perhaps, Sunday as well, because the Lipstick Killer case that they had been pursuing for months might, just *might*, culminate in an arrest by then. She quickly summarized their progress since they had last spoken. 'And hence, the expletive, sorry.'

'Not a problem. I'm there for work so we'll see how it goes. If you're tied up … I don't mean literally—'

Rita groaned.

'So,' Ash went on, 'I'll ask them to book me into a hotel and we'll see how it goes when I get there. Okay, sweet cheeks? And by the way, I'm talking about the cheeks on your face.'

Ash at his sleazy best. Was he a member of some exclusive kinky online club as well? Rita wondered as she ended the call.

Ash picked up two coffees from Costa and walked into his office. Handing one of the brews to his secretary he asked her to change his Mumbai ticket to Friday morning. If Rita was going to be busy on Saturday the twelfth, he would surprise her on the eleventh.

'There are no available flights on Friday, the eleventh,' his secretary called him on the intercom.

'Thursday?'

She put him on hold for a minute. Then: 'You're booked for Thursday, the tenth.'

'Thank you, Jenny.'

He had hardly replaced the phone on the cradle, when it rang again.

'Ash Mattel.'

'Ash, it's Katie.'

He had recognized the voice anyway, but the voice conveyed that something was badly amiss.

'Hi Katie, everything all right?'

'Ash, I lost my job ...'

When Katie and Ash were married, Katie was a finance honcho in an accounting firm, making money hand over fist. They had dated for two years before getting married. The cracks in the relationship began to appear within a year of married life. Katie was ambitious, but then why wouldn't she be? She was amazingly bright and head-hunted by employers both within the country and across the Atlantic. Their marriage eventually disintegrated and Katie moved to New York. That seemed a lifetime ago.

'How?' *And why call me*?

'The audit caught some inconsistencies that the Board had known about all along, but they had to find a scapegoat, so it was my neck this time.'

'I'm so sorry to hear this.'

'I was asked to leave immediately. Can I come home?'

'Home?' *The* home *you forced me to pay for your share when you walked out on me*?

'I don't have any money, Ash. No salary, no car.'

'What happened to all that money you were making? Don't tell me you bought Jimmy Choos with all of it.'

'Stop being a cold-hearted bastard, Ash. Could I live with you for a short period until I figure things out … please?'

'Look, Katie, I don't think it's a good idea – you moving into my apartment.'

'Why not? Are you dating someone?'

Typical Katie. She had no business to ask or be answered. Ash could feel his ire rising. She needed a favour and was demanding it.

'If you need some money, I'll be happy to—'

'And where do I keep all my stuff?'

I don't care would have been a perfect response.

'How long do you need a place to stay?' he asked.

'A couple of weeks, at least.'

'Okay. I'm going abroad on Thursday. Why don't you collect the apartment keys from my office and move in. And we'll see how best to manage the situation when I return.'

'Why can't I move in now? I'm in trouble, Ash, please help me, for old times' sake. I promise I won't seduce you.'

He wanted to tell her she couldn't even if she tried, but he didn't want to start an unnecessary argument. 'Okay.'

'I always knew you would help me, Ash.'

Shit!

INTERLUDE
Present

I'm a sharp guy, I know. I also know this is blowing my own trumpet, but I am what I am. If you don't believe me, ask Nutty-me.

I made three observations that an ordinary human would fail to notice. One: the gate to Alka Dixit's apartment block is open to drive in and drive out. Two: the watchman is lousy or a fucktard or lazy or incompetent – whichever he may be, he doesn't bother with stray cars just driving in and parking in the bays. And three: and the most important one, there's a To Let sign for an apartment in the very same building.

The question is: do I need to hire it? There's little point in revealing my identity to an estate agent in the vicinity. Why leave behind any footprints? Considering the security in the building, it would be a lot easier to break into an empty apartment, isn't it? What are lock picks for?

Obviously, I would need to put on a disguise to get into the building. Sitting still in the car on a rainy night in Mumbai and watching is one thing but moving around in the building on foot could raise eyebrows. However, this could just be a figment of my imagination. This is Mumbai – no one has time to even know their neighbours, so another face might not raise eyebrows, but why risk it?

First, I need to pick another lock. Someone's inconspicuous car that they won't miss for the day. I know just the place to pick up such cars. Any car parked outside any of Mumbai's numerous stations where people left their vehicles for the day. It's not simple these days with all this electronic gadgetry, but it's not terribly difficult either.

'*Come on, hurry up*,' says Nutty-me, all fired up.

Nutty-me is a glutton, always hungry for more. More blood, more sex, more violence. His needs have always been more urgent than mine. He overwhelms me like a tsunami that doesn't recede until it inundates everything around. I could say I'm a mere spectator watching from the sidelines, but no – I enjoy it too much to stop him. Nutty-me is the one who leads me to a strong, heart-pounding release, like a jolt of electricity shooting through my body. Always. There is some sort of occult communication between him and me. Psychomancy, it's called. And if there's a term for it, it surely exists, right?

Right from the start, as soon as I saw Tina, it has been our mission – Nutty-me and mine – to provide the best orgasm to women of her ilk. Nothing less, nothing more. You see, asphyxiation heightens the orgasm. And if the woman is looking to play beyond the boundaries of her marriage, we would like to reward her with the best orgasm of her life. But it is also their last. With the rod buried deep inside their womanhood – deeper than ever before, deeper than any man would ever reach – the garrotting guarantees that her fatal, final orgasm is worth dying for, even if it was momentary.

Nutty-me and I aren't the monsters that we are made out to be. We provide the ultimate pleasure. Unfortunately, it comes at a price.

We're certain it's worth dying for.

Maybe our desire to quit has never been strong enough to leave it all behind. They say no one is congenitally twisted; it's not in the genes, it is bad nurturing. But who knows whether there was some strange and warped DNA in Nutty-me and me that loved moribund women? When we reach the part where they are on the verge of extinction at our hands, it makes both of us ecstatic. We're not perfect, but then who is?

In the end, I didn't need to do anything petty. Late last night, Nutty-me whispered to me a simple and brilliant idea. He's wicked.

Around nine in the morning I picked up one of my untraceable mobile phones and called the telephone number I had memorized on the To-Let sign. It was some small-time estate agent, Ravi-something.

'Ravi Estates, Ravi speaking, how may I help you?'

'Mr Ravi, this is … Anand. I was looking for an apartment in Versova and saw a To-Let sign in one of the buildings that I visited yesterday—'

'Which building?'

'I think it was Rajdoot—'

'Yes, we have one left,' he was either rude, impatient or just busy; he doesn't let me complete my sentences. Either way, it sounds good, if you ask me. Impatient muttonheads like these register very little, so this conversation is almost as good as private. Just the kind of chap I want on the line.

'Is it two or three bed—'

'It's a two-BHK,' Mumbai parlance for two-bedroom-hall-kitchen.

'Are there any three-bedroom ones available in the building?'

'Oh, sir, you just missed out. We had a beautiful three-bed, and it was only recently let out.'

'Oh shame,' I feign. 'What are the rents like—'

'For two-bedroom?'

'Yes.'

He quotes the rent and deposit.

I whistle. 'Wow, that's really expensive, so how does anyone afford a three-bedroom one in that building?'

'Oh, these tenants have moved in from abroad somewhere. Singapore, I think.'

I was dead on target.

'Oh, which flat was it?'

'406'

'Must be a large family …'

'In fact, it's just husband and wife, but they wanted the space.'

'Is it the Dixits?' I couldn't stop myself.

'Yes, do you know—'

I had no intentions of listening to his irritating voice anymore. I hung up. Mission accomplished: Alka Dixit lives in flat 406.

Three-bedroom apartment for a couple sounded a bit over-the-top extravagant. Especially when the husband, as Alka Dixit told me, travelled a lot. Why? That, and the fact she's agreed to see me at her home for unbridled sex within the first few months of her moving to Mumbai, and only after a few chats with me, a stranger on FB, fascinates me. Either she's a total nymphomaniac or there's something I've certainly missed. My sixth sense has switched on a warning light. With police so hot on the trail of the Lipstick Killer – not me, of course – what if they're circling around all single adulteresses. But how could they possibly find all these women – they don't have access to a database, do they?

'*You worry too much*,' Nutty-me says. '*The police are no closer to you today than they were a year ago*.'

I have a plan.

TWENTY-ONE

Wednesday, 09 December.

All police work started with a theory. Then you played the odds. At this point in time the odds were stacked high against them. The unsub, so far, had always been two steps ahead of them, leaving no clues behind. This was the first time that they had witnessed a movement on the installed cameras, but this activity, too, had been revealed only after he had left the party.

The CCTV footage was analysed by Rita and the taskforce several times over before being forwarded to the experts who would tear it down scene-by-scene and examine it frame-by-frame to see if the primary taskforce had missed anything. Nothing gave except the car make. They reconfirmed that it was a VW Passat. If anything, the colour of the car came into question. It may not have been a black Passat after all. The experts opined that the vehicle could well have been navy blue or dark green. Another spanner in the works. As if finding the black car wasn't difficult enough, adding other colours into the fray muddied the waters even further. In any event the finding was moot, because Rita & Co. had decided that they weren't going after the car anyway.

Had they missed or misinterpreted any clue, was Rita's biggest concern. Had the team failed to spot a logical discrepancy somewhere that might have steered the investigation in some other direction? Any witness statements that were contradictory or inconsistent? Was there anything they could do between now and Saturday evening to nab the bastard before he came to see Ruby aka Alka Dixit? Despite the security and all the other arrangements, the rendezvous wasn't Rita's first preference. Didn't Sun Tzu say: *The greatest victory is that which requires no battle*? And this could well turn into a battle, both ugly and bloody. A thousand plus things could go wrong. Who knew what weapons the unsub carried or how he would react when he was as high as a kite on his lust for blood? What if a neighbour got caught in the crossfire?

The last-ditch effort for a crime investigator was to shake enough trees to see if something fell out. Documents, witness statements, investigator notes, scene of crime photographs, forensic and autopsy reports were read and re-read by other teams to pick up anything the first set of eyes might have missed. Nada. Rather than a miss on the part of the investigating team, it was the cunning of the unsub that got highlighted. By all accounts, they were dealing with a criminal mastermind here, whose intelligence and imagination were both off the charts.

Reinterviewing any witnesses now would only confirm the Loftus and Palmer theory: memory was often distorted by the information acquired after the event. That would cause a mix-up of epic proportions, as the original memory would merge with info they had picked up from other sources, which in this case was all over the media. Initially, the dhobi said that he had seen a big black car, but if they went back to ask him if the big black car was in fact a navy blue Passat, the answer would have been an emphatic 'yes'. It was a no-go place. As such, there was no fresh intel.

And they had to be particularly cautious. They needed to totally blackout the media until the operation was complete. One leak and it would be all over. If the unsub even got an inkling that he was about to poke the wrong beehive, it could turn nasty. Even fatal.

By the evening, Rita was exhausted like she had never been before. More than the physical fatigue it was the overwhelming stress which resulted in acute insomnia. She realized coffee wasn't doing the trick anymore. If she needed this operation to be successful, the key players needed to be at their highest alert. If they lost focus for any reason, they could end up paying the price.

Harry and Akhil '*Takla*' Mathur were assigned the responsibility of taking over the Facebook account for twenty-four hours while Rita, Vikram, Jatin and Ravi '*Chota*' Mathur took a twenty-four-hour break. It was agreed that they would return to the Ops Room Thursday evening and remain there until they brought the unsub down on Saturday. This was their twenty-four-hour break before the forty-eight-hour non-stop duty from Thursday evening. Harry and *Takla* Mathur would take their break on Thursday night and return at noon on Friday. Friday night, they were all to stay on duty, monitoring everything, taking power breaks in turns.

'Guys – stay alert, stay safe,' Rita said before she checked out of the Operations Room.

Rita went home, showered, changed into a skirt for the first time in a long time, and then called a cab to Versova. She wanted to sport a different look from the work Rita, and she certainly didn't want to take the car. She had called Ruby. This could well be the last time she would get some time with Ruby – her erstwhile, temporary flatmate – before Saturday. Best to have some conversation over dinner to calm her down in case her nerves got the better of her. Rita decided to refrain from telling Ruby that they might have sighted the unsub sniffing around in her building already. They weren't sure if it was him, first of all; all they had worked out was purely circumstantial – an unrecognized car that was suspicious in itself; nothing that could ever be proved in a court of law. Secondly, it would have put paid to whatever little sleep the poor lass was getting.

Ruby was maintaining a façade of normalcy, but Rita could sense that the girl was on edge. Credit where it was due, she was putting on a brave front; Ruby had lived a hard life and wouldn't crumble easily, although she was probably questioning the prudence of the task she had signed up for. Should she have given it some thought before agreeing to fall in with Rita's scheme? Whichever way one looked at it, it was a frightening predicament. It was one thing to be caught up in a maelstrom, but quite another to anticipate it.

'Will it be okay?'

Rita nodded.

'Is Saturday definite?'

Rita guessed that Ruby had given herself a timeframe. *It would all be over by the weekend.* It was normal, natural to look beyond the tunnel.

'Yes,' Rita responded. After a pregnant silence, Rita asked, 'How did you—'

'Get into this mess? It's a long story.'

'I have all the time in the world,' Rita smiled at the girl who had put her head on a block – quite literally.

If a psychiatrist like Ash had been around, he would have analysed the situation in medical terms, but Rita could appreciate Ruby's rationale. When one encountered a difficult or dangerous situation, the mind drew parallels with previous trauma. In Ruby's case, the reality was shocking. A deep melancholy filled her as she time-travelled to all those years ago where her innocence was exploited by the animal in the man she had once loved. His betrayal hurt more than the physical pain.

She was sixteen when she fell in love with Ajay, a twenty-two-year-old company executive who had recently moved into the neighbourhood. Little did she know that her love story would soon mutate into a horror show. When Ajay proposed the ultimate intimacy, starry-eyed Ruby couldn't wait to give her virginity to the man she loved.

On that ill-fated day, Ajay took her to his Borivali apartment where he not only screwed her, but also took pictures of her in flagrante delicto. From that point on, she got called upon to service his so-called friends. Then clients. More photographs of depraved acts were taken trapping her in a quagmire that she couldn't escape. Her appalled family disowned her, and she had no one to turn to for help. A puppet to primal needs, unwittingly sold into the world's oldest profession before the realization dawned. Her life, as she once knew it, was over; like someone had torn out a page before it had been read.

Intercourse with an endless parade of men culminated when a politician's son, a young married man, took a fancy to her and wanted her exclusively. He moved her into an apartment on Marine Drive, which was within driving distance for him and easier to reach. The hiatus lasted all of six months before he wanted someone else. Initially, he only allowed his close friends to use her but, over the course of time, she became a high-class escort.

'Do the original photographs still exist?' Rita asked. Stupid question, she knew, but she didn't know what else to ask.

'I'm sure they exist somewhere. A lot more were taken consecutively, and probably circulated as well. But I stopped caring after a while because it didn't matter. I was a whore. Every man who had money fornicated with me and used my body, so why bother about the original pictures? It wasn't like I was someone's girlfriend or wife that I would be discovered …'

'How long ago was this?'

'I'm twenty-eight now, so it has been almost ten years.'

'Ever met Ajay after you moved?'

'Yes, he came to see me recently. He gleefully told me how great I was in bed, and how he had "shaped" my career …'

'Give me his full name and address, I'll find him.'

'I no longer crave for revenge, Rita, but I'm worried he could be luring other girls into this vile "career",' she confessed.

'I wish I had been there to save you then. I cannot change what happened, but I promise I'll get his ass hauled into prison for a very long time.'

'Thanks, Rita,' Ruby turned away so Rita wouldn't see her tears.

'Let's order some food,' Rita changed tack.

'Pizza?' Ruby responded like a child.

'Why not?'

TWENTY-TWO

Thursday, 10 December.

The Best Laid Plans – hadn't the famous novelist Sidney Sheldon written a book to demonstrate how ironical that phrase could be? Ash Mattel took the Thursday late-afternoon flight from London and arrived in Mumbai, early Friday morning. The stewardess served fresh orange juice even before the aircraft began trundling down the runway. He was flying earlier than his original schedule, but his plan had been far from successful.

Despite his immaculate planning, his ex-wife Katie had arrived at his place with bag and baggage, a day prior to what he had agreed. A blue-eyed blonde, petite and gorgeous, Katie didn't think it would be an issue because they had once been married. Perhaps she had had an ulterior motive. That night, Katie and Ash sat on the small balcony of his flat enjoying the views. The snow hadn't melted, the clouds still stood their ground and the temperature had risen making it a beautiful weather. Cool, but not cold. Their conversation had been stilted to begin with, but quickly led to the raunchy and the far from formal. As wine got the better of them, sentiments flowed uninhibitedly. Katie soon discarded her boots and socks and moved her bare foot on Ash's jeans-clad calves. A show of love and companionship. The proverbial one thing led to the proverbial other. The two retreated from the balcony, the clothes didn't take long to come off, the intimacy they had once shared came returned with a vengeance. The lovemaking was primal like they had been kept in separate cages and prevented from consummating.

Lying naked with Ash on the living room carpet, she had asked him if he was seeing anyone else and he hadn't responded. Lying by omission was better than an answer.

Ash, now sipping his third drink, thirty thousand or so feet above the ground, pondered: where did his loyalties lie? He had booked an early flight to be with Rita, but … now, he didn't know. Couldn't figure it out.

Procrastination was one strategy. Although, in the long run, it would, he knew, come back to bite him in his ass. At any rate, he would be living a lie and end up hurting Rita who had never deceived him, and simultaneously play Katie false. Between a rock and a hard place. There was no future with Rita, was there? She was as good as married to her job. Sex was good, amazing in fact. But it had been equally amazing with Katie. Rita and he were on the same mental plane but so were Katie and he, at least in the initial years when they were married, before everything started coming apart at the seams. Rita had once hinted that if they were both still single at forty, they'd 'get together'. A promise of sorts. However, one couldn't live one's life on a standby. What if either of them didn't live to be forty? What if Rita found someone else while he was away?

Katie was now.

Rita might be then.

For the first time in his life he was confused. A specialist in human psychology was as good for himself as a lawyer fighting his own case. It had 'lose-lose' written all over it.

It was not so much about taking a wrong decision, but *not* taking the decision. As always not taking a decision was a decision too. Should he let it go? Not talk about Katie to Rita on this trip and let time make the decision?

'What would you like for dinner, Mr Mattel?' Ash's reverie was shattered by the stewardess.

'My apologies,' he said. 'I'm not sure I saw the menu – what's on offer?'

Friday, 11 December.

It was quite early in the morning when the pilot announced their descent. The tailwind, he mentioned, had been strong and they had reduced their flying time by an hour.

Just when I could have spent more time thinking, thought Ash wryly. If he wanted, he could simply check into a hotel and not call Rita. How would she know? She wasn't expecting him until Saturday morning anyway. Perhaps that was what he should do.

Out of the aircraft, he went swiftly through the immigration before collecting his bags and walked straight to the taxi rank.

'Where to, *sahib*?'

'Bandra.' He had arrived two days early to surprise Rita, and that was precisely what he would do. He had convinced himself, after six drinks some thirty thousand feet above sea level, to come clean and face the consequences.

Rita was still in bed when the doorbell rang.

She had spent most of the previous night in Crawford Market, in the Ops Room with the men. There had been no communiqué from Gautam. His silence was unnerving. Rita had – from Alka's account – sent a hello, which hadn't been acknowledged. Facebook Messenger showed that the recipient hadn't seen the message. Gautam seemed to have vanished into thin air. Had he changed his mind? If he didn't turn up at Alka's apartment on Saturday, their entire stratagem would come to nothing. Had he somehow figured out that it was a trap? How could he? The plan had been carefully contained within the small coterie of officers working on it. Even the officers in the immediate outer circle didn't know what the inner group had planned. No, it couldn't have leaked.

Groggy from lack of sleep she went to the door. Whoever it was she would shoo him or her away and tell the person to return at a less ungodly hour.

'Who is it?' she growled from behind the door.

'The one and only, Ash Mattel.'

'But you were supposed to come later.'

'Sorry, but I'm here early.'

No wise retort, Rita wondered. Under ordinary circumstances, a cheesy line would have answered her innocent question. Something wasn't right. She looked down at the well-worn comfortable tee that she liked to wear to bed – it was barely decent.

'Are you alone?'

'Yes.'

If Ash expected an outburst or waterworks, Rita certainly disappointed him. She was mature enough to understand his dilemma. On her part she had never given him any assurance of a long-term relationship. They had been friends with benefits, nothing more. A standby when they got to forty was just a joke, wasn't it? Who knew whether Ash would be single again by then or if she herself would still be single? Perhaps she would find someone in the next year or the one after that? Where did that leave Ash? He couldn't wait around forever. Neither could she. Perhaps she could change the situation if she told him right then that she wanted to be with him for the rest of her life. But could she?

What had he been thinking? Why did he come to her apartment with his bags, two days earlier?

'I had changed my ticket to Thursday before Katie called. But when she moved into my apartment earlier, there were no seats available, in any class, to move my travel ahead. My hotel reservation is from noon onwards today, so I thought I'd come here and talk to you.'

'Good for you.' Rita didn't want to break down, but she was fighting an emotional tide. Something was wrong with her if all her relationships disintegrated before they matured. Was she was looking for something she would never find?

'You okay?'

'The fact that you're telling me this means you've already taken a decision. Is there any point in my trying to convince you otherwise? I love you, and I know you well, Ash. I respect your decision. We should remain as friends and professional colleagues. Of course, I'm okay. How much have you told Katie about us?'

'Nothing.'

Fuck you very much, she wanted to say, but she just smiled. *How convenient.*

'Why don't you take a shower in the guest room while I fix us breakfast?' She made it amply clear he wasn't going anywhere near her bedroom. That chapter was over and done with.

'Sure.'

An awkwardness permeated the room all through breakfast. Neither of them knew how to address it. Rita, on her part, did not want to let her mind wander into the emotional space today, because she had a big task ahead. She needed to be clear-headed for the day after tomorrow, Saturday.

Ash, somehow reading her mind, made an excuse and called for a cab. It was best for both of them if he moved out.

They agreed to remain friends, but both knew it would never happen. A professional relationship could continue but there wouldn't be very much on the personal front.

INTERLUDE
Present

I don't log into my Facebook account since I don't want Mrs Alka Dixit to change her mind or the date. If she can't contact me, she will be expecting me. I've been watching her building for the last few days now. And I know she has lied to me. None of her friends have visited her. So why lie to me? I don't like lies. Why did she want me to come on Saturday? Why did she make me wait?

'*She wants it hard*,' Nutty-me whispers.

'*I know that, damn it*,' I snapped, but why make me wait when there's no reason?

Or is there some reason?

Is there someone I missed who had gone into her apartment and taken her before me? I could have been blindsided thinking she was expecting a female friend, but it could well have been a male. What if she was entertaining someone before me? Cheating slut.

'*Teach her a lesson*,' Nutty-me orders.

How?

'Let's visit her tonight, an evening before the date.'

But what if someone is there?

'*Do you care?*'

No.

'*Tonight it is then.*' Nutty-me makes an executive decision and I get into preparation. It's still six hours to darkness. Why not tonight?

We start planning.

Going around eleven p.m. will be a safe bet. The neighbours will be safely tucked in and there is no chance that anyone will see me in the building. The watchman is a joke anyway.

However, going that late will necessitate a break-in.

Why would Alka Dixit open her door to an unknown man that late at night?

Going around eight-thirty p.m. is ideal. It would be dinnertime for most people. With my baseball cap worn low and dressed as a pizza delivery boy, I could knock on the door. Surely she'll say she hasn't ordered a pizza, but will undoubtedly open the door to talk to a harmless delivery boy at that hour. Worst case, I'll walk away if someone else sees me. Nothing will be lost. I can always go back later. This way, I will also confirm the apartment number that the idiot estate agent had given me.

Yes, I'll go at eight-thirty. It's seven now Time to get ready.

TWENTY-THREE

It was meant to be a long day for DCP Rita Ferreira and the entire team. A mission like this made for a truckload of paperwork. Everything needed to be documented and approved by the commissioner himself before Saturday. The plan had to look perfect and foolproof on paper, although anyone who's ever been in the defence forces knows that plans were only good at the start. The opponent's reaction could turn everything topsy-turvy, therefore planning was purely theoretical because one could only plan for some, not all, contingencies. No one, not even a computer, could work out every possible scenario and the events that unfolded could fly in the face of everything that the police thinktank had imagined. For instance, what if there were two killers working in tandem? What if the unsub already knew about the sting operation and was all set to handle any interruptions?

Then, there was the risk factor to the other residents in the building. The police couldn't evacuate the building at short notice. If they did, the unsub would smell a rat. He was far from stupid. He had already been in the building – supposedly at least – and he could be watching it. At any rate, a mass exodus from the building would attract too much attention, and then where would the 'covert' in their covert strike go?

Nevertheless, the paperwork had to be duly processed. All the police weapons for the core teams were tested and put on record. If any were used, they would have to be properly registered. Unlike the cowboys in the movies, the police couldn't randomly turn up with whatever personal armaments they had at the scene of crime.

Rita, having risen early to receive the news of Ash Mattel moving on with his life, was concentrating hard to not let her mind wander. There was too much at stake here for her to allow her emotions to run riot and impede her judgement.

There was still no message from Mr Gautam on Alka's Facebook Messenger. Was there any point in sending another *hello*? They decided against it. It could look like Alka was desperate, and in the worst case, ring some invisible alarm bells for the unsub. Why do that? The date had been fixed, so in all probability he would turn up to see Alka tomorrow.

Fingers crossed.

Leaving Harry in the Ops Room for the first half of the shift, Rita decided everyone else could take a powernap elsewhere in the office. The only two things to galvanize everybody into action at this juncture were (a) signs of activity on Alka's Facebook Messenger and (b) if the team watching the concealed cameras at Rajdoot Apartments reported anything suspicious in the vicinity.

'Why don't you go home, ma'am?' Harry said.

Had he read her mind? Did her face reflect that she had been dumped today?

'I'm fine. I'll be in my office.'

'Actually, Harry's right – there's no point in your hanging around,' agreed Jatin, 'we can take care of this, and you can return early tomorrow morning.'

The two Mathurs and Vikram supported this suggestion, and it did indeed make sense. What was the point of six people milling around in the office when they weren't required?

'Why don't we all leave?' Rita asked. She didn't want to be the only one going home to her bed when the entire team remained in the office.

'Yup, we could do that as well ...'

Despite their original decision of everyone camping in the office, it was decided that only Harry and Jatin would stay behind, taking turns to watch for any activity from Gautam and the other four would go home to return bright-eyed and bushy-tailed the next morning.

'We'll get him tomorrow.'

The decision made, Rita, the Mathurs and Vikram left the office a little after eight p.m.

Ruby aka Alka Dixit was in her bedroom when she heard a soft knock on the door. She wasn't expecting anyone, but then she hadn't expected Rita to drop by yesterday either. She glanced down at herself. She was in her night suit, but it didn't matter. Gone were the days she had to be dolled up to entertain rutting clients.

'Who is it?' she asked from behind the door, looking through the peephole. Someone wearing a baseball cap and holding a rectangular box stood there. The face was only partially visible.

'Your pizza, madam.'

'I didn't order any.'

'Are you sure?'

'What apartment number does the order say?'

'Wait, let me check again.'

Alka unlatched the door. Rita had ordered pizza yesterday. Perhaps it was the same company delivering the pizza, and there had been some mix up in the address.

The guy put his foot in the doorway the moment she opened it and shoved her back. Before she could shout or scream, he dropped the pizza box on the floor – the thud sounded a lot louder than a mere cardboard box; it definitely carried something heavy – kicked the door shut in one swift motion, spun her around and covered her mouth. All in the space of ten seconds. It was a gloved hand. She heard him slide the bolt home. It couldn't be unlocked even if the police arrived with the spare key they had for the door.

'Shhhh ... don't make any noise,' the man whispered. 'And don't turn around until I tell you to or I'll hurt you.' He slowly dragged her away from the front door, away from the panic alarm that had been installed by the police. Shit! Why hadn't she pressed that immediately?

'Do as I say, and everything will be all right, okay?' the man said in harsh monotone. No emotions.

Alka nodded.

'I'll remove my hand from your mouth, but if you try to scream, I could be forced to kill you.'

A chill went down Alka's spine. She nodded again. All the blood had rushed to her head, clouding her thoughts. What on earth had she signed up for? And where the hell was Rita now?

'Who are you?' she asked the moment he removed his hand.

'Gautam.'

She felt the rug had been pulled from under her feet. How had he gotten here? Wasn't he supposed to come tomorrow? Had Rita made an error?

Before she could say anything, he pulled out a rag from his pocket, pushed the rag into her mouth and swiftly placed a tape over it. She heard the rustle of fabric like he was putting on something.

'Now turn around,' he ordered.

He wore a ski mask now, with cut outs for eyes. His voice came from behind the knitted black fabric. Who wore that in Mumbai? Even in December? Where does one even buy such an outfit? Real panic set in now; she had missed the two panic buttons installed in the living room. A leaden sensation of hopelessness seized her. She felt cold as the direness of her predicament dawned on her. Although her hands were free, she didn't dare to even try to prise her gag off. The guy was big and carried a six-inch serrated knife.

'Hmmm … mmm … mmm … mmm,' she didn't know what she wanted to say.

'Why am I here a day early?' he seemed to be reading her thoughts. 'Because you lied to me, you harlot. Because you do not have any friend visiting you today, so why did you ask me to come tomorrow evening?'

Her eyes were beginning to fill with tears. He had deliberately come a day early; it wasn't that Rita had miscalculated. That being the case there would be no police coming over. No one would just drop by to save her.

'Take off your clothes slowly, one item at a time,' he intoned. 'Let's get this party started.'

His accent sounded educated. His black jeans looked expensive. He wore a long-sleeved, black, knitted T-shirt. Black leather shoes. Oxford brogues. She couldn't glimpse any of his skin at all. All she could hear was the voice. There was not much body odour either. Would he rape her? For years she had endured consensual rape for money or out of lack of choices. Why had she voluntarily taken the lead role in this psychodrama? Her fear turned to horror.

As Kuldeep drove Rita home, her mind ran through a collage of emotions. From the Lipstick Killer to Ash Mattel's decision this morning. At another time, another woman had stolen her boyfriend, Karan, from her. The last thing Rita wanted to be was the other woman who had come between husband and wife. Okay, ex-wife, but they had reunited, hadn't they? One of life's greatest lessons was to learn to let go. The car was still moving like the slowest snail on earth, stuck in the vast car park that was Mumbai's roads at this hour. Another kilometre, she assured herself, and then they would be on the Bandra-Worli Sea Link, and they could dart through to get on to the road home. The December sun had set, and the dark sea seemed calm on the surface as they ascended the flyover. On her right, Mumbai's lights shone bright. To erase the pointless thoughts, she forced her mind on the case at hand. She went over the evening she had spent with Ruby and made a note to start the search for the douchebag who had ruined the poor girl's life, and so many more that she wasn't aware of yet. She marvelled at Ruby's resilience despite her circumstances. Also creditable was the enthusiasm of Mr Ash Mattel, who flew down to Mumbai two days before she had expected him, to announce he was getting back with this ex. If only he had come early without the heartbreaking newsflash. Why did only bad things arrive before their time? Why did … her mind suddenly stopped mid-thought.

'Holy fuck!' she almost screamed.

How would Gautam, whoever he was, figure out which apartment Alka Dixit lived in? If her memory served her right, she had only given him the building's name, not the apartment number. And if the assumption was correct, that it was indeed him in the dark VW saloon, scouting the building, what were the chances he hadn't already figured out which apartment his prey occupied. Was that why he wasn't responding to Alka's messages, because he didn't need any more information?

'Harry,' she called the Ops Room, 'go through the entire chat history between Alka and Gautam – did we accidentally give him the apartment number?'

'Wait a minute, ma'am.' Then a minute later: 'No, ma'am. He never asked for the apartment number. How does he intend meeting Alka then?'

'He already knows it.'

'How?'

'I don't know, but it can't be the most difficult thing to find out.'

'If he knows the apartment, he could easily be there tonight.'

'My thoughts exactly – he could be there a day early. Get the team to Alka's apartment immediately. Call the local Versova police station to get the cavalry there and ask them to wait for me or until they see someone from our team. What vehicle do you have?'

'A motorbike, ma'am.'

'Here's what you do: check with the surveillance team if they've spotted anything unusual; leave the Ops Room to Jatin; get the spare key to Alka's apartment and meet me there, asap.'

'Roger that, ma'am.'

'Kuldeep, blue light and siren on, and zip; we need to get to Versova.' If Kuldeep heard the panic in her voice, he didn't show it. He switched on the cherry on top and floored the pedal.

Jatin called back in four minutes.

Watching CCTV is a known skull-numbing activity. Nothing happens for hours. And sometimes you missed something because it was so mundane, so ordinary. Nothing extraordinary had occurred, Jatin reported. The residents had all long ago been identified, and hence ruled out. No one else – no single male guest – had come visiting any apartment the entire evening, except a pizza delivery man.

'In Alka's block?' Probably an insignificant event, but Rita still asked.

'Yes, ma'am.'

'At what time?'

'At 20:28 hours.'

'At what time did he leave?'

The car, with its red and blue light flashing and siren screaming, was turning right from Juhu. Another ten minutes.

'The surveillance team didn't think it was critical to note the time of his departure. He could have slipped out sometime when they weren't looking at the screen, ma'am.'

'Check. If they missed him going out, they might have also missed someone coming in. I'll hold.' Rita's voice was a decibel higher than normal. She was sweating. It could be nothing, but something in her gut told her something wasn't right.

'The pizza guy hasn't left yet,' Jatin reported, after checking.

'What?' She instinctively looked at the time. 'What has the pizza guy been doing in the building for the last thirty minutes?'

'Look at you,' the madman let out a low wolf-whistle seeing Alka in her undergarments. Were you Miss Mumbai? Wow. I've never seen someone as good as you. Now the bra.'

She shuddered.

'D'you want me to cut it?' he brandished the knife, 'it could accidentally cut some skin. You wouldn't want that now, would you?'

As Alka fumbled with the hook behind her back, she realized the madman was talking to himself. He was mumbling '*Yes, yes, just like Tina*,' to someone invisible. Alka could feel the bile rise in her throat.

'*Hold on*,' the madman said to someone, like he was trying to stop them from doing something, then he spoke to her: 'Your heat is burning my loins. I'll have so much fun pleasuring you. Now the rest,' he pointed indicated the lace panty.

Alka, her mouth still taped, pleaded with her eyes.

The psycho intermittently spoke to someone, called him 'Nutty'. He yelped in ecstasy as Alka stepped out of her last garment.

'*A sight for sore eyes, isn't she*?' he asked someone. Then tilted his head like he was actually listening to the invisible someone. '*Yes, Nirvana*,' he agreed. Was he carrying a hidden camera and microphone and broadcasting this to someone?

He transferred the knife to his left hand and moved the right one over her. 'Most people underestimate the pleasure of sight and miss taking in the scent of a body like this. Flawless.' He gripped her around the waist and walked with her to pick up a slim briefcase from within the pizza box. 'Don't try anything cute or you will be real sorry.'

Alka didn't need to be told that he meant every word.

'Now, where's the bedroom, gorgeous?'

The pizza delivery man still hadn't left the building when Rita's car screeched to a halt outside the building at 9.16 p.m. She had told Kuldeep to switch off the siren to avoid sending any kind of signal to the unsub *if* he was indeed in there. She jumped out of the car and looked around for a second. The local police hadn't arrived yet. Were they getting fucking pedicures?

As she ran towards the apartment, she heard the rumble of a motorbike. Thank heavens, Harry-Mr-Idiom had arrived, so they had a spare key to sneak in if need be.

All Alka prayed for now was a painless death. She had complied with his every command. He had tethered her to the bed, face-down, spread-eagled. She hadn't had a chance to press the panic button that was under her bed. If only she could work her right hand loose, she could reach it.

And then suddenly, he walked out of the bedroom, leaving her in a lather.

He returned after apparently taking a quick tour of the apartment.

'Strange,' he stated, 'this place doesn't feel like a home for someone like you. I see no photographs – neither yours nor your husband's, no personal touches at all. I'd have expected something better from someone as hot as you. Or are you a total slut, purely focused on sex?'

He sat on the bed beside her. The knife moved from her buttocks to the perineum to her inner thighs to the pubis and back up the same route. Not cutting the skin but the sharpness of the steel still hurt. It left reddened weals in its wake. She winced. But the psycho seemed impervious to her pain. From whatever she had read about the Lipstick Killer, she knew what he was capable of. And he appeared to be in no rush to carry out the carnage.

'Wait until it goes into you,' he murmured. Then spoke to someone only he could sense, '*Yes, we're going to have a long night, Nutty; don't worry. We'll enjoy every second.*'

Alka sensed a slight noise, like someone had knocked on the main door. But her tormentor heard it first.

'Expecting another lover?' he asked. 'The more the merrier.' He rose and left the bedroom once again.

'The door's bolted from inside,' Harry whispered to Rita. The duplicate key turned the lock, but the door remained shut.

'Fuck! Why did we leave the bolt on the door?'

'Shhh ... I hear someone coming, ma'am.'

'Quick, let's move. If it's Alka, she'll ask, if it's someone else, he might just peep through the eyehole. We shouldn't be visible.'

They flattened themselves against the wall on either sides of the door. Someone came to the door. They saw the peephole darken like someone had their eye glued to it. Then light shone through again. Then the steps sounded like they were walking away from the door.

'Should we break the door?' Harry asked. 'Fire a bullet through the wood?'

'If he is inside, he'll take Alka hostage. Worse still, he might kill her.'

'What then?'

'Let's go up a floor.'

Rita rang the bell on the apartment directly above Alka's. An elderly man opened the door. Rita showed him her ID, motioned him to maintain silence as both she and Harry went into the old man's apartment.

'What do you want from me?' asked the old gent.

'We'll explain everything to you later.' The last thing Rita wanted to do was to cause panic. The residents hadn't been told about the sting operation, and this wasn't the time for getting into details.

'The balcony ...' Rita pointed out.

The apartments were replicas of each other. Alka's balcony was directly under this one. One good thing about new-build apartments was that the ceiling heights weren't more than ten or twelve feet. A jump from that height wasn't too much of a challenge.

'I'll go,' Harry said.

'No. You go down and shoot down the door. That will distract him, and I'll come in from the balcony.'

The balcony was in the living room with floor to ceiling glass windows. Breaking the glass to enter would be child's play. Rita checked for her gun, and then stepped over the balcony. She grasped the grill and lowered herself. She slipped down holding the grill until she dangled six feet from the floor of Alka's balcony. Not a difficult feat, but the thump of her shoes would alert anyone in the apartment, so she stayed suspended until she heard Harry shoot the main door.

Bang! The sound was deafening. In that second, Rita let go of the grill and jumped, landing on her feet. The drawing room curtains had been drawn, so there was no visibility.

'Arrrrrrgh ...'

She heard a scream inside. She took out her Smith and Wesson and shattered the glass with the butt of her gun.

'Hello, DCP,' said a man in a ski mask. Harry writhed on the floor, bleeding. The assailant had anticipated Harry after he broke the door. Rita looked carefully and saw a knife stuck in Harry's thigh, and the Lipstick Killer held Harry's gun aimed at Harry. 'Welcome.' He didn't take his eyes off his target.

'Surrender yourself. You cannot escape. Versova Police will be here any minute. How many will you fight?'

'Who says I'm running away? I'll kill this bastard who interrupted my session with my lover. Then I'll strip you, tie you next to my lover and pleasure both of you. Sounds like a good idea?'

'Shoot him,' Harry yelped.

'Oh yeah, you find the idea of my fucking your boss so revolting that you don't mind dying? How about I make you fuck her before I kill you?'

Rita smiled.

'What are you smiling at, bitch?'

With his attention was divided between Harry and Rita, his back was towards the main door. He was facing Rita who had come in through the balcony which was opposite the entrance. Ergo, Rita saw what he had missed. As they say, everyone eventually runs out of aces.

The bullet hit the back of his head, the blood splatter contained within the ski-cap as the man fell forward in the middle of the room, his face crashing against the glass coffee table and smashing it. Vikram had arrived and had seen the tableau. Left with no alternative, he shot point blank.

While Vikram confirmed that the man was dead before he attended to Harry, Rita rushed into the bedroom to check on Ruby. She immediately covered Ruby's modesty before anyone else came in and then untied the blue nylon cords. If that obliterated some evidence, so be it – although from past experience she knew there was nary a chance of any physical evidence. In the small leather case lying open by the bed, she found Maybelline Jewels Refined Wine lipstick, the leather belt, the strong bleach – all the accoutrements that the Lipstick Killer had previously used on other victims. The serrated knife in Harry's leg seemed the shape and size he had inserted into his previous murder victims.

Had they finally brought the curtain down on one of the most heinous of psychopaths in recent times? In all probability the answer was yes, but a first-year law student would argue that the evidence was, at best, circumstantial. If the police witnessed a man holding a knife, and then came across a homicide three kilometres away that had occurred using a similar knife, it did not necessarily mean that the person seen with the knife earlier was the killer. By law, the police would have had to discover some evidence that linked the two events. The accused and the victim should somehow fit in the same frame. Or find the knife that killed the victim and find prints of the killer on it. Arresting a killer and proving his guilt were two separate beasts. The defence lawyer would argue that this was only a copycat, imitating the Lipstick Killer, even if his MO and toolkit matched.

But it was all moot. It wasn't like the corpse in the living room could rise up and claim he wasn't the killer that they were looking for. In any event, Ruby had been stripped and restrained, which was a crime. The killer had stabbed Harry, and that was enough to warrant a bullet.

POSTLUDE

The bullet had been fired from quite a close range, and hence obliterated the face of the killer. The coffee table glass, on which he fell, completed the job: what was left of his face had a million shards of glass embedded in it. If identifying the Lipstick Killer were to be solely dependent on facial recognition, it would prove tenebrous at best. The corpse did not have a single hair on its body – just eyebrows and eyelashes, which explained why no hair was ever found at the scenes of the crimes. The only uncovered parts of the body were his eyes.

After the ambulance had taken Harry and Ruby to hospital, Rita and the team remained in situ until the local police arrived to take over the crime scene. The residents had congregated on the ground floor. Some were disgruntled that they had not been informed that the police would carry out such a perilous operation in their building; others were relieved that the dreaded killer was finally dead, allowing them to sleep in peace.

The psychopath's body had been thoroughly searched for anything that would provide some clue to his identity, but he carried nothing on him that revealed anything. No wallet with credit cards or a driving licence. The search for a black or navy blue or dark green VW Passats in the vicinity did not yield any results either. How had the perp travelled to Versova? His mode of conveyance could have been a cab – he could have been dropped off somewhere nearby and then he would have walked the rest of the way. Although they realized they might never know the answer to that one, they didn't let it bother them, because the more important challenge was to find out where he had travelled *from*? His home?

After a successful event like this, it was quite normal for most police officers to convene at some place to dissipate the anxiety that had built up leading to the chase. It was time for the adrenaline to settle. They sat around, relaxing and evaluating the operation. Assessed the rights and wrongs, what could have been done better. It was not a celebration per se, but a return to normalcy. Rita & Co. had moved to the only tea stall open in the early hours near Crawford Market.

'Has anyone reported a missing person yet?' Rita asked, although she didn't sound too convincing. What were the chances that the Lipstick Killer lived with someone who would rush to the nearest police station to report him missing when he or she didn't find him at home in the morning?

Fingerprints, DNA, dental records were all unique to an individual, but what good were they? If their unsub had a prior police record in Mumbai, they could find a match although even that could take months. Rita anticipated the media's question long before sunrise, and she wasn't wrong.

'Who was the Lipstick Killer?'

Virtually every news channel, every newspaper asked the same question. Twelve hours after the operation, the police were none the wiser.

Sexy, with Vinay Joshi in tow, came down to the Ops Room and congratulated the whole team. They contributed generous amounts into the collection pool for flowers and cards for Harry and Ruby.

'Our next priority is to name the Lipstick Killer,' declared Joshi, the master of the obvious, before the bigwigs returned to their ivory towers.

How? Rita wondered.

Three Days Later.

'DCP Rita Ferreira?' asked Chavi Nair, star reporter from *Mumbai24*.

It had taken her a couple of days since her boyfriend had gone missing to actually go looking for him. When he stopped answering her calls, she had gone to his luxury penthouse apartment and rung the bell, then knocked on the door, but didn't get any response. Afraid that something untoward could have happened to him she asked one of her office boys to summon a locksmith. It was only when she entered his study, a territory she had never stepped into before, that she realized who her boyfriend truly was. The computers, the violent porn magazines, photographs of the women he had supposedly killed and cases that she herself had covered on her shows. The evidence was all there. It only took minutes to comprehend that her boyfriend had been the dreaded Lipstick Killer himself. She passed out on the floor of the study. She was parched when she came to. The shock of her discovery had left her dehydrated. She had been dating a very sick psychopath all along. And she, an investigative journalist! She wondered whether it was her profession that had drawn him to her. She wondered why he had never attacked her. If he had done so, she would have been blindsided. It was then that she decided to make the call. She was sharp enough to know that the police would be able to trace her call, so she called from his penthouse's landline. She covered the mouthpiece with a thick kitchen towel to disguise her voice as much as possible. Her personal loss aside – she knew she would never recover from the horror of dating a serial killer – she had no intention of revealing her personal hell to anyone, at least for now. She hadn't known about her boyfriend's nefarious activities at all, and she wasn't going to sacrifice her career by submitting herself for pointless questioning by the police. The police, she knew, would come at her from several angles. *How could you miss it? Were you his accomplice – his partner-in-crime?*

'Yes, it's Rita Ferreira,' answered the voice at the other end.

'I think I know the identity of the corpse that you have in the morgue, the one the world knows as the Lipstick Killer.'

'Who are you?'

'Who I am is of no consequence, and I'd like to keep my identity private.'

'How do we know—'

'I'll give you the name and address, and you can send your team there. There's enough evidence here to charge this person many times over.'

'Okay, go on, then.' There was resignation in the voice of the DCP, like she would take whatever she could get to confirm the identity of the killer first. The rest could come later.

'Rajat Khanna.'

'Now where have I heard that name before?'

'PMC,' Chavi said, her voice trembled with the overwhelming flood of emotions and tears. She slammed the phone down, wiped her prints from the phone and quickly left the building. She was aware that someone, somewhere would know of her relationship with the deceased. This wasn't the end of her nightmare. But she had done the right thing by making the call.

Rajat Khanna, CEO, Personal Machines Corporation. The pieces of the puzzle clicked into place almost instantly. Isha Thapar, the high-profile defence lawyer, hired to defend Ranbeer. There had been no Initial Public Offering from the company; Ranbeer was lured out into the open by the offer to reimburse him for his final assignment with the company, and then killed in cold blood. If the police had tracked the company, the alarm bells would have pealed. But they had missed it. Well, even the so-called best detective was human and hence prone to errors. With all eyes on the ball, they had missed the goalpost by a mile.

The police raid followed and Rajat Khanna's penthouse in Worli was sealed off. His computers were seized. Rajat hadn't had a chance to erase anything from them and it was a simple case of hacking into the system. The last conversation Rajat, aka Gautam, had with Ruby, aka Alka, was there in his Facebook Messenger. Other chat history proved that he had been in touch with all the other victims. His MO was already known to the police: he befriended women and lured them to open their homes to him.

It took them less than six hours to discover the person who had telephoned Rita to point them towards Rajat Khanna. Although Rita could empathize with Chavi, in accordance with police protocol, she was kept under surveillance, until further inquiries could be carried out. She ensured that no one contacted Chavi at the moment. If any evidence was discovered of Chavi's involvement in any of the killings, they would have to immediately take her into custody. Otherwise, Rita decided to speak one-on-one to Chavi in a couple of days. This would give the girl some time to mourn.

The police turned Rajat Sharma's penthouse upside down and inside out. The documents found there established that he had changed his name after coming to Mumbai. He was originally Ashish Sharma, born in New Delhi and raised in Vasant Kunj. Further investigation brought forward a cold case of one Tina Aggarwal, over fifteen years ago. Not much evidence was found, but it didn't need waking up too many grey cells to infer who could be responsible for it, although Rajat, aka Ashish Sharma, would have been in his early teens back then. All the neighbourhoods he had ever stayed in, however temporarily, were checked out. Nothing untoward had occurred during his stays. Okay, he may have indulged in voyeurism, but no one ever noticed or reported it, but definitely no homicides. As always, the past neighbours were shocked when they heard he had been identified as the Lipstick Killer, the serial killer who had set Mumbai by the ears: '*He seemed to keep himself to himself.*' '*Always said hello, with a smile.*' '*I can't believe it was him.*'

Rita visited Harry and Ruby in the afternoon. Harry's right thigh was impressively bandaged. Fortunately, his injuries were more muscle and flesh, and no vital veins had been damaged. He had started hopping around with the help of a walking stick. Rita felt she was responsible because she hadn't taken into account Harry's lack of experience. Anyone familiar with such nasty face-offs – they could easily turn fatal – wouldn't have entered the apartment straightaway after shooting the door down. The noise would have afforded ample time for the assailant to prepare for the imminent attack. After doing his part, all Harry had needed to do was wait and let Rita attack from the other side, blindsiding the unsub. Instead he had walked right into the trap.

Harry admitted he had jumped the gun in his rookie enthusiasm. 'And once I got in it was like *come-buffalo-hit-me*.'

After wiping away the tears of laughter, Rita pointed out, 'I think the actual idiom has a bull not a buffalo.'

'It's actually an ox in the original idiom, ma'am. But buffalo sounds more interesting, don't you think?'

Still smiling, she said, 'Welcome to the Crime Branch, Harry'. Of course, she would take him into her team. Harry had shown indomitable courage in the face of potential disaster, which was the right attitude for the job. Everything else, Rita knew, could be taught.

'Thank you, ma'am.'

'Take rest, and we'll see you soon.'

Harry would be on leave for a while until he was declared physically and emotionally fit to resume duty.

Ruby was still hyperventilating, and justifiably so. She had come within inches of undergoing live dissection by the monster. Rita assured her that they would start work on her new identity as soon as she was ready to leave the hospital. Jatin Singh was given the responsibility for all her security arrangements while she stayed in the hospital, and then she would move into Rita's apartment once again. Rita promised to find Ajay – Ruby's unconscionable ex, who had pushed her into hell.

By the time Rita got home, she was more exhausted than she had ever been in her life. The last few days had been particularly stressful – finding the Lipstick Killer, but not knowing who he was had been unnerving. Until they comprehensively knew they had got the right guy, it was the proverbial sword of Damocles over their heads. But it was all over now.

It was only then that she realized that Ash Mattel had inadvertently helped her, once again, by arriving a day before he had said he would. It was time to be mature.

'I wanted to thank you,' she said when she telephoned him. He was at the airport. *On his way back to Katie.*

'For what?'

She told him. 'You coming in prior to the appointment made me change tack in my thinking and that's how I suspected the killer could arrive early too. That set the ball rolling, so to speak …'

'That was a mere coincidence.'

Then there was silence. Neither knew how to continue the conversation. Nor did they know how to conclude it without being abrupt.

'Hey,' Rita finally said, 'remember your promise? If both of us are single when we're forty, we get together.'

'Yeah!' Ash uttered, but the response lacked his usual verve.

'I don't mean you should break up with Katie by then. In fact, I wish you all the very best, but, just in case …'

'I know. I'm sorry, Rita. I'm sorry for doing this, but I hope you understand.'

'I do, my friend. I do. Let's just be friends again.'

'Not friends with benefits?'

'That's the Ash I know, with the tacky one-liners.'

They chuckled, wished each other well and disconnected.

These past few years she had settled into the warm uncertainty of Ash's visits. She fixed herself a drink from the bottle of Jack Daniel's he had brought on his previous visit. She remembered her dad who always quoted some famous political cartoonist by the name of Dr Seuss: '*Don't cry because it's over; smile because it happened.*' She promised herself that she would endeavour to keep Ash as a happy memory. After all, Cupid could always come calling with his little bow and arrow, couldn't he?

Adios, she murmured to herself. Rita stood with the drink in her hand for the longest time. Seconds. Minutes. An hour? How could someone win and lose in the same instant? She smiled and had just decided to put on some music, when there was a knock on her door. She looked through the peephole and couldn't believe her eyes.

'Hi,' she said, opening the door wide to her visitor.

'I hope I'm not disturbing you,' the guest said.

'Come on in.'

'I knew you would immediately guess the identity of the person who called you about Rajat Khanna. I thought I should come and speak to you and tell you all.'

'However evil he was, I'm really sorry for your loss, Chavi. Care for a drink?'

ABOUT THE AUTHOR

Vish Dhamija is the bestselling author of eight crime fiction books. He is frequently referred to in the press as the 'master of crime and courtroom drama in India'. In August 2015, at the release of his first legal fiction, *Deja Karma, Glimpse* magazine called him 'India's John Grisham' for stimulating the genre of legal fiction in India, which was almost non-existent before his arrival on the scene. Vish lives in London with his wife, Nidhi.